Teaching Beauty
in
DeLillo, Woolf, and Merrill

Teaching Beauty
in
DeLillo, Woolf, and Merrill

Jennifer Green-Lewis and Margaret Soltan

palgrave
macmillan

First published in 2008 by
PALGRAVE MACMILLAN™
175 Fifth Avenue, New York, N.Y. 10010 and
Houndmills, Basingstoke, Hampshire, England RG21 6XS.
Companies and representatives throughout the world.

PALGRAVE MACMILLAN is the global academic imprint of the Palgrave
Macmillan division of St. Martin's Press, LLC and of Palgrave Macmillan Ltd.
Macmillan® is a registered trademark in the United States, United Kingdom
and other countries. Palgrave is a registered trademark in the European Union
and other countries.

ISBN-13: 978-0-230-60124-6
ISBN-10: 0-230-60124-3

Library of Congress Cataloging-in-Publication Data is available from
the Library of Congress.

A catalogue record of the book is available from the British Library.

Design by Scribe Inc.

First edition: April 2008

10 9 8 7 6 5 4 3 2 1

Printed in the United States of America.

In memory of our mothers:
gardeners, lovers of beauty.

Contents

Acknowledgments

This book grew out of a course that we teach together at the George Washington University in Washington, D.C., and its greatest debt is to our students, whose passion and responsiveness convinced us that there was more to be said on the subject of why teaching beauty matters.

Jennifer Green-Lewis thanks the friends whose interest in the project made her bold enough to persuade them to read bits of it: Allyson Booth, Harriet Chessman, and John Elder responded generously to the pieces they saw. Many colleagues at the Bread Loaf School of English graciously put up with longwinded accounts of the book at otherwise pleasant social events: special thanks to Dare Clubb and Bryan Wolf for memorable conversations on the topic of beauty. Thanks of course to the Scathing Online Schoolmarm, Margaret Soltan. Above all, thanks to Craig Lewis. And to Phoebe, Max, and Oliver Lewis: sorry this took so long.

Margaret Soltan would like to acknowledge, first, the hard work, love, and friendship of Jennifer Green-Lewis. She thanks David Kosofsky, friend and intellectual companion of a lifetime. She was inspired every day by Karol Edward Soltan, whose physical and metaphysical beauty deepens over time. To mark her gratitude to her daughter, Ania, Soltan will poach Christopher Lasch's Shakespearean tribute to *his* daughter in his great book, *The Culture of Narcissism*: "For she is wise, if I can judge of her, / And fair she is, if that mine eyes be true, / And true she is, as she hath prov'd herself; / And therefore, like herself, wise, fair, and true, / Shall she be placed in my constant soul."

Parts of Soltan's chapters have appeared in earlier versions under the following titles: "An Oblivion that Knows its Limits," in *Message in a Bottle: The Literature of Small Islands*, eds. Laurie Brinklow, Frank Ledwell, and Jane Ledwell (Prince Edward Island: Institute of Island Studies, 2000, pp. 101–21); "Hoax Poetry in America" in the journal *Angelaki* (vol. 6, no. 3, pp. 43–62); "No Field, No Future," in the online journal *Inside Higher Ed* (December 6, 2005). Thanks to each for permission to republish. Parts of Chapter 6 appear as "Loyalty to Reality in Don DeLillo's *White Noise*," in *Approaches to Teaching DeLillo's White Noise* (New York: Modern Language

Association of America, 2006, pp. 158–68), reprinted here by permission of the Modern Language Association of America.

Both authors are grateful to the fearless Annie Lowrey, cite-checker extraordinaire; to Christina Mueller for computer expertise; to Lisa Rivero for taking care of the index; to Tracy Gibbons at Farrar, Straus and Giroux; to Yvette Chin for her painstaking work; and to Farideh Koohi-Kamali and Julia Cohen at Palgrave Macmillan.

A Note to the Reader

This book has two authors. In order to write it, we each assumed individual responsibility for certain chapters and then we exchanged, reviewed, and edited each other's work. We speak as two people in agreement with each other. Our "we" is, therefore, literal rather than royal or coercive. The things we argue in this book are things that the two of us both believe.

At times in our writing, however, a first person voice also emerges, as when we describe our own responses to reading and teaching a work or when we are moved to express something that has peculiar appeal to our own, and not necessarily to each other's, ears or eyes. We could have made these sections more uniform, of course, for the sake of a smoother syntax, but to do so would have been to play down the discrete, idiosyncratic, and *personal* nature of the aesthetic experiences we all—which includes you—have as we move through the world.

Our belief that we can usefully and affirmatively share these private experiences—that we can move in fruitful ways between the "I" and the "we"—is the foundation of this book.

JGL
MS

Preface

"How shall the heart be reconciled / to its feast of losses?" asks Stanley Kunitz in his poem "The Layers."[1] As Kunitz clearly knew, there are actually a few things available to us in a time of grief that, if they cannot reconcile the heart, at least may turn the shapelessness of loss into the consolation of elegy. This book is about one of them. It is intended, first and foremost, for our students who, after their early morning encounters with the world via CNN, appear in our classrooms to talk about Ruskin or Thackeray or Nabokov. How shall *their* hearts be "reconciled" to the world in which they find themselves? Why, they might well ask, should they study literature amid the ongoing global feast of losses?

Our response to that question, and the starting point for this book, is our belief that beauty, and specifically the beauty to be experienced in literature, is one of the things that can offer our students consolation, can give them forms in which shape their own present and future grief and joy. There have been times—on September 12, 2001, for example, while the sky visible from our classroom still bore traces of smoke over the Pentagon—when as teachers of literature we have felt ourselves at an almost grotesque remove from the misfortunes of the world. But our recognition of that remove also recharges our daily awareness of the extraordinary privilege that it is to be in the classroom with our students. As teachers of literature, we are not only intellectually excited but also ethically obliged to make the beauty of litera-ture—the reconciliation to our world that a written work may offer—a part of our discussion of a work.

And certainly there is plenty of thinking about beauty going on, unfash-ionable as it has been in recent years to acknowledge it. Notwithstanding the shifting tastes of literature departments, beauty has never abandoned the province of literature, nor have readers failed over past decades to appreciate it. Our argument in this book, however, is that in its evolution into literary and cultural studies, what used to be called "literary criticism" failed to bring along with it what was once also part of its purview: namely, an appreciation of, and the skills to describe, the aesthetic life of a work. As teachers of literature started to move beyond the textually prescribed boundaries of close literary analysis to pursue historical, political, and theoretical approaches to literary works, we stopped making time to let our students talk about beauty, and we failed to teach them a formal vocabulary with which to do it.

The conclusions we draw in this book result from our own experience as teachers of literature—as people, that is, who like to read and who teach other people how to read and how to write about what they read. In another age, we might have said that we were literary critics, but in academia today that term has a quaintness about it that brings to mind worthy but impossibly tweedy figures such as the Leavises. Today's successful literary critic writes for a periodical, such as the *New York Review of Books*, and is rarely found in the halls of the English department.[2] We don't often teach literary criticism at universities any more—at least, not the kind of literary criticism involving the kind of close reading, evaluation, and judgment that are required for writing a decent book review.

This may be because, as with so many things in America, the thing that once was literary criticism has grown much larger in the past twenty-five years, while, paradoxically, in their various conceptual expansions, English departments have simultaneously made less and less space available for serious study of aesthetic questions—those questions pertaining, that is, to beauty. We believe that a relentless focus in the college classroom on the work of art as cultural production or on the creation of its readership and an emphasis on what or whom a text may represent and whose rights or interests are slighted by it have led to a culture of criticism full of its own special interests, while its neediest practitioners—our students—have been too often starved of the pleasures—the *reconciliations*—of the work itself.

Why does a work move us? How do we explain the pleasure, or discomfort, given us by a particular couplet, or arrangement of words, or indeed any literary device? What is the nature of our aesthetic response and can we identify what has elicited it? Open questions such as these that offer a grounded point of entry into the discussion of a work of literature or art have been asked far too rarely over the past thirty years, while other questions have become, as a result, burdened with complexity and often regarded as off limits. For example: How do we justify the choices we make when we judge between works, as judge we must?[3] What does it mean to say that something is well or poorly written? How can students of literature and art—how can *anyone*—identify any artwork as definitively bad—or good?

To this last question concerning the possibility of evaluation, students are often uniform in their answer that there is, in fact, no difference between good and bad and that there are no better and no worse works. Students are, in our experience, frequently poised to meet questions regarding the worth of a work with a flat (but very *polite*) refusal to explore their implications: "What is Good for me," they say, "may be Bad for you." (Or, as we heard it recently expressed, "If I disagree with you about the value of a work, I am criticizing you." Since it is rude to criticize, the disagreement and therefore the evaluation must be abandoned.) The question of *how* to judge is confused and ultimately effaced altogether by the sense that one *ought not* to judge at all, that judging, in fact, constitutes bad manners and results in divisiveness, elitism, and hierarchies.

Thus questions attending to the life of the work that might seem to be a necessary starting place for a discussion of its merits have been largely shunted aside in favor of questions that attend instead to the lives, habits, and rights of *readers*. The study of literary texts in recent years has seen the university student unleashed on an extraordinary array of material, on a vigorous hunt for social justice and injustice, tracking political motivations and consequences, sniffing out historical and cultural ramifications, exploring traces, in fact, of just about anything that pertains to the production of any given work and its consequences in the lives of its readers.

Such foraging has, predictably and as intended, produced volumes of publications, some rich, fascinating, and instructive, some of doubtful interest to anyone but the original authors. And much of what has been published is, as the popular press is so fond of noting, largely unintelligible to an educated and literate public. As terms to describe literary criticism, indeed, "serious" and "accessible" seem to have parted company, the latter now bearing in academic circles a faint whiff of insult. There are book reviews in the magazines and Sunday papers that anyone may read, and then there is what academics do, which, increasingly, only a very few of them can understand.

Moreover, while book reviews continue to make space for the consideration of the craft of writing (reviewers fortunately still feel it useful to note that a book is beautifully or poorly written, for example), academic writing of recent years has too often neglected the primary and obvious fact of aesthetic response. Aesthetic questions that speak to the formal life of the work of art and that usually begin life as the more general kinds of inquiry suggested above are actually of much wider interest and greater import than their infrequent formal airing by English departments would suggest.

This last is a more important point than one might at first suppose, since the most common charge leveled against the celebrant of aesthetic experience is one of elitism. While we will not shy away from this thorny issue, we wish to note from the outset that, despite the frequently solitary nature of the aesthetic experience, in writing this book we are motivated by a desire to bring back into public and shared debate the aesthetic pleasure that drew our students (and, once upon a time, drew us) to want to read literature (or hear music, or stare at paintings) in the first place.

For our appreciation of the beauty of a work has, it seems, become an increasingly private experience on campus. In the classroom it rarely provides the starting place for a discussion of our reading of books but now seems to enter the conversation rather surreptitiously or by accident (as when, for example, a student interjects "oh, I loved that bit!" and then subsides). It's likely that students have as many aesthetic experiences—as many pulsations, as Walter Pater puts it—as they did in the days when hundreds of them showed up to hear what Lionel Trilling had to say about Jane Austen or in the nineteenth century when benches were crowded with working men come to hear John Ruskin talk about J. M. W. Turner. We know that students are having extremely powerful aesthetic experiences, good and bad, with the works assigned them and probably many more with the various objects they discover in their travels. But if you ask students to discuss how a novel or poem or essay moves them, if you ask them to explain why something is beautiful or whether—a tougher question—its beauty is indexed to its value, it is as though a little sign marked "private" goes up, and you hear only scrupulously cautious self-reflections of the "it is beautiful to me" order. You almost never get to hear any reasoned argument, let alone passion, in defense of the work itself. And should students dislike a work, or find it offensive or worthless or flat-out boring, negative responses dictate that they will rarely give something another go but will simply reject it because "it doesn't speak to me"—and therefore nothing remains to be said on the subject.

This damping down, or shrinking, of aesthetic experience is a learned response. We have, it seems, in recent years disregarded or discounted or somehow rendered obsolete Stendhal's "promise of happiness": the future as it may be discerned or imagined or dreamed in and through contemplation of what is beautiful. If beauty is a promise, then it is beyond our grasp; it moves us to reach beyond ourselves, a reach that extends across time, through space, continent, culture, gender, race. It moves us to imagine ourselves as other selves, in worlds other than our own. Richard Rorty claims that the refusal to "indulge," as he puts it, "in utopian thinking," is a Foucauldian legacy, a direct consequence of Michel Foucault's "unfortunate inability to believe in the possibility of human happiness, and his consequent inability to think of beauty as the promise of happiness."[4] To this we would add that we find utopian thought itself to contain the seeds of happiness, premised as it is in a desire to look forward and beyond the exigencies of obsessive presentness that currently dominate literary studies in universities and high schools across America.

This book seeks to make clear the price of such presentness and argues that as teachers of literature the one thing we are really obliged to teach—whatever our theoretical approach; regardless of our political beliefs—is beauty. To make clear the academic context within which students of literature find themselves on campus today, the first two chapters offer a somewhat bleak analysis of recent practices in literary scholarship and of their wider expression in and implications for the classroom and indeed for American culture generally. Later chapters, however, develop a more optimistic response to the work of such contemporary thinkers and writers as David Denby, Denis Donoghue, Ihab Hassan, Alexander Nehamas, Richard Rorty, and Elaine Scarry, to cite only a few—critics and philosophers whose very different kinds of work have all helped to redirect attention to the power of aesthetic response and whose efforts to describe the nature of that response have both inspired and encouraged us.

Our book evolved from a course that we teach together, a course in which our selection of formally complex modernist works is, we happily confess, deliberate: we like, at least initially, to direct discussion away from meaning in order to ground it as far as possible in form, something we have found much easier to do when students are more obviously confronting difficulties of language and stylistic experiment. In the works of Eliot, Joyce, Nabokov, Lawrence, and Woolf, and more recently, DeLillo, Kundera, and Merrill, we find frequent occasion to consider our aesthetic responses, and we use those responses throughout the class as the ground on which to reconsider specific problems in aesthetics. The central part of this book reflects our enthusiasm for complexity of form in both modernism and postmodernism by offering a brief selection from those readings: here we consider works by Woolf, DeLillo, and Merrill, each in light of specific questions on evaluation, judgment, taste, understanding, and emotion to which our students have persistently returned us. As important, however, for a discussion of aesthetic response is the admittedly personal bias involved in our selection. In this book, as in our classes, we have chosen to discuss literature that we love, and, in the generative tradition of beauty (and with a nod to Wordsworth), we want our students to love it too.

But this is not a book on modernism or its descendants, and it makes no claims about any literary movements as such, other than to note in passing that complex works of overt and self-conscious formal ingenuity invite and indeed welcome the kind of scrutiny we hope to encourage in our students because these works offer frequent cause for aesthetic reflection without necessarily or initially distracting us with questions of content or moral import. Works of "self-conscious formal ingenuity" are, of course, hardly confined to the twentieth century, and for our literary sources we could have drawn on Victorian or medieval or romantic writings to make our case. We thus consider this book to be a starting point but hardly the conclusion to the wider work of returning aesthetics to pedagogy, of bringing beauty back into the classroom.

One further addendum: the reader may notice in later chapters that, while we argue that an informed attention to beauty must be returned to the formal study of literature, we also celebrate signs of what appears to be its imminent return. The liturgically sensitive ear may pick up an echo of desire for a holy communion with art, but in fact the desires of this book are fully rooted in this world and not in any other. While the book marks a faith, it is cheerfully secular: faith in a shared, communicable world in which identity politics have little to teach us about the value of the aesthetic experience. This book marks our faith in a world in which who we are, or once were, can fade to insignificance beside what beauty may help us—and our students—to imagine and to become.

INTRODUCTION

Teaching Beauty

In the sky outside an English department office at George Washington University, in Washington, D.C., a white blimp suddenly appears.[1] It's a clear early autumn afternoon, and the professor in the office puts aside her lecture notes for the modern novel class she's preparing and gazes at the thing at her window. What does it mean?

The White House and the World Bank are nearby, so air space here is restricted, especially since 9/11. Maybe the zeppelin is a military or espionage or security vehicle—a high-tech way to survey the streets around the capitol for terrorists. Maybe the blimp can see and hear her office in Academic Center, any of its lazy circlings keeping track of her e-mail messages, her chats with a dissertation student, her call home to her daughter. These rather anxious thoughts draw her away from what she's been doing: preparing a class on Don DeLillo's novel *White Noise*. Yet how far away, really? Her students never have trouble picking up on that novel's satirical nuances, its send-up of bright, happy postmodern American affluence; but the darker shadings it brings to its white-noise world sometimes elude them. The blimp—as much an aesthetically compelling as a disturbing sight—conveys that duality.

Interestingly, the professor is not thinking much about obvious Orwellian overtones as she looks out her window; rather, she is struck by the blimp's strange elegance as it passes lightly by her window and through the flaky clouds and blue sky. Its soft curves make it human and funny somehow—quite the opposite of unnerving. The power of the white zeppelin's image is such that she takes it in as—the metaphor comes to her from the sixties—a surrealistic pillow.

Surrealistic Pillow is Jefferson Airplane's best-known album, the one that includes the druggy "White Rabbit."[2] Sitting at her desk, tracing the slow turns of the spy ship, the English professor thinks of the blimp as the bright white dome of Thomas Jefferson's memorial—lifted, levitated, and set going gently around her head.

Whatever their particular stream of associations, many Washingtonians that day, gazing at the white ship, probably did something like this. They found a personal way to tuck it into consciousness. They found an order—possibly an aesthetic one—through which to understand it, just the way in which (as the English professor explains to her class later that day) DeLillo finds an aesthetic frame within which to place and order otherwise raw fear in *White Noise*.

To live and work in any major city in our time is to do this sort of thing pretty regularly, to assimilate unsettling enigmas via an essentially aesthetic activity. The novel the professor was about to teach, in this still-fraught post-9/11 landscape, a few miles from a once-burning Pentagon, helps her students overcome their all-American sense of immunity and removal from reality by riveting their attention to the truth of their lives in one of the only ways they can stand to be riveted: aesthetically.

Other novels also work to disturb American complacency and restore the reader to the real world, but DeLillo in particular has anticipated this strange form of consciousness, paradoxically stuffed full of postmodern confections and hollowed out by submerged fear. As we will suggest in a later chapter, DeLillo's genius lies in his ability to capture and reveal, beautifully, the complex contents of our particular postmodern consciousnesses. To read him is to find reassurance on a number of levels: reassurance that despite the sometimes out-of-control feel of the post-9/11 world, great writers can still shape coherent narratives out of it; reassurance that despite the tendency toward the uniformity of experience, individuality survives; reassurance that despite the dumbing down even of university culture, challenging philosophical and moral complexity still exists; and that despite the gaudy and superficial theatricality of so much experience in a postmodern setting, a quiet and constructive human interiority survives. Among other things that they do, aesthetic objects educate our students by appealing to their interiority, their capacity to complicate their own consciousness.

All of this the university professor gazing at the zeppelin is keen to convey to her students, whose avid and still-unencumbered consciousness is, she hopes, well suited to receive it. And isn't this, she wonders, one important way of understanding the pedagogical transaction in many humanities classrooms: an instructor, newly aware of the urgency of aesthetic receptivity, and a group of students, acutely responsive to aesthetic efforts to bridge the distance between their complacency and their fear?

In order to get this crucial classroom transaction going, contemporary professors need to take seriously their students' aesthetic responses. Yet literary study in our time is very much about the belittling or denial of just this responsiveness. In Europe and America in the last twenty years, the study of art in general, and literature in particular, has been dominated by social and political, rather than aesthetic, questions. The overwhelming question asked of artwork has been: how does this cultural production reflect or resist its ideological atmosphere? The very category *art* has been called into question by theorists who claim that elites have simply labeled certain forms of writing "art" in order to privilege them and the hegemonic values they express. Indeed, since there is no way to distinguish certain human expressions as art and certain others as non-art, this argument continues, we must learn to regard all cultural expressions formerly considered aesthetic as social and political documents and to judge them according to their social and political utility.

But just as there will always be those who believe art's thrilling intimation of an untapped plenitude within us and in the world represents a perilous unraveling of our civic will, so there will always be those who believe the intoxicating power of art inclines us toward civic virtue by invigorating our faith in humanity, clarifying our spiritual and ethical particularity, and inspiring us to do great and good things. For its champions, art discloses both the vulnerability and the vigor of people and institutions; however depressing its manifest content, its ability to move us to a condition of ecstasy as we lose ourselves in its particular forms of beauty offers an immensely important reassurance: beneath the mundane life of daily consciousness lies a deep source of meaning, a motive to action, and joy. Leonard Bernstein says of Mahler's Ninth Symphony that it is "a sonic presentation of death itself . . . which paradoxically reanimates us every time we hear it."[3] "The more pessimistic the book, the more pulsating energy, life energy, I felt beneath its surface," writes Aleksander Wat, recalling what it was like to get hold of writers like Proust in Lubyanka, a Soviet prison.[4] Wayne Koestenbaum writes of the operatic diva that she "interrupts our ideas of health, because what she produces is unnatural but also eerily beautiful. The diva, when she sings, exposes *interiority*, the inside of a body and the inside of a self; we may feel that the world of the interior that the diva exposes is a diseased place, but we learn from the diva's beautiful voice to treasure and solicit those operatic moments when suddenly interiority upstages exteriority."[5]

These observations touch upon not only the paradox of art's vitalizing effect upon us even (especially?) when its surface presents morbidity and distortion, but they touch also upon the oddness of the best art—its tendency to display behaviors, sounds, human types, and emotions that we've never before encountered and that often seem "eerie" or "unnatural." "There is no excellent beauty that hath not some strangeness in the proportion," writes Francis Bacon.[6] A sufficiently great artist may convey the odd, convoluted, unsayable substance of any person's emotional life. In Chopin's piano music, for instance, Edward Said hears a "speechless, contentless eloquence [he] find[s] very difficult to explain . . . there is, inexplicably, pathos and a sense of loss."[7]

Although difficult to explain, beauty's complex expressiveness and our response to it can be approached. In his 1973 lectures at Harvard University, later published under the title *The Unanswered Question*, Bernstein talks about how art conveys the ultimate human contradiction:

> [A]s each of us grows up, the mark of our maturity is that we accept our mortality; and yet we persist in our search for immortality. We may believe it's all transient, even that it's all over; yet we believe [in] a future. We *believe*. We emerge from a cinema after three hours of the most abject degeneracy in a film such as *La Dolce Vita*, and we emerge on wings, from the sheer creativity of it; we can fly on, to a future. And the same is true after witnessing the hopelessness of *Godot* in the theater, or after the aggressive violence of *The Rite of Spring* in the concert hall.[8]

Bernstein is trying to account for the particularly powerful impact of contradiction in art, for the odd exhilaration we feel on encountering in one complex aesthetic expression a full acknowledgement of death and a fiercely charged life energy—much, in fact, like Henry Miller's *Tropic of Cancer*. Miller's presentation of the pointless ghastliness of life becomes positively lyrical because of the writer's obvious formal and affective relish in the sordid spectacle—or, perhaps, because of his unsinkable all-American energy in the face of a world he describes as totally desiccated. It is the sheer durable force of Miller's outsized ego, his bold and transformative personal vision in a cancerous world, that delights us and that inspires George Orwell to call Miller a "Whitman among the corpses."[9] Indeed, after William Blake, it is Walt Whitman who most famously articulates both the aesthetic power of contradiction and the power, for the individual, of the acceptance of contradiction in life as much as in art. "Do I contradict myself?" Whitman writes. "Very well then I contradict myself, / (I am large, I contain multitudes.)"[10]

On one level, this commitment to contradictoriness is simply mimetic, a reliable vehicle of the truth of our lives, as the American poet Randall Jarrell, in an appreciation of Whitman, suggests:

> When you organize one of the contradictory elements out of your work of art, you are getting rid not just of it, but of the contradiction of which it was a part; and it is the contradictions in works of art which make them able to represent to us—as logical and methodical generalizations cannot—our world and our selves, which are also full of contradictions.[11]

the film features the rapid and complete wipeout of a perfectly inoffensive family (the two children are killed in a car crash; four years later, the father is also killed in a car crash; and shortly thereafter, the mother commits suicide), it might seem that, on the contrary, the film stares shit in the face. Yet the very fact of every member of this family dying violently within four years stacks the deck to compete with the dark imaginings of Sophocles and Shakespeare, while it leaves the film with a tragic human reality for whose deeply disturbing, nihilistic sweep it does not even try to account. Instead, the film lifts us up right away into a trite technicolor heaven where all that has been lost is gloriously recovered.

What is offensive in kitsch like this is one's realization that complex, profound, perennial ideas and images foundational to culture (death, love, heaven, and hell) have been travestied, reduced, tarted up, and expressed via a superficial and denigrating imagination. Whatever our religious or secular affiliations and convictions, we are liable to find the inadequacy of this attempt to render a plausible meditation on, and representation of, the deepest of human themes either appalling or funny or both. Kitsch is not merely outrageously inadequate, but in fact it is an outright lie, a denial of fundamental, anguishing, ugly human truths.

A focus upon bad art is one way of entering, in the classroom, into the question of what it is in great art that we love, that compels our attention, that moves us, that sustains an appropriate focus and seriousness upon complex and abiding realities of life. What do we look for in the best art? What precise effects does powerful art have on us? "I have more than once been surprised and embarrassed to find myself beginning to weep watching Fred Astaire dance, which is for me a strong aesthetic experience," writes Stuart Hampshire. "I have had the same somatic experience listening to Victoria de Los Angeles singing Schubert naively and without the familiar mannerisms of lieder singers."[27] "I was a crisis worker at an AIDS organization in the mid-'80s," writes Patrick Giles, when "some of us discovered not a treatment, but at least a balm: a 1977 album of music by an Estonian classical composer with the peculiar name Arvo Pärt, [music whose] relentless, severe, repetitive and deeply inspiring sound had a powerful impact on my dying friends . . . the music brought comfort."[28]

Certainly one central claim made about the beautiful, both in art and in the natural world, is that beauty discloses the most private, painful, unalterable human truths in a gorgeous way; it transforms distress into something glorious. Iris Murdoch believes that "beauty in art is the formal imaginative exhibition of something [deeply and perhaps disturbingly] true."[29] Mark Doty speaks of loving the art of "Hart Crane and Cavafy, Billie Holiday,

Chet Baker, Joseph Cornell, film noir: lush surfaces spread over difficult material, art marked by the transubstantiation of pain into style. Art full of anguish and pleasure in the racked beauty of the world . . . true to the world's comminglings of gorgeousness and terror."[30]

Unlike kitsch, art does not prettify heaven and downplay hell; it is that mode of human expression that both fully acknowledges the vile realities of mortal, fallible life and at the same time somehow uses those very realities as the basis for something enormously attractive and pleasurable. And one of the reasons that we feel invigorated by it, regardless of any tragic content, is that this sort of art encourages us to express, or at least accept, our own wounded interiority without fear. As Harold Bloom notes,

> The reception of aesthetic power enables us to learn how to talk to ourselves and how to endure ourselves. The true use of Shakespeare or of Cervantes, of Homer or of Dante, of Chaucer or of Rabelais, is to augment one's own growing inner self. Reading deeply in the Canon will not make one a better or a worse person, a more useful or more harmful citizen. The mind's dialogue with itself is not primarily a social reality. All that the Western Canon can bring one is the proper use of one's own solitude, that solitude whose final form is one's confrontation with one's own mortality.[31]

Powerful responses to aesthetic expression turn out to have something to do with courage—the courage to face up to what is most frightening, unharmonic, and mysterious in the world and in yourself. Murdoch writes that "art is close dangerous play with unconscious forces" which we enjoy "because it disturbs us in deep, often incomprehensible ways."[32] The power of art to make beauty out of terror somehow conveys to us that human beings have not only a complex unconscious that art can rouse in simultaneously disturbing, pleasurable and enlightening ways, but also some degree of control over their lives, despite the primal power of unconscious drives and despite the fearsomeness of the world outside ourselves. Art, with its passion and control, suggests that we can impose form upon flux, meaning upon chaos. As Murdoch puts it, "[a] deep motive for making literature or art of any sort is the desire to defeat the formlessness of the world and cheer oneself up by constructing forms out of what might otherwise seem a mass of senseless rubble."[33] Bernstein and Roger Scruton, two writers on music who disagree on much, use similar language to describe great music; writing about Brahms's Fourth Symphony, Scruton describes its evocation of "tragic feeling that is nevertheless utterly controlled, and utterly in control."[34] Mozart's G Minor Symphony, writes Bernstein, is "a work of utmost passion utterly controlled."[35]

All of this offers, oddly, one way of making sense of the following quotation from Richard Klein in his book on smoking: "Kant calls 'sublime' that aesthetic satisfaction which includes as one of its moments a negative experience, a shock, a blockage, an intimation of mortality. It is in this very strict sense that Kant gives the term that the beauty of smoking cigarettes may be considered sublime."[36] Klein's book is partly about how enormously difficult it was for him to quit, and it attempts to account for the aesthetic charge of lighting up. The beauty of smoking, if we follow the Kantian line, presumably lies in its morbid expressivity, its seductive acknowledgment of sickness and compulsion, its transgressive contempt for the healthy-minded strictures of the larger culture.

To get at the complex workings of the aesthetic, then, we need to understand the smoky ambiguity that compellingly beautiful things contain, their somehow exhilarating play between life and death, unconscious and conscious, disease and health. The most potent aesthetic experiences, we would suggest, are often provoked by those works of art that, like Purcell's "Music for a While," are essentially what Bernstein calls "mismatchings," which display simultaneously—in music, for example—a brooding, insistent mournful "ground" or latency with a "higher" more obvious line of ringing affirmation. The artist can make these mismatches match or make them play compellingly and fulsomely to our ear, even as their mismatch remains apparent to us. *Waiting for Godot*, for instance, manages to be hysterically funny in a slapstick sort of way while registering infinite despair about the human condition. The best art, as Bernstein argues of great music, "hovers between something and something else."[37]

Another American composer, George Rochberg, says something similar in his essay, "Indeterminacy in the New Music":

> It is said that after one has studied Zen Buddhism, "then mountains look like the mountains again and rivers like rivers." This implies a new simplicity which will undoubtedly come. But now, at a time "when mountains do not look like mountains or rivers like rivers," before we can be certain again, we shall first have to learn to be certain of the uncertain, to feel and to love where there is no apparent reason to feel and love, to live and act because living and acting are all that human beings are capable of. The composer is no more exempt from this than any other creative artist. This is the condition of our subjective freedom—now stripped of the old value forms—and therefore the material of our art and music.[38]

Instinctively we go toward art that offers us, in one beautiful, mysterious conveyance, the irresolvable complexity of our lives. In affirming aesthetic power and ambiguity, one affirms one's own complex interiority, as Koesten-baum suggests; one discovers the confidence to dismiss reductive attempts to flatten one's self and to flatten the world. As Alexander Nehamas writes,

> It is possible that spending a life, or part of a life, in the pursuit of beauty—even if only to find it, not to produce it—gives that life a beauty of its own. For in the end the standard by which I can judge whether my choices of what to pursue were the right ones or not is whether they turned me into an indi-vidual in my own right. That is a question of style. If there is coherence in my aesthetical choices, in the objects I like, in the groups I belong to, in my reasons for choosing as I do, then I have managed to put things together in my own manner and form. I have developed, out of the things I have loved, my own style, a new way of doing things.[39]

It is arguable that the contemporary American is less able to be receptive to serious aesthetic creation than ever. Even if we don't want to assent to the recent assertions of two French political scientists that the American is "no longer curious about the outside world or capable of aesthetic enjoyment," we would probably agree that there is—or that it feels as if there is—"no time to wander freely, no time to waste in wonderment, reflection, or diver-sion. . . . The imperatives of power and success, of hyperprofessionalism and the total mobilization of personal energies to a single project, sound the death knell not only of dilettantism but also art. Only the most utilitarian ways of thinking can triumph within such narrow forms of activity."[40]

If "experiences of the beautiful are distinguishable from those of desire or lust which 'hurry us on' to the possession of certain coveted objects . . . [because] we are caused to respond to particular things in a purely contem-plative frame of mind," then frenetic overwork in the service of materialism is not exactly conducive to aesthetic response.[41] And perhaps there's a causal connection in this picture of current American conditions, because our cul-tural moment, as we know, displays its own ambiguity, if a gross and obvious one: America has the world's highest standard of living and the world's high-est depression rates, the shiniest, happiest people and the busiest pharmaco-logical laboratories. One noted political scientist has called our extensively depressed America "the joyless polity."[42]

One film that has attempted to bring some aesthetic depth to this mis-match has received a lot of attention; its name is convenient for our purposes, but the characters of *American Beauty* (1999) conform almost too perfectly to the description of Americans that the French political scientists offer.[43] The wife in the film is a driven professional whose personal aesthetic is one

of beauty should be unafraid to acknowledge its powerful ability to move us away from matter of factness and toward social hope.

If, in the larger culture, people's fundamental disposition is one of conformist passivity and hyperconsumption, the beauty-lover's quirky openness to intense experience for its own sake will certainly seem bizarre. Many decades ago, social critics like Lewis Mumford had already decried the diminishment of "time to converse, to ruminate, to contemplate the meaning of life,"[8] but as Alexander Star notes, it is only lately that "technological consumerism has created a culture of privatized distraction."[9]

In the particular case of the American university classroom, what was once indeed a haven for wonderment and reflection for many has been invaded by distracting personal computers, cell phones, and other technological devices as well as by a worldly ambition, even in the early undergraduate years, at total odds with the unworldly quietness and patience real thought demands. Even the Ivy League now exhibits enough indifference to focused meditation to have prompted a flurry of protest on the campus of Princeton University: in response to a letter signed by eleven student leaders decrying the "lackluster intellectual culture" there, the university has formed a faculty committee to consider the problem. At Harvard, a student comments, "There is no reflection time whatsoever. I don't even account for reflection in my schedule."[10]

Outside the classroom, the "overworked American" (a phrase that is also the title of economist Juliet Schor's much-discussed book on the subject) exists in a state of manic exhaustion, a condition most in evidence on the roadways.[11] "What does it say about the United States," asks Gregg Easterbrook in an article about SUVs,

> that there are now millions of people who want to drive an anti-social automobile? Huge numbers of Americans will pay thousands of dollars extra for vehicles that visually declare, 'I have serious psychological problems.' . . . The antagonistic environment of the modern road is linked, of course, to the more general psychological predicament usually called stress. We are all stressed for time or money or achievement or sex, or at least we all view ourselves as being thus stressed; and the road is experienced as both an obstacle to the things that we are in such a hurry to fail to get and an arena for the cathartic release from this strain.[12]

In this sort of setting, in which road rage rather than encounters with beauty provides catharsis, closeted aesthetic experience is acceptable, if enigmatic; but testimonials to one's love of beauty and to the transformative effects of encounters with it are likely to be dismissed as naïve, sentimental, or crypto-religious. As Schjeldahl puts it, "Beauty . . . has been quarantined from educated talk . . . commerce travesties it and intellectual fashion demonizes it."[13] "Since the nineteenth century," writes Denis Donoghue, "in literature as in conversation, the concept of beauty has fallen into disuse."[14] Among art historians too, writes Jeremy Gilbert-Rolfe, "beauty is what serious people want to get beyond as quickly as possible when discussing works of art." The current "eagerness to get beauty out of the way," Gilbert-Rolfe continues, has to do with "the contemporary art world having de-aestheticized art and replaced it with a species of cultural anthropology."[15] The best policy when it comes to one's sense of beauty would thus seem to be don't ask, don't tell.

Nor does any degree of effort toward objectivity in aesthetic description and analysis make much of a difference. The "failure of the notion of beauty," writes Susan Sontag, "reflects the discrediting of the prestige of judgment itself, as something that could conceivably be impartial or objective, not always self-serving or self-referring."[16] Sontag alludes here to the now-familiar attitude that any position a person takes relative to something in the world expresses merely his or her socially constructed "subject position" rather than anything generalizable or rationally founded. Thus, oddly, the more lucid and informed the aesthetic testimonial—as, for instance, in the impressive work of the art historian Michael Fried—the more likely one is to draw the "metaphysical buzzword" objection (the phrase is from T. J. Clark, a Marxist art historian with whom Fried has tangled on this issue): the claim that one is projecting powerful metaphysical needs onto the aesthetic realm, that one's very language (words like purity, depth, fullness, authenticity, coherence, and presentness are commonly invoked) betrays submerged belief.

These essentially religious needs, Clark explains, arise out of Fried's inescapable class position as a bourgeois: "The bourgeoisie has [an] . . . interest in preserving a certain myth of the aesthetic consciousness, one where a transcendental ego is given something appropriate to contemplate in a situation essentially detached from the pressures and deformities of history. The interest is considerable because the class in question has few other areas (since the decline of the sacred) in which its account of consciousness and freedom can be at all compellingly phrased."[17] Wallace Shawn's narrator in his performance piece, *The Fever*, expresses this bad faith with utter clarity:

> You see, *I* like Beethoven. *I* like to hear the bow of the violin *cut* into the string. *I* like to follow the phrase of the violin as it goes on and on, like a deep-rooted orgasm squeezed out into a rope of sound. . . . I love the violin. I love . . . music . . . [I love] the city with its lights, the theaters, coffeeshops, newstands, books. The constant celebration. Life should be celebrated. Life is a

gift. . . . I like warmth, coziness, pleasure, love . . . nice plates—those paintings by Matisse . . . Yes, I'm an aesthete. I like beauty.

So far so good. But Shawn's narrator, unfortunately, doesn't stop there:

Yes—poor countries are beautiful. Poor people are beautiful. It's a wonderful feeling to have money in a country where most people are poor, to ride in a taxi through horrible slums.

Yes—a beggar can be beautiful. . . . Why not give her all that you have?

Be careful, that's a question that could poison your life. Your love of beauty could actually kill you.[18]

Here, the affluent American displays an infantile, passive emotionality that generates a blandly promiscuous notion of the beautiful: everything's beautiful, including beggars if you look at them with complacent eyes as just one more manifestation in the world designed to please you aesthetically. Shawn thus suggests a moral and conceptual equivalence between the aesthetic experience of listening to Beethoven and the act of perceiving poverty, with the obvious implication that the only legitimate thing to do under these circumstances is to stop listening to Beethoven. Under current cultural conditions, aesthetic experience *in itself* is suspect; it enables one to maintain a cozy, morally evasive life relative to a world of suffering. For Clark and Shawn, the very act of loving, deriving inspiration from, and seeking to explain experiences of beauty is an exposure of oneself as a bourgeois in bad faith, for as long as you *are* a bourgeois, you will not really be having aesthetic experiences but rather morally reprehensible narcissistic gratifications. This is a large part of the reason why beauty has, as Susan Yelavich puts it, "for almost a century [been] reviled as the province of the petit bourgeois."[19]

This is not to say that a straightforwardly religious apprehension of beauty represents a better place to be in a secular culture. Theological interest in aesthetics absolves you of bourgeois bad faith only to land you in what plenty of people will dismiss as pious delusion. Still, either way, one can hardly blame critics for their suspicion that aesthetic experience is often profoundly allied with religious. Personal accounts attesting to an original experience of the beautiful as key to the disclosure of the sacred are legion, as William James discovered in his research for *The Varieties of Religious Experience*.[20] More recently, the British monk Bede Griffiths writes in his memoir, *The Golden String*, "It was through beauty that I believed that one could make contact with reality, and a form of truth which could not be expressed in a form of beauty meant nothing to me."[21] A George Herbert poem and other forms of beautiful religious language propelled Simone Weil toward the church: "The proof for me," she wrote, "the miraculous thing, is the perfect beauty of the words of the Passion, joined with a few stunning words from Isaiah and Saint Paul: that is what forces me to believe."[22] The Reverend MPF Cullinan, in the 1997 newsletter of the Latin Mass Society, writes that "earlier ages with more instinct for beauty produced a liturgy that reaches parts of the soul unreached by the new liturgy."[23] "Salient in my memory is an experience of 'depth' that I had the morning I left Siena for France," the Christian philosopher Robert C. Roberts recalls in another typical sequence. "It was cool, and the sun was just preparing to rise over the city and the surrounding countryside. The streets were deserted. . . . As I walked to the train station with my bags, the glowing sky and the stone city below it seemed to speak of something permanent and profound, which I was on the verge of glimpsing."[24]

Aesthetic bliss discloses a world made radiant and vital by a mostly unseen but occasionally glimpsed sublime coherence—unattached in the mind to any particular divinity or creed—underlying the seeming contingency of the world. "I am sure that far from feeling myself degraded by my intercourse with art," William James tells his skeptical father, "I continually receive from it spiritual impressions the intensest and purest I know."[25] In Victor Segalen's *Essay on Exoticism: An Aesthetics of Diversity*, he describes the heart of aesthetic pleasure as involving a vision of "the diversity of forms and of things [as they] rise from some unfathomable abyss of unity."[26] Though the source and nature of this unity remains enigmatic, its effect on the observer involves the sudden conviction that there is more to the world than we have ever sensed before, that beneath the flux and immanence of daily experience, the world is animated by a steady source of meaning and value. The observed beautiful thing is the emblem of that somehow reassuring submerged coherence in its utter unanswerable reality, its stupendous presentness. Standing in the bedroom where his lover has just died, gazing at his face, Mark Doty writes of the moment's beauty: "All things which are absolutely authentic are beautiful. Is there a luminous threshold where the self becomes irreducible, stripped to the point where all that's left to see is pure soul, the essence of character? Here, in unfailing self-ness, is not room or energy for anything inessential, for anything less than what counts."[27] "What does it mean to say that an equation is beautiful?" asks Graham Farmelo in his introduction to a book about the greatest scientific equations. He answers that equations "can evoke the same rapture as other things that many of us describe as beautiful." They contain "universality, simplicity, inevitability, and an elemental power. . . . [They represent] something monumental in conception, fundamentally pure, free of excrescence."[28] The biologist Paul M. Wassarman clearly has similar attributes in mind when he writes, wonderfully, that "[t]he Graafian follicle of the mammalian ovary is a thing of beauty."[29]

James Agee, describing the houses of tenant farmers in *Let Us Now Praise Famous Men*, expresses the same equivalence between beauty and a purity that seems to convey unmediated, ingenious, and even somehow *mended* reality: "There can be more beauty and more deep wonder in the standings and spacings of mute furnishings on a bare floor between the squaring bourns of walls than in any music ever made: that this square home, as it stands in unshadowed earth between the winding years of heaven, is not to me but of itself, one among the serene and final, uncapturable beauties of existence . . . in this uncured time."[30] "I stand as though in the mind of some young, wide-eyed god, extravagantly in love with detail, and grieved by nothing under the sun," writes James Merrill of a visit in his youth to San Vitale. The details of the church "become steps in an argument so daring yet so crucial to the rest of my life that I know I must get it by heart. . . . I sit by myself . . . brimming with insights, free associations that sparkle my way from remote crevices of the past. . . . 'Childhood is health,' said Herbert, and here is mine, along with Christianity's. Merely to know that these early, glistening states are still attainable . . . !"[31] Rorty recalls his own "Wordsworthian moments in which, in the woods around Flatbrookville . . . I had felt touched by something numinous, something of ineffable importance."[32] Even the aggressively secular beauty-epiphany of Stephen Dedalus, in *A Portrait of the Artist as a Young Man*—his revelation of his artistic vocation as he gazes transfixed at a young woman wading in the Irish Sea—is permeated with this sort of religious imagery and feeling.[33]

***

The monk, the scientist, the poet, the composer, and the novelist all recognize the centrality of beauty to the profundity of human experience. They are a formidable chorus, and they are proof that despite the sense conveyed in university departments of literature that beauty is a topic whose time is past, one does not have to look far for evidence to the contrary.

Most telling, perhaps, are those voices among the chorus for whom beauty has recently come to seem more urgently necessary than ever. In the wake of September 11, writes David Patrick Stearns in "The Sound of Consolation," New Yorkers rushed to certain musical events, like the performance of a solo Bach piece that "embodied a feeling of being dwarfed by the enormity of recent events. [But it also expressed the] spiritual power that can be generated by the properly focused energies of a lone individual." The piece, importantly, both acknowledged the overwhelming nature of the catastrophe *and*, in the music's "spiritual power," conveyed something reassuring about the capacity human beings retained after the attack to generate meaning and order through "focused energies."[34] It was the kind of art that Doty describes as "marked by the transubstantiation of pain into style. Art full of anguish and pleasure in the racked beauty of the world."[35] Stearns, after September 11, wants "music that seems more infused with the divine . . . which means pretty much anything by Bach, lots of choral music. . . . [W]hat's needed isn't validation of sadness and rage—that comes through the news media—but something that aids in the adjustment to and acceptance of a world that's forever changed."[36] "Only those who are positively wounded," writes Peter Conradi in his biography of Iris Murdoch, "have the chance of learning wisdom."[37] The most beautiful art—for instance, the singing of Maria Callas— Wayne Koestenbaum writes, always has an injury in it: "The steel and wobble [of Callas's upper register] announced a predicament: we loved the mistakes because they seemed autobiographical, because without mediation or guile they wrote a naked heart's wound."[38]

This process of adaptation to a broken world involves both direct confrontation with the morbid and horrifying force of the instigating event and, just as importantly, reassurance that individual and communal abilities to overcome injury and reorder the world remain intact. In an essay of September 2001, titled "Mahler Was There Ahead of Us—How Art Helps Us Face the Unfathomable," Joshua Kosman writes that artists "take our ragged, inchoate emotions and reflect them back to us in more coherent form"; they help us "replace raw terror with a sense of awe."[39] "When we say a thing is unreal," writes the novelist Don DeLillo of the World Trade Tower attacks, "we mean it is too real, a phenomenon so unaccountable and yet so bound to the power of objective fact that we can't tilt it to the slant of our perceptions. First the planes struck the towers. After a time it became possible for us to absorb this, barely. But when the towers fell. When the rolling smoke began moving downward floor to floor. This was so vast and terrible that it was outside imagining even as it happened. We could not catch up with it. But it was real, punishingly so."[40]

Yet if it is incomprehensible, it is not, DeLillo suggests, omnipotent. Although the terrorists have temporarily seized the "narrative" of the world, "it is left to us to create the counternarrative" by letting the event twist our hearts rather than tie our hands. "We need," he writes, "the smaller objects and more marginal stories in the sifted ruins of the day. We need them, even the common tools of the terrorists, to set against the massive spectacle that continues to seem unmanageable, too powerful a thing to set into our frame

of practised response." "The writer begins in the towers," he continues, "trying to imagine the moment, desperately. Before politics, before history, and
religion, there is the primal terror. People falling from the towers hand in
hand. This is part of the counternarrative, hands and spirits joining, human
beauty in the crush of meshed steel. . . . The writer tries to give memory,
tenderness and meaning to all that howling space."[41]

In *Minima Moralia: Reflections from a Damaged Life,* Theodor Adorno
writes that in the wake of World War II and the concentration camps, "there
is no longer beauty or consolation except in the gaze falling on horror, with-
standing it, and in unalleviated consciousness of negativity holding fast to the
possibility of what is better."[42] Leonard Bernstein finds this strange new beauty,
evoked and shaped for us by the artist, in Mahler's work. "Ours is the century
of death," Bernstein writes in *The Unanswered Question,* "and Mahler is its
musical prophet."[43] Bernstein describes the finale of the Ninth Symphony:

> [This is] the closest we have ever come, in any work of art, to experiencing
> the very act of dying, of giving it all up. The slowness of this page is terrify-
> ing: *Adagissimo,* he writes, the slowest possible musical direction; and then
> *langsam* (slow), *ersterbend* (dying away), *zögernd* (hesitating), and as if all those
> were not enough to indicate the near stoppage of time, he adds *äussert langsam*
> (extremely slow) in the very last bars. It *is* terrifying, and paralyzing, as the
> strands of sound disintegrate. We hold on to them, hovering between hope
> and submission. And one by one, these spidery strands connecting us to life
> melt away, vanish from our fingers even as we hold them. We cling to them as
> they dematerialize; we are holding two—then one. One, and suddenly none.
> For a petrifying moment there is only silence. Then again, a strand, a broken
> strand, two strands, one . . . none. [In] ceasing, we lose it all. But in letting go,
> we have gained everything.[44]

Unalleviated negativity under the control of the artist, rendered as beauty,
conveys a disturbing, thrilling, and ultimately reassuring truth to us.

But it isn't a truth, according to a larger ontological argument against
aesthetic experience. All humans, John Gray argues, "think they are free, conscious beings, when in truth they are deluded animals."[45] "Autonomy," Gray
continues, "means acting on reasons I have chosen; but the lesson of cognitive science is that there is no self to do the choosing."[46] Clark's ironclad class
consciousness becomes in Gray an ironclad biochemical consciousness. Gray
cites the scientist Jacques Monod's summary of the contents of the modern
liberal humanist's mind: "'A disgusting farrago of Judeo-Christian religiosity,
scientistic progressism, belief in the "natural" rights of man and utilitarian
pragmatism.' Man must," Gray continues, "set these errors aside and accept

that his/her existence is entirely accidental. . . . 'He must realise that, like a gypsy, he lives on the boundary of an alien world; a world that is deaf to his music and as indifferent to his hopes as it is to his suffering and his crimes.'"47

Gray's nihilistic account of humanity in his book *Straw Dogs* is the latest in a long line of post-Heideggerian, postideological assurances that we are pointless animals whose delusions (that we *have* consciousness, that we can *attain* relative degrees of autonomy) and whose aspirations (that by putting into play thought and freedom we can change ourselves and the world) are in fact destroying the world. Because it provokes and sustains these delusional aspirations, beauty is an especially toxic cultural poison—it keeps us thinking we're humans rather than animals.

***

Given dehumanizing philosophies such as these, given the dismissive attitude toward emotionality they express, how can teachers not merely explain but also *convey* the sheer affective intensity of responses to beauty? They can stress, in their lectures, first of all, the reiterated testimonies of beauty lovers, one of whom we will cite and discuss here.

Powerful efforts to suppress the force and meaning of aesthetic experience constantly push up against the overwhelming felt reality of this experience, whether instigated through nature or art—a reality so transformative that it often provokes, as we have seen, dramatic testimonials on its behalf. These testimonials speak to what Elaine Scarry calls the "generative" nature of the beautiful: we want to describe, to copy, and ultimately to share our aesthetic discoveries. In the aesthetic moment, we are, as Dave Hickey puts it,

> for once, at home with ourselves in the incarnate world, yet no longer in tune with the mass of people who do not respond as we do. We now belong to the constituency of people who *do* respond—if such a constituency exists. Thus the urgency of our vocalization: "Beautiful!" Thus our willingness to accost strangers with our enthusiasm, to venture among them in search of co-conspirators. Thus, beautiful objects or events are defined by their ability to reorganize society by creating constituencies around them, and to represent for those constituencies both who they are and what they want—and in a free society the question of what a group of citizens wants is always political.48

Our intuitive sense that the experience of beauty is in some profound way allied with morality and politics accounts for the emergence, for instance, of what Allen Carlson has proposed calling a "pastoral aesthetics" movement, in which "an objective basis for aesthetic appreciation of nature holds out promise of some direct practical relevance in a world increasingly engaged in environmental assessment."[49] In other words, we should be able to harness our emotional conviction of the beauty of the natural world to environmental "caretaker" activism. And although some critics, like Rorty, will disagree that aesthetic experience has—or should have—a necessary relationship to the realm of the political, most everyone agrees with Denis Donoghue that "Beauty is a *value*, to be perceived in its diverse manifestations."[50]

We know in any case that we invest beauty with value when we recognize our intense responses to those few people who don't. When the composer Karl-Heinz Stockhausen called September 11, 2001, "the greatest work of art ever," and when the artist Damien Hirst echoed him by describing the attack as "visually stunning. . . . So on one level [the terrorists] kind of need congratulating, which a lot of people shy away from, which is a very dangerous thing," we recoil at the total disconnect between beauty and value that the comments reveal.[51] When Shawn's narrator in *The Fever* reveals that for him "beauty" is tantamount to anything that increases his sense of his immunity from suffering, we recoil. We sense, to return to the subject of emotion, that these people have trained themselves up in utter emotionlessness, in a fully realized matter of factness that allows them to make anything, even massive carnage in the case of Hirst and Stockhausen, aesthetic. Their vocalization, "Beautiful!" repels us; indeed it helps us understand the features of the constituencies with which we *are* affiliated.

Although many writers seem to agree that a central component of the experience of the beautiful in art or nature is a conviction of the *clarification* of life in a moment of frozen time, analysis of the experience itself tends to be, as Clark complains, fuzzy.[52] Testimonials, as we've seen, abound, but they tend to remain personal and therefore difficult to translate into shared experience. One modern critic, however, has examined his reactions to beauty with great care, and his account jibes so well with so many other accounts that it is worthwhile to follow closely a crucial passage of his on the subject, pausing to amplify his observations with the observations of others.

"In my experience," writes the art critic and poet Peter Schjeldahl, "an onset of beauty is marked by extremes of stimulation and relaxation. My mind is hyperalert."[53] This initial attentiveness, this tendency to be riveted by the precipitating object, recurs throughout the history of descriptions of beauty. Consider Henry in *The Tropic of Cancer*, who attends a Ravel and Debussy concert entirely by accident (he could never have afforded the ticket on his own) after noticing and picking up a ticket for the event that someone dropped in the Paris Metro. As the music begins, Henry reports: "My mind is curiously alert; it's as though my skull had a thousand mirrors inside it. My nerves are taut, vibrant! the notes are like glass balls dancing on a million jets of water."[54] Our tendency to sleepwalk through our lives is suddenly suspended by aesthetic experience, and afterward we are receptive to new ideas and sensations. The distracted American college student—distracted even in the context of the university classroom—should hear this about beauty first: it has a peculiar and characteristic power of riveting an otherwise wandering eye.

"My body is at ease," Schjeldahl continues. "Often I am aware of my shoulders coming down, as unconscious muscular tension lets go. My mood soars." Mind alert, body at ease, Schjeldahl documents the way in which beauty creates its particular form of mental focus by suspending not only customary forms of semiawareness but also customary anxiety and self-consciousness about the body. Iris Murdoch, among others, broadens this aspect of the experience of beauty out toward a moral argument, for in its prompting of an awareness that "something other than oneself is real," she argues that this experience moves us toward love, the very basis of human morality.[55] She later adds that "Art (good art) used to silence and annihilate the self. We contemplated in quietness something whose authority made us unaware of ourselves."[56] Here is a possible antidote to the narcissism that makes so many students resistant to the "unselfing" of aesthetic experience. But let us for the moment remain in the realm of, if you like, clinical description.

Like Merrill in San Vitale, "grieved by nothing under the sun," Roland Barthes, in describing his response to a canvas by Cy Twombly, registers a dramatic lifting of his mood: "[A] certain smudge at first seems to me hurried, poorly formed, inconsequential: I do not understand it; but this smudge works in me, unknown to myself; after I have left the canvas, it returns, becomes a memory, a tenacious memory. . . . [T]he canvas makes me happy, retroactively."[57] The staying power of aesthetic experience, its tendency to work its way under your skin and make you almost too happy, appears in one of Samuel Pepys's diary entries. On February 16, 1668, he writes of a performance of *The Virgin Martyr* by Thomas Dekker and Philip Massinger: "That which did please me beyond anything in the whole world was the wind musique when the Angell comes down, which is so sweet that it ravished me; and indeed, in a word, did wrap up my soul so that it made me really sick, just as I have formerly been when in love with my wife; that neither then, nor all the evening going home and at home, I was able to think of anything, but remained all night transported."[58] Likewise, Albert Schweitzer reports that when he was young something as simple as the two-part harmony in the song *In the Mill by the Stream*, "thrilled me all over, to my very marrow, and similarly the first time I heard brass instruments playing together I almost fainted from excess of pleasure."[59] The onset of aesthetic experience focuses our consciousness, suspends mental and physical distraction, and exhilarates.

"I have a conviction of goodness in all things," Schjeldahl goes on. "I feel that everything is going to be all right." We now move out of the realm of somatic experience (although we're not finished with that yet) and into generalizations about value: in the grip of aesthetic experience, the world presents itself as intrinsically good, as if it is reassuring us that despite its horrors human life is fundamentally okay. This is clearly what Rorty has in mind by beauty's "inspirational" nature. In *Within a Budding Grove*, Proust describes the same conviction of comprehensive goodness. Traveling by train to Balbec, Marcel sees a peasant girl walking toward the station in the early morning, offering coffee and milk, and says: "I felt on seeing her that desire to live which is reborn in us whenever we become conscious anew of beauty and of happiness."[60] Beauty kicks the world into alignment, prompts in us something that seems as far removed from the experience of alienation as it is possible to get, even as it retains the reality of anxiety: "Something connecting our bodies to our minds vibrates like a tuning fork [in the experience of beauty]," writes Dave Hickey, "and the sudden, unexpected harmony of body, mind, and world becomes the occasion for both consolation and anxiety."[61] For the Hungarian writer Georg Konrad, a beautiful view catalyzes the same happiness:

> Everything I see is mine, everyone I think of with affection is mine. The view from Chain Bridge or Saint George Hill is so beautiful, so satisfying that I can't begin to give it its due. But even just greeting a new day, taking a deep breath and stretching, pouring something nice and warm into your stomach, knowing that you can still move, that you haven't been downed by a bullet, thrombosis, or an oncoming car, that the horsemen of the Apocalypse have missed you this time round—even these things are enough to warrant thanks to Creation and Creator for being and letting you be, now, at this very moment.[62]

This sense of ownership of the world recurs in Hickey's recent account of the beautiful in the journal *Daedalus*, when he writes that "[w]anting to buy the whole world is the first condition of cosmopolitan paganism," an attitude of open, avid attraction to the entire world and its objects. "Beauty arises out of that desire."[63] In a similar way, Segalen describes his embrace of the tropics to a friend: "I told you I had been happy in the tropics. This is violently true. During the two years I spent in Polynesia, I could hardly sleep for joy. I would awake and cry in drunken joy at the break of day. . . . I felt exhilaration flowing through my muscles. . . . The whole island came to me like a woman."[64]

Aesthetic bliss may not express itself with straightforward happiness, however; in fact, tears—not of sorrow, but of intense emotion overflowing—are just as likely. "I have more than once been surprised and embarrassed to find myself beginning to weep watching Fred Astaire dance, which is for me a strong aesthetic experience," writes Stuart Hampshire. "I have had the same somatic experience listening to Victoria de Los Angeles singing Schubert naively and without the familiar mannerisms of the Lieder singers."[65] "If a performance of Couperin's *Troisième Leçons de Ténèbres* doesn't make you cry with its beauty, the singers are doing something wrong," writes a BBC Radio reviewer.[66]

One of the most potent triggers for this somatic response, as Adorno's notion of postwar beauty would suggest, is the simultaneous juxtaposition of horror and beauty. "The most beautiful Christmas I had ever seen," wrote a German soldier to his family during the Russian winter of 1942, was "made entirely of disinterested emotions and stripped of all tawdry trimmings. I was all alone beneath an enormous starred sky, and I can remember a tear running down my frozen cheek, a tear neither of pain nor of joy but of emotion created by intense experience."[67] The soldier's emotions are "disinterested." They lift him out of himself and his vile immediacy into what many of the writers on the subject, as we've seen, insist on calling a purer realm, and yet the achieved purity is possible only *because* the scene of devastation in which it takes place continues to assert its own reality. "Not a single house has remained undamaged in the town," writes Robert Graves of a destroyed French village during World War I. "It is beautiful now in a fantastic way."[68] "My dissertation adviser eons ago confided to me," one of James Elkins's respondents writes to him, "that he had cried when first seeing the Brueghel collection in Vienna, because he saw them in the still bombed-out museum. The entire scene really overpowered him."[69]

Tearful release from self and circumstance in the presence of the beautiful may be just as potent in one's private life. Grieving his grandmother's death, Proust's character Marcel experiences a consoling catharsis when he sees a spectacular orchard of apple trees: "full bloom, unbelievably luxuriant . . . [they] glittered in the sunlight; the distant horizon of the sea gave the trees the background of a Japanese print; if I raised my head to gaze at the sky through the flowers, which made its serene blue appear almost violent, they seemed to draw apart to reveal the immensity of their paradise. . . . [I]t moved one to tears because, to whatever lengths it went in its effects of refined artifice, one felt that it was natural, that these apple trees were there in the heart of the country."[70] Once again, what's expressed is Schjeldahl's "conviction of goodness" in all things—a conviction that the natural world is ultimately benign and that even at its most twisted, the world can eventually straighten itself out.

"Later, I am pleasantly a little tired all over, as after swimming," Schjeldahl writes. In *The Tropic of Cancer*, after the Ravel and Debussy performance, Henry puts it this way: "[T]here follows an interval of semiconsciousness balanced by such a calm that I feel a great lake inside me, a lake of iridescent sheen, cool as jelly; and over this lake, rising in great sweeping spirals, there emerge flocks of birds of passage with long slim legs and brilliant plumage."[71] Aesthetic experience dissolves you; the intensity with which it grips you exhausts as much as it exhilarates. "Mind and body become indivisible in beauty": Schjeldahl here echoes Hickey's comment about the harmony of body, mind, and world in aesthetic experience. He continues, "Beauty teaches me that my brain is a physical organ and that intelligence is not limited to thought but entails feeling and sensation, the whole organism in concert. Centrally involved is a subtle hormonal excitation in or about the heart—the muscular organ, not the metaphor." Here is the confirmation of the centrality of the realm of feeling in the evolution toward wisdom; here are the stark somatic aspects of aesthetic experience.

According to Schjeldahl, "Beauty is a willing loss of mental control, surrendered to an organic process that is momentarily under the direction of an exterior object. The object is not thought and felt about, exactly. It seems to use my capacities to think and feel itself." The supremely important displacement of the self in aesthetic experience is now affirmed; it is *the* key component of the production as well as the reception of beauty. "You submit to the text," writes Frank Lentricchia, "you relinquish yourself, because you need to be transported. You know with complete certitude that when you are yourself, you are only, at best, half alive. Even if you can't say what it is, you know when you're in the thrall of real literature."[72] "To understand a work, then," writes Georges Poulet, "is to let the individual who wrote it reveal himself to us in us. . . . to live, from the inside, in a certain identity with the work. . . . [thus] the act of reading has delivered me from egocentricity."[73] "Only [the pianist] who sinks himself in the emotional world of Bach," writes Schweitzer, "who lives and thinks with him, who is simple and modest as he, is in a position to perform him properly."[74]

In hearing beautiful music, we undergo a self-emptying and a correspondent flooding by the power of the exterior object. Leontyne Price's voice, writes Koestenbaum, "exposes the listener's interior. Her voice enters me, makes me a 'me,' an interior, by virtue of the fact that I have been entered. The singer, through osmosis, passes through the self's porous membrane, and discredits the fiction that bodies are separate, boundaried packages. The singer destroys the division between her body and our own, for her sound enters our system. . . . Am I listening to Leontyne Price or am I incorporating her, swallowing her, memorizing her? She becomes part of my brain. And I begin to believe—sheer illusion!—that she spins out *my* self."[75] This confusion of realms, Barthes suggests in describing what it feels like for him to play Schumann piano pieces, can be akin to madness:

> Schumann's music goes much farther than the ear; it goes into the body, into the muscles by the beats of its rhythm, and somehow into the viscera by the voluptuous pleasure of its *melos*: as if on each occasion the piece was written only for one person, the one who plays it. . . . Schumann's music involves something radical, which makes it into an existential, rather than a social or moral experience. This radicality has some relation to madness. . . . Madness here is incipient in the vision, the economy of the world with which the subject, Schumann, entertains a relation which gradually destroys him, while the music itself seeks to construct itself.[76]

Barthes here describes the ultimate self-displacement, having in mind Schumann's descent into madness; but just as importantly he describes the "existential" nature of aesthetic experience, the way it seems to transcend society and morality and move one toward fullness of being. Indeed, teachers of beauty should not shrink from suggesting that a growing receptivity to beauty over the course of a student's lifetime may well give the student a more valuable life. In his Orpheus poems, Rainer Maria Rilke was concerned to isolate precisely the quality of "voice" capable of producing this existential music:

> Real singing is a different breath.
> A breath for nothing. A wafting in the god. A wind.[77]

Much of Barthes' work in aesthetics, in fact, elaborates upon existential beauty's fundamental *negligence* ("a breath for nothing"), as he sometimes calls it, whether he finds it in Twombly's paintings or in Beethoven's music, in which, he writes, "there is something *inaudible* . . . [his music] is endowed, one might say, with sensuous intelligibility, with an intelligibility somehow perceptible to the senses."[78] Here it all is again, a willing surrender of the self to a powerful force outside of it and, in place of self-generated explication, a somatically felt conviction of an underlying, vitalizing, existential truth that flourishes independently of our perceiving selves but depends upon those selves to actuate it, to give it shape and meaning, to celebrate it.

"Beauty is never pure for me," Schjeldahl observes. "It is always mixed up with something else, some other quality or value—or story, even, in a rudimentary form of allegory, 'moral,' or 'sentiment.'" Although the charge of aesthetic experience typically involves, as we have seen, a conviction of the pure existence in the world of some world-transcending vital truth (the perpetual humanity of Doty's lover; the sacred vulnerability of the tenant farmers for Agee), the sense of the beautiful that has prompted this conviction is always generated *out of* the worldly—simple stories, sentiments, and morals. (This worldliness suggests a way out of the "metaphysical buzzwords" conundrum.) There is something here of Yeats's "foul rag and bone shop of the heart," the lowly origin of beauty's highest expression; it is an idea echoed in Merrill's Yeatsian poem "After Greece," in which, having returned from Greece to his American home, he longs retrospectively for Greek essentials— "salt, wine, olive, the light"—but realizes that "I have scarcely named you" when, instead of gorgeous universals, the grubby particularities of Merrill's own suffering life arise.[79] This disappointment prompts him to grab a drink, a drink that becomes a wry sort of celebration:

> Perhaps the system
> Calls for spirits. This first glass I down
> To the last time
> I ate and drank in that old world. May I
> Also survive its meanings, and my own.[80]

Beauty, in this sense, is the radiance given off by the "spirited" transmutation of contingent debilitating grief into an aesthetic "essential" that may, as Merrill writes at the end of the poem, help him survive both his personal meanings and the universal meanings embodied in "Greece." Beauty registers those moments in which we sense ways to become reconciled to the world; indeed, it registers moments in which we sense the possibility that we live—or can work it so that we may one day live—in a world naturally reconciled to us.

"Nothing in itself," concludes Schjeldahl, "beauty may be a mental solvent that dissolves something else, melting it into radiance." One way of thinking about the mental solvency of beauty would be to suggest that, when encountered, what it "melts" is the customary self and its customary methods of making the world intelligible. Beauty in art, for instance, *defamiliarizes*, as Roman Jakobson argues.[81] It makes things odd, or it reveals the essential oddity of things. When Harold Bloom asks what makes artworks canonical, he finds that the answer "more often than not, has turned out to be strangeness, a mode of originality that either cannot be assimilated, or that so assimilates us that we cease to see it as strange."[82] Looked at in this way, talking in the classroom about the ineffability of aesthetic experience is not a religious dodge, but rather a reasonable description of the way intense beauty feels and of the strange newness of the world that it discloses. Thus Segalen argues that the beauty that derives from the experience of exoticism "is not the perfect comprehension of something outside one's self that one has managed to embrace fully, but the keen and immediate perception of an eternal incomprehensibility."[83]

The ecstasy of experiencing beauty would then be the keen and immediate conviction both of the ultimate unreachability of the world's truth *and* the conviction of having just had powerful, if always partial, access to that truth. Beauty is the shimmer, the radiance, given off by the world as it lives its complete life beyond our perception. Highly charged aesthetic objects carry with them this sense of underlying complete life, which is why, for instance, Poulet writes that after years of looking at Tintoretto's paintings, "I had suddenly the impression of having reached the common essence present in all the works of a great master, an essence which I was not able to perceive, except when emptying my mind of all the particular images created by the artist. I became aware of a subjective power at work in all of these pictures."[84] It is why Fried writes that a sculpture by Anthony Caro, in its "continuous and entire presentness, amounting . . . to the perpetual creation of itself . . . [that] one experiences as a kind of *instantaneousness*," makes him feel as though "if only one were infinitely more acute, a single infinitely brief instant would be long enough to see everything, to experience the work in all its depth and fullness, to be forever convinced by it."[85]

However we want to characterize it, the realm of fullness and reassurance that beauty seems to disclose is, more than ever today, drawing us into its orbit. Its consoling, exhilarating, and clarifying truths—truths that were always there—now stand in profound and important resistance to darker realities. The contemporary humanities classroom should acknowledge and honor this ultimately political resistance.

CHAPTER 2

Beauty Barred

When humanities professors get down to the business of structuring syllabi and lectures around beautiful literature, they are likely to be discouraged. The discipline of literary studies in the United States, after all, has pretty much collapsed. The designation *English department* no longer corresponds to any institutionally organized activity involving written texts in English whose words intend to have much more than the pragmatic function of, say, political speeches designed to get out the vote. The very properties distinguishing literary from nonliterary language—metaphor, rhythm, formal coherence, complex individual points of view, thematic ambiguity, and so forth—have disappeared as subjects of discussion from much of the intellectual work that people who continue to call themselves English professors produce. Instead of this model of activity, we remain today within a determinedly content-driven analysis of a wide range of texts (only some of which are written) that takes place in essays and books whose function is frequently political: these works intend to shore up support for a range of politically and psychologically liberatory trends, and the literature the works consider often exists as little more than a verbal bolster for political positions.

Our department of English recently gave a colloquium that it titled "The Futures of the Field." The tension in that plural ("Future*s*") carried the weight of much of what has gone wrong in the discipline. We and our colleagues, first of all, are situated in what has long been called, and continues to be called, an "English" department. The name "English" designates a primary activity in our offices and classrooms involving the reading and interpreting of literary texts in English. (This would include foreign literature translated into English.) If we want primarily to involve ourselves with historical texts, we go over to the history department, philosophical, the philosophy department, and so forth. What distinguishes our department, as

Judith Halberstam says on the first page of her essay, "The Death of English," are the "appraisals of 'aesthetic complexity' through close readings"—not philosophical or historical, but *aesthetic* complexity.[1]

This model of the English department, and the canon of great aesthetic works that comprised its content, has collapsed in most colleges and universities. The value and nature of our reading (that is, when English departments feature reading at all—film, television, music, and material culture courses have displaced to some extent written texts in many schools) has radically changed, and the inclusion of cheap detective novels and poorly written political essays, for instance, is now routine in departments that used to disdain prose that exhibited little aesthetic complexity or stylistic distinction.

On the other end, there's also now the inclusion of notoriously over-complex—to the point of unintelligibility, never mind stylistic ugliness—advanced critical texts in our courses. A character in Don DeLillo's *White Noise* says of his university's English department, "There are full professors in this place who read nothing but cereal boxes." But there are as many professors too who read nothing but the densest, most arcane, and most poorly written critical theory.[2]

All of which is to say that there is no "field," so there cannot be any "future" or even "futures." That "s" in our series title tries to reassure us that instead of a profession-killing chaos, what we have now is a profession-enhancing variety, richness, flexibility, ferment, inclusiveness . . . choose your reassuring adjective. Yet when there's not even a broadly conceived field of valuable objects around which we all agree our intellectual and pedagogical activity should revolve, there's no discipline of any kind.

Instead, there is a strong tendency, as Louis Menand says, toward "a predictable and aimless eclecticism."[3] A young English professor who has a column in the *Chronicle of Higher Education* newspaper puts it this way: "I can't even figure out what 'English' is anymore, after ten years of graduate school and five years on the tenure track. I can't understand 80 percent of *PMLA*, the discipline's major journal. I can't talk to most people in my own profession—not that we have anything to say to each other. We don't even buy one another's books; apparently they are not worth reading. . . . [We] complain about how awful everything is, how there's no point to continuing, but nobody has any idea what to do next."[4]

The "English" department is typically, then, a utilitarian administrative conceit, and the "profession" exists only as a hiring, firing, and credentialing extension of that conceit. If we wish to say that we've retained disciplinary integrity based on our continued close attention to texts of all kinds, aesthetic and nonaesthetic, that sharpen our ideological clarity about the world (or, as Menand writes, texts that allow us to "[examine] the political implications of culture through the study of representations"⁵), then we have already conceded the death of the English department, as Halberstam notes. Indeed, since highly complex aesthetic texts tend to be concerned with personal, moral, and spiritual, rather than political, matters, we shouldn't be surprised to find in Halberstam an outright *hostility* to precisely the imaginative written texts in English that have more or less from the outset comprised the English department's objects of value and communal study.

Menand (who is himself a professor of English) notes that the "crisis of rationale" described here has had serious negative consequences. Among a number of humanities departments that are losing disciplinary definition, English, he says, is the most advanced in this direction: "English has become almost completely post-disciplinary." Menand has pointed out earlier the inaccuracy of another reassuring word—*interdisciplinarity*: "The collapse of disciplines must mean the collapse of interdisciplinarity as well; for interdisciplinarity is the ratification of the logic of disciplinarity. The very term implies respect for the discrete perspectives of different disciplines." The absence of disciplines means the "collapse of consensus about the humanities curriculum," and this comes at a time when rapidly escalating outside scrutiny of the intellectual organization requires justification of the expensive American university.

Further, "the discipline acts as a community that judges the merit of its members' work by community standards." When there is no self-defining and self-justifying community, English departments, Menand continues, become easy marks for downsizing:

> Administrators would love to 'melt down' the disciplines, since this would allow them to deploy faculty more efficiently—and the claim that disciplinarity represents a factitious organization of knowledge is as good an excuse as any. Why support separate medievalists in your history department, your English department, your French department, and your art history department, none of them probably attracting huge enrollments, when you can hire one interdisciplinary super-medievalist and install her in a Medieval Studies program, whose survival can be made to depend on its ability to attract outside funding?⁶

Halberstam acknowledges these effects and proposes that we "update our field before it is updated by some administrations wishing to downsize the humanities."⁷ By "update," though, she means provide a decent burial: "I propose that the discipline is dead, that we willingly killed it," and we must "now decide . . . what should replace it." In place of the "elitism" inherent in close readings of aesthetically complex works, Halberstam proposes an education in "plot summary," a better skill for making sense of what Halberstam sees as our totally reactionary political moment. Indeed, throughout her essay, Halberstam conflates religious seriousness with politically reactionary positions.

Now, a huge amount of Western culture's high literature involves religious seriousness. If, like Halberstam, you regard contemporary America as a fundamentalist nightmare and if your very definition of the American university is that it is, as she writes, "the last place in this increasingly conservative and religious country to invest in critical and counter-hegemonic discourse," then you have a problem. You either want to steer your students away from much of this literature, since, though perhaps not fundamentalist, it assumes a world permeated with religious belief (or, as in much literary modernism of Kafka's sort, as suffering from an absence of belief), or you want to present this literature in a way that undermines, to the extent possible, its own status as a document that takes religion seriously.

It's just this sort of cognitive dissonance relative to the body of knowledge English professors have been trained to teach that in part accounts for the death of English. Halberstam's primary motive as a university professor is political and social—she has situated herself in an American university because that location is our last, best hope for changing the politics of the country. Indeed, if there is a "consensus" about anything in many English departments, it lies here, in the shared conviction, articulated by Halberstam, that our primary function as teachers and scholars is to focus upon and change immediate political arrangements in this country; that is, one assumes a socially utilitarian attitude toward what one teaches.

This attitude is played out straightforwardly in a letter a Tufts University adjunct English professor wrote the student newspaper. In the aftermath of a drunken Tufts student's violent and bigoted attack on a policewoman, the professor expresses her bitterness against students in her classes who don't like her self-described "insist[ence] on raising issues of social inequality and cultural politics in our classrooms, perhaps ad infinitum to some of your ears."[8] Students must stop resisting her "overtly, perhaps uncomfortably, political discussions in the classroom." Apparently this form of student resistance is a general source of faculty irritation in her department: she describes herself recently "sitting in my East Hall office with some of my colleagues, discussing Tufts students' resistance to conversations about racial, class, gender, and sexual inequalities." The professor concludes: "The next time you are sitting in class, rolling your eyes when your professor 'whines about feminism' or, in analyzing ongoing racism and colonialism 'blows things out of proportion' or 'overreacts,' or (most cardinal of American sins) says something 'communist,'" students must remember that they too are part of the same sick country that produced the drunken racist. "Take advantage," she pleads, "of the opportunity we present to understand the world that shapes you," the violent bigotry that "characterizes our culture."

Similarly, a professor of French and Italian at another university complains that her "attempts to introduce contemporary politics into classroom discussions meet with blank stares." When she touches on the subject of the Iraq war, for instance, she encounters "mostly silence," which she interprets as "a mix of paralysis and anxiety." Students resist "'wakeful' political literacy," she concludes, "because they drink from the same pool of Lethe we all do." But since this professor is teaching a class on French literature, it is, once again, more likely that the students' silence represents a certain confusion or resentment that a class described as a discussion of *Madame Bovary* is actually going to talk about troop levels in Baghdad.[9]

There was nothing inevitable about this turn outward to the immediate exigencies of the political and social world, by the way. As Theodor Adorno writes in *Minima Moralia*, the intellectual is, more often than not, "cut off from practical life; revulsion from it has driven him to concern himself with so-called things of the mind." But this withdrawal also drives the intellectual's critical power: "Only someone who keeps himself in some measure pure has hatred, nerves, freedom and mobility enough to oppose the world."[10]

No one is arguing here that we return to a very narrow canon, to an uncritical piety concerning the literature of our culture, and to a monastic withdrawal from the world. Instead, what we would like to suggest is a return to the one discrete thing that our discipline used to do and, in certain departments, still does.

A few years back, in the *New York Review of Books*, Andrew Delbanco, an English professor at Columbia, announced "the sad news . . . that teachers of literature have lost faith in their subject and themselves. . . . English today exhibits the contradictory attributes of a religion in its late phase—a certain desperation to attract converts, combined with an evident lack of convinced belief in its own scriptures and traditions."[11] Delbanco writes that students still go to university "with the human craving for contact with works of art that somehow register one's own longings and yet exceed what one has been able to articulate by and for oneself." This craving now, more often than not, goes unfulfilled, because the teachers of these students have lost faith. In similar language, Robert Scholes writes, "As our Romantic faith in the spiritual value of literary texts has waned, we have found ourselves more and more requiring knowledge *about* texts instead of encouraging the direct experience *of* these texts."[12]

Notice the language here: direct experience, contact. The political and more broadly theoretical abstractions that have been thrown over the artwork from the outset, as it is often presented in class, block precisely this complex, essentially aesthetic experience. This experience, triggered by a patient engagement of some duration with challenging and beautiful language, by entry into a thickly layered world that gives shape and substance to one's own inchoate "cravings" and "longings," is the very heart, the glory, of the literary. Students—some students—arrive at the university with precisely these powerful ontological energies. Certain novels, poems, and plays, if they let them, can surprise these students, both with their anticipation of particularly acute states of consciousness and with their placement of those consciousnesses within formally ordered literary structures.

One of the noblest and most disciplinarily discrete things we can do in the classroom is to take those ontological drives seriously, to suggest ways in which great works of art repeatedly honor and clarify them as they animate them through character, style, and point of view. One of the least noble and most self-defeating things we can do is avert our students' eyes from the peculiar, delicate, and enlightening transaction we're trying to describe here. When we dismiss this transaction, as Fredric Jameson does, as merely "moral"—or, worse, as protoreligious—rather than political, when we rush our students forward to formulated political beliefs, we fail them and we fail literature. Humanistic education is a slow process of assimilation without any clear real-world point to it. We should trust our students enough to guide them lightly as they work their way toward the complex truths literature discloses.

**

The degeneration of literature into boilerplate for content-driven professors—into a sort of benevolent propaganda—has not only meant the destruction of any disciplinary integrity in English studies. It has also meant that American students of the novel, poetry, and drama, who bring to college an inchoate but often passionate love for aesthetic values, learn to view this passion as naïve, irrelevant, and shamefully apolitical. Students beginning to work their way out of adolescent self-absorption and toward a broader, more nuanced, more empathetic sense of the complexity of human experience are brought right back into narcissism by professors who value literary texts only to the extent that they affirm the student's ethnic or gender identity. Likewise, students beginning to discriminate between excellent and mediocre literature are handed horrible as well as exquisite writing as if there were no difference between the two.

The fate of a novel like *The Awakening*, its prose often indistinguishable from that of a romance novel, illustrates the point as well as anything else. Because many English professors read Kate Chopin's work as an inspiring fable of liberation from sexual repression, it has been canonized. No one appears to notice that, because it is badly written, it flattens the complexity of its moral and emotional situation. The obvious fact of its inadequacy to the real complexity of human consciousness is never mentioned, although students must be registering the weirdly undermotivated and overromanticized suicide at the end, for example. The same can be said of any number of stylistically crude but politically useful artworks: their absence of much discernable literary quality is ignored or unnoticed by a critic or teacher who cares nothing for stylistic and intellectual discrimination and everything for the prompt delivery of the right message.[13]

Likewise, when the beauty-phobic literary critic analyzes an uncontroversially *great* work of art—the example we'll use is Shelley's "Ode to the West Wind"—he or she ignores or minimizes the manifest glory of its form in order to exploit it for purely content-driven ends. Stylistic intensity and brilliance, far from representing the core of what makes English studies great, bespeak a threatening personal passion that the critic will disdain as at best naïve and at worst fascistic. This sort of critic presents us with the peculiar spectacle of a literature professor analyzing the best poems ever written by diverting his or her attention from everything that makes them great.

Consider Barbara Johnson's treatment of Shelley's poem. Like many academics, she rejects what Marjorie Perloff describes as "the idea of poetry as a language construct, poetry as delight, poetry as itself a form of knowledge and not necessarily a conduit for ideology."[14] Mark Edmundson has argued that, in a Platonic gesture, critics like Johnson have thrown out poetry because they regard its untamable spiritual energies, its lessons in finitude and impurity, as threatening to the sovereign controlling intellect.[15] Just how uncompromising that expression of conceptual power over the poem's passionate beauty can be becomes clear in Johnson's essay, "Apostrophe, Animation, and Abortion."[16] In a consideration not only of the Shelley poem but of a number of modern poems on the subject of abortion, Johnson displays the dominant characteristics of academic criticism directed toward poetry—the reduction of poetry to the critic's political agenda, which almost always means an attack on late capitalist ideology; the denial of autonomy, agency, and subjectivity; and a disembodied and circuitous prose that attempts to submerge under words the dry knowingness of the writer's philosophy of life.

Johnson sees her contribution to the debate on abortion as emerging out of her "problematizing" of the dominant cultural rhetoric that revolves around the issue. That rhetoric decides "who will wield and who will receive violence in a given human society."[17] Like Foucault, Johnson believes that culture is intrinsically about violence; it is really a matter of what form of violence you find yourself consorting with. The violence of abortion may be imperative when your personal development is at stake: "The choice is not between violence and nonviolence, but between simple violence to a fetus and complex, less determinant violence to an involuntary mother and/or an unwanted child."[18] Women poets who write about their abortions are in a position to subvert this dominant rhetoric with a poetry that represents a violent, metaphorical expulsion of the fetus for the sake of the poet's aesthetic and social freedom.

The clutch of poems on the subject of abortion Johnson considers are, she suggests, superior to Shelley's Ode, which she ignores as an object of beauty and scorns as an expression of the sort of babyish maternal dependency one would expect of a man. Just as Henry David Thoreau put himself out there in the woods, demanding of Mother Nature that she return to him his boyish sense of vitality and power, so Shelley in this poem—unlike the mature women poets who must deal with Nature as a real, life-threatening force—is unable "to achieve a full elaboration of any discursive position other than that of child."[19] All Shelley does, after all, is pray to a bunch of dead leaves to reanimate themselves and thereby the poet, whereas woman *is* mother, life-giver, and life-taker, and her poetry is therefore deeper and finer than that of men. Romantic male poets are stuck in what Johnson calls the "mama! mama!" mode of relationship to the world, in which they persist in futile demands for fulfillment, self-realization, and authenticity, whereas the literal mothers of the world, so long seen as powerless relative to language-bearing men, are in fact the world's unacknowledged legislators.

Johnson's bizarre insistence on the deathliness of Shelley's riotously vivid lyric, and her equally strange implication that a group of inferior poems are superior to it, is made possible by her seeming indifference to aesthetic values and her overriding commitment to political position taking. If the experience of beauty, as so many commentators have suggested, resides in large part in a sense of defamiliarization and expansion, of new worlds opening up, this essentially didactic criticism, which reads poetry primarily in a utilitarian way in order to reinforce an established liberatory social project, is beauty's enemy.

The cultural devaluation of beauty and the accompanying overvaluation of the self and its immediate circumstances are only deepened by the enormously popular and ever-growing Creative Writing minors and majors at American colleges and universities. Here the embryonic writing of undergraduates is treated reverentially as if identity affirmation and dramatic position taking matter more than mature emotion, style, and form.

In fact, Creative Writing courses are strangling other more serious, difficult, and substantive university courses. We review applicants each year for the English department's honors seminar in literature, and we have seen a steady decline in literature courses among our strongest students. Instead of studying Virginia Woolf, they are studying themselves and the writing of their fellow students. They've chosen to spend the little time they have in college reading stories written by fellow undergraduates instead of reading and studying the very best literature.

The implicit message that extensive university-level attention to students' creative writing sends is actually destructive: It tells them that they are already so talented that a large and growing portion of their university's faculty ought to spend a large and growing portion of its classroom time analyzing it, to the detriment of the literary tradition that forms the aesthetic foundation of all good and great writers. It tells students that they needn't spend most of their time reading and studying the prose of writers who have everything to teach them about style and content—that it's just as valuable to pore over their classmates' often immature efforts. The humility and patience that all serious writers need to have relative to the literary tradition is replaced, in overgrown Creative Writing programs, with a facile sense of one's own peer group's centrality.

But it is of course the onrush of theory in its many forms in the academy that has powered most of the acceptance of ugly writing and the univocal focus upon social values; and now that theory has begun to recede, or at least to be used more stringently and with greater skepticism, we need to be clear about the damage it has done to aesthetic understanding. We need to suggest ways in which a sense of beauty, and with it a sense of the "literary" itself, may be returned to literary studies.

***

There's one thing you can say for literary and critical theory in its heyday during the 1970s and 1980s: at its best, it took seriously the idea that the connection between various forms of imaginative discourse and social realities was tenuous, subtle, and difficult to access. The work of a theorist like Roland Barthes always acknowledged the fragile and enigmatic nature of writing, as well as the delicate linkage between the world of writing and the world of politics and social change. Barthes was an individualist who did not see the experience of reading as a corporate activity engaged in by likeminded activists looking for validation of their politics. Barthes recognized and hon-ored the essentially private transaction that takes place between a reader and a literary text; he saw the payoff of serious literary experience as primarily individual, having more to do with the clarification of human particularity and with forms of sensibility and repose than with the discovery of politically correct stances.

But the playfully subjective portrait of the act of reading that Barthes (as well as Jacques Derrida) offered, a complex and elusive act that left open the question of politics, has now degenerated into simple-minded, ear-nest accounts of literary experience as an act of ego building and position bolstering. The faculties of university English departments today gener-ally break down according to which ideological enthusiasm they are going to be promoting through the reading of inspiring novels: Asian American identity, Native American identity, and so forth. Professors often structure their courses in terms of the particular social movement they support. Many announce right away, on syllabi and in introductory comments, that they are "coming from" a particular political position and that the readings will reflect this. Moreover, classroom activity may involve breaking students into groups to talk among themselves about what they are reading, thus undermining efforts toward private engagement with aesthetic complexity. The popularity of "peer reading" exercises—in these courses and, of course, in creative writ-ing classes—means that students become accustomed to thinking of writing and reading as exclusively public acts, in which their work will immediately be judged according to how well it plays to an audience, how well it conforms to certain approved public stances.

Of course, identity- and politics-driven professors are unlikely to choose aesthetically and intellectually complex texts; they avoid authors like Henry James or André Gide because such writers are hard to read, hard to under-stand, and hard to categorize in terms of political and social positioning. But the difficulty of an author like James or a poet like Rilke resides pre-cisely in the *interiority* we are trying to evoke here, in their commitment to the clarification, exemplification, and deepening of private experience. The more successful a writer's grasp of actual individual human consciousness, the less useful his or her rendering will be for politically minded people, ever in search of broad consensus, policy conclusions, and goads to action.

Theory degenerated in America from the slow and nuanced investigations of consciousness and personal morality to slapdash sermonizing for other, more specifically national reasons as well. America is the land of attention deficit, the land of what DeLillo in *White Noise* calls "brain fade."[20] Social commentators now routinely characterize the country as "a-literate," which is to say that although most Americans have the ability to read and write on a fairly high level, they simply prefer not to. They neither read nor write very much, even in settings and during chapters of their lives when those activities are supposed to be primary. A small but significant number of college students, for instance, plagiarizes rather than writes research papers, and even some of their professors avoid the task of writing their own words.[21] The problem, writes Richard Posner in regard to proliferating instances of plagiarism among some of America's most esteemed and high-profile scholars, "is that we no longer have a culture of writing. Writing is now a specialty. So judges, politicians, businessmen, lawyers—and now it seems law professors—increasingly hire ghostwriters (whether they're called ghostwriters, law clerks, or research assistants) as specialists in writing." Posner adds that he is "one of the dinosaurs who still does all [his] own opinion writing (and of course book and article writing as well). But let's face it: we're on the road to extinction."[22]

In a postmodern society of the spectacle, where people are either busy being passively entertained by visual amusements or busy overworking, few have the time, interest, or ability to settle in for the lengthy act of intense focus upon language and consciousness that reading or writing a serious novel or monograph demands. In a culture where most activity is thought of in terms of its market value, more and more people take the attitude toward reading and writing of the hack, regarding their engagement with books and articles exclusively in terms of profitability and self-promotion. Can a book advance my career? My policy goals? Can it make me more money? How can I get it written most quickly? These are not the sorts of questions that move one toward the creation of serious literature. Such questions may be the necessary precursor of promotion to full professorship, but they do not guarantee works of scholarship that will be of interest to anyone beyond one's own exclusive and tiny field. Nor do such questions promote the sustained and selfless act of feeling and thought that enable receptivity to aesthetic experience.

DeLillo, among other important American novelists, has argued that the novel is one of the few truth-telling vehicles left in a profoundly mediated and stage-managed atmosphere; but even as authentic expressivity in the novel becomes terribly difficult for the writer to achieve amid the sophisticated baffles of our environment, the ability of people to read and make sense of that authenticity has seriously dissipated. Indeed, the fate of literature has been to *join* our simulacral world rather than contest it. Many theorists, like Jacques Lacan and Jean Baudrillard, have been allies of the simulacrum, deepening the damage yet more by assuring us that incomprehension and inauthenticity are inescapable elements of our psyches and our world.[23]

The retreat from interiority has meant the triumph of a grand, theatrical exteriority of manner in America: everyone is "out there," "up front." Experiences of beauty, as subsequent chapters in this book suggest, demand the cultivation of privacy, the appreciation of one's own and others' individual particularity, and an ability to elude the simplifying maw of popular culture. "I have my own cosmology of pain," complains the novelist at the center of DeLillo's *Mao II*; "Leave me alone with it."[24] Everything in our therapeutic, exteriorizing, solution-driven culture exists to deny that writer his own cosmology of pain; yet he knows that he will never write an authentic word or attain any real understanding of existence without somehow protecting his peculiar form of solitude from the perverse solicitude of a postmodern world.

***

One of the privileged, protected places for the cultivation of one's own cosmologies of feeling is the university. Nick Bromell writes that "the most fundamental value of higher education is the perspective a student gains by stepping outside the play of market forces and inhabiting, if only for four short years, what former Yale president A. Bartlett Giamatti called 'a free and ordered space.'"[25] Within that intellectually serious free and ordered space, the reading of novels and poems is arguably the quintessential act of intellectual seriousness, for they alone allow sustained and organized access to states of interiority. They and they alone manifest free consciousness, freely considered, freely structured by the novelist's own consciousness at serious play with the self in the world.

One way of understanding the experience of beauty, as we have already suggested, is as the disclosure of a radiant and exhilarating fit between the self and the world. For many people who have testified about their experience of the beautiful, it involves primarily this glimpse of an underlying coherence, of a seemingly natural alliance between the self and the world at a time when an utter alienation between the self and the world is assumed. "How," asks Czeslaw Milosz, "can one still the thought that aesthetic experiences arise out of something organic and that the union of color and harmony with fear is as difficult to imagine as brilliant plumage on birds living in the northern tundras?"[26] It is this complex intuition of an organic fit between the self and the world, primarily disclosed through the experience of beauty, through the careful reading of novels, and through observation of paintings, that liberal arts study should help students begin to grasp.

And it should not aim to do so merely for formal reasons. To sense the rightness of certain forms of being in the world is to begin establishing a sense of what forms seem wrong. The encouragement and reassurance we feel in the presence of beauty is easily contrasted with the misery and anxiety we feel in the presence of the ugly. Elaine Scarry suggests in *On Beauty and Being Just* that we can intuit things about justice, mutuality, and freedom from the experience of beauty. In *Reading Lolita in Tehran*, Azar Nafisi's account of life in the mullahs' Iran, she writes, "Unable to decipher or understand complications or irregularities, angered by what they considered betrayal in their own ranks, the officials were forced to impose their simple formulas on fiction as they did on life. Just as they censored the colors and tones of reality to suit their black and white world, they censored any form of interiority in fiction: ironically, for them as for their ideological opponents, works that did not carry a political message were deemed dangerous."[27] But this is not really ironic, and it is not new. As Orwell and others have noted, it's the novel of complex interiority, the artwork of human ambiguity, that affirms the existence of immense stretches of inviolable free thought and eccentric experience and that most threatens repressive political regimes.

The benevolent, repressive regime of the current American university classroom finds the elusive thickness and obstinate contingencies of the powerful work of art similarly threatening. This regime would apparently prefer to dismiss seriously beautiful novels as a form of escapism; its proponents imply that it is frivolous and indulgent and even reactionary to while away hours of solitary silence on Proust. But these hours in fact represent precisely the respite from exteriority and groupthink that American students need if they are to continue thinking of the world as comprehensible and themselves as subjects with agency.

It's important not to confuse the withdrawal from the public world of the contemporary American college student, wired to an iPod outside of class and riveted by a laptop screen in class, with the aesthetically charged experience of interiority that beauty catalyzes. A professor at Emory describes his visit to a wired classroom there:

> Throughout the class the students took notes on the computers, creating a ceaseless keyboard clatter and making it difficult for anyone to hear the teacher's voice. Worse, as they faced their screens they looked away from the professor and away from one another. The class had no sense of communal purpose, and some students scarcely gave the professor a glance.
>
> The PowerPoint remote control didn't work quite right at first—tinkering with it caused a delay—and students periodically whispered to one another about technical problems when they should have been learning the day's topic. One rogue was covertly checking his e-mail messages; another was browsing supermodel Web sites.[28]

Certainly the wired, PowerPointed classroom drives people in on themselves, but this is a mere atomized withdrawal, a suspension of consciousness fully at odds with the highly charged consciousness of beauty.

Yet the protection from strife and fear that all of that swaddling technology represents is well worth pondering in the context of our subject. Students at our Washington, D.C., university attend class only a few miles from the Pentagon and four blocks from the White House. In the back of at least a few minds here are images of the smoking Pentagon (visible from our English department offices) and of the plane that reportedly intended to fly into the White House. One can understand why the temptation would be to shut out all of that, to have a constant stream of loud music or images of supermodels with you at all times. On our campus, the American tendency toward distraction combines with a localized fear to create a particularly thin and disengaged consciousness.

One way to think about how to overcome that brittleness is again in terms of experiences of beauty. Beauty doesn't force a confrontation with the horrors of 9/11; rather, it offers an aesthetically coherent response to it that conveys, *in a way we can stand*, the complexity and magnitude of that event. This is why Terry Teachout, writing about the intense aestheticism of New York City in the wake of 9/11, can argue the following: "[A] few days [after 9/11], musicians in New York and elsewhere began giving memorial concerts to which the public flocked. . . . 'One greatly needs beauty when death is so close,' old King Arkel sings in Debussy's *Pelléas et Mélisande*. What Americans wanted in their time of need was beauty, and they never doubted for a moment that such a thing existed." Teachout argues, however, that this turn to beauty had already begun before the fall of 2001:

> It was already in the wind, just as postmodernism itself was not so much an era as an episode, a gradual transition from one cultural epoch to the next. What we are now seeing, by contrast, is the emergence of a genuinely new style for which no one as yet has coined a better name than "post-postmodernism." It was evident, for instance, in the growing willingness of independent-minded American filmmakers to engage directly—and beautifully—with the problem of postmodern relativism. . . . This suggests that when it comes to post-postmodern art in America, it doesn't much matter where you do it or what you call it, so long as the results are beautiful. And it is no coincidence that post-postmodern artists are increasingly willing to use that word without encasing it in the protective quotation marks of irony. "Trying to compose beautiful things, I say what I mean and mean what I say," explains Paul Moravec. . . . "The irony in my work is not glibly postmodern, but rather the essence of making audible the experience of fundamental paradox and ambiguity."[29]

In concluding, Teachout makes the political implications of this clear: "Osama bin Laden and his cronies, the ones who banned secular music from Afghanistan, would scarcely have approved of such talk. For them, as for every other zealot who murders in the name of a false god, earthly beauty is a mere illusion, a distraction from the One True Cause. But if September 11 taught us anything, it was that beauty is real, as real as evil, and worth fighting for."[30]

Paradox and ambiguity: how glibly contemporary literary critics have dismissed these words as holdovers from the New Criticism, as an evasive, apolitical attitude rather than a direct ideological struggle. But cultivation of one's sense of paradox and ambiguity is precisely what is needed to deal with a dangerous world. The ability to grasp both the privileged calm of campus life *and* the imperiled reality of much of the human race is precisely what an education in meaningful, beautiful objects strengthens. It is, in short, one of the claims of this book that, *pace* Jameson, postmodernity doesn't have to mean living in an unmappable world. The best novels and poems, the most inspiring creations of sculptural or musical beauty, stand there as they always have, as powerful modes of apprehending and ordering the world, even as the world seems increasingly complex and out of our control.

CHAPTER 3

"Aside from a Pushing World": Making Space for Beauty in the Classroom

"Good causes are regularly damaged by exorbitant claims for them, and by excesses in their practice. . . . The good cause, in this case, is the beautiful, which can be apprehended only by standing aside from a pushing world."[1] What does Denis Donoghue mean by this? How might the cause of beauty be furthered by "standing aside" from the world? Why does he think that beauty can indeed be apprehended *only* by standing aside?

Although Donoghue speaks in general rather than specific terms, we understand him to be saying something germane to both the reading and the teaching of literature in the twenty-first century. Our focus in this chapter is first on what it means to stand aside from the world, and why it might be helpful or even necessary to do so in the study and teaching of literature, and second on *how* one might stand aside or allow one's students the space to do so and what the benefits might be.

We begin with the simple assertion that some literary works need more space than others. They require concentration; they cannot necessarily be made to do what we want them to do. These works have an existence that is independent of our desires, although unless we are unusually selfless readers, our desires inevitably shape our understanding of them. These works are also often extraordinarily demanding of our time and attention. Here is the first reason why one might have to stand aside from the "pushing world" in order to read them: reading demanding works takes time, and it is time spent in solitude.

But true solitude is very hard to achieve; silence, albeit only an internal silence that allows for concentration, must be consciously cultivated if one is really to carve out a space for reading. Standing aside, settling down to read and only to read—not to make notes for an essay, or to skim for the plot, or to use the work in some previously determined way—marks a decision to step out of time and to suspend belief, as it were, in the world around us.

Another reason that one might have to stand aside from the pushing world is that it is this very world (we mean our own contemporary American culture) that nurtures the kind of self-absorption that actually hinders us from being able to read effectively at all. An example of this would be the notion, surprisingly widespread among teachers, that readers are best served by works about situations with which they are familiar or people to whom they can "relate" and that they are in fact either incapable or unwilling to read works that ask a lot of them imaginatively.[2] From this perspective, reading amounts to little more than a shoring up of the self, a reaffirmation of what one already knows to be the case. But it is our belief that "the anxious avaricious tentacles of the self," as Iris Murdoch puts it,[3] must be resisted if, in our forays into literature, we are to discover what a work, in itself, really is.

Of course, the paradox (like the Arnoldian echo) is obvious: we say that we want to know what the work in itself is, but at the same time we acknowledge that our readings of any work are shaped by our own reading selves; by our historical moment; by our various contingencies. There is, we often say to our students, no such thing as a naked reading—we always bring something to bear upon a book. Those anxious tentacles that bind us to the world are sticky and grasping and we cannot, at least on this side of sanity, fully get rid of them. At the same time, we can insist that the literary work "is what it is, and not another thing,"[4] and in order to learn what it is, or what it might be, and in what ways it might be different from all other works, we must first learn how to really look at it. To do this kind of looking requires space; it requires less, rather than more, interference on our part. In fact, it also initially requires both silence and solitude, although it is likely that silence—the silence necessitated by reading—like solitude will be followed by a desire for discussion and community.

Sometimes on college campuses it seems as though the necessary first part of the experience, the quiet and solitary reading, has been overlooked, undervalued, or simply not given enough time and space, while the second part of the experience, the discussion of the work and its public consideration, is too often in reality no discussion of our primary experience at all, but rather a broadcast of received opinion. Our discussion of the work frequently becomes the occasion for airing our expectations for it, expectations that have arisen from previously held notions about a period, a genre, or an author. Such discussions tend to flatten out and even minimize works in that they begin and end with an affirmation of the self. Students come away vindicated, perhaps even energized, not by the work itself but by our abilities to make the work conform to our notions about it. Such discussions are unlikely to result in much that is painful or evolutionary since their ultimate purpose is the affirmation rather than the expansion of the self. Their conclusion leaves students in a position of authority over the text, enjoying what Richard Rorty calls a "knowingness" about it that stems from their having somehow managed to deal with it and tidy it away.[5]

Of course, this is a far more comfortable position for students to enjoy than feeling that they have been somehow altered or knocked off their easy and virtuous paths or that they are troubled in ways we cannot articulate. David Denby recalls Professor Edward Tayler at Columbia University saying in an introduction to his undergraduate "Literature Humanities" course that the material the students would read in that class offered them the opportunity to build a self, because you "create a self, you don't inherit it. One way you create it is out of the past."[6] This seems like an honest beginning in that it foregrounds the essentially selfish nature of studying literature. It also asks the students to assent to two propositions: first, that the self is indeed to be constructed, and second, that literature can have an enormous amount of power over that self. The first proposition requires a degree of humility, notwithstanding its postmodern twist (the self as constructed rather than purely innate). It also brings with it a promise of danger, or at least of change. The second proposition, that literature is capable of changing a person, requires a resignation of control, as well as an acceptance that in fact a book might be more powerful than a person. It is not a position we are necessarily predisposed to assume, and it is not one contemporary culture invites or nurtures. (Discussions about whether the world is better off for the kind of selves that might be built as a result of such reading will have to wait.)

Approaching a work in the spirit of humility is not, however, the same thing as approaching a work in the spirit of veneration. Veneration is as dangerous as knowingness; indeed, it is its own kind of knowingness, a smug and also preconceived knowingness that the work is a great and implacable object, a monument around which one might tiptoe without danger of being sucked in. Instead, in clear distinction from veneration, it is the possibility of being surprised and moved by extraordinary things—what Stephen Greenblatt calls the spirit of wonder[7]—that we wish to evoke here and that we hope to nurture in our students.

In this chapter we will discuss some of the ways in which we think it is possible to create or enlarge the space within which the spirit of wonder, which is also the spirit of beauty, might be apprehended—ways, that is, to keep the pushing world at bay in order to allow the work of building the self to proceed—and ways that allow for the unforeseen to occur and for every class, like every reading, to unfold in unexpected ways. Before we do that, however, we must first consider what Professor Tayler might have meant by his phrase "building the self," and ask whether that is really the goal of the kind of teaching practice we mean to promote.

***

What does it mean to build a self? There's something vaguely repellent about the phrase, at least in the context of contemporary American society, in which changing the self is generally a matter of responding to social pressures. But building a self differs from toning the abs or working on self-esteem in that, like reading, it is at base a solitary activity, and one that has ultimately nothing to show for it. A lot of reading may not make you feel better about yourself and in fact will probably make you look worse. Building a self does not equate with self-improvement. The self is a private thing, and building it is a profoundly personal activity. Let us propose, simply, that building a self involves exposing one's mind to ideas about the world emotionally, spiritually, and practically. What happens as a result of that exposure is hard to say. Building a self does not have an ending place, since neither self nor building is ever complete. Moreover, while reading is a primary tool in this kind of building, it is far from the only one. One can attend to the world through all the senses, as long as one is mindful. We will confine ourselves here, however, to the role that literary study might play in building the self.

The phrase "building a self" implies a certain utility, and its metaphorical appeal—and perhaps the reason it gets trotted out on occasion—lies in its hint of practicality. The word "building" makes us feel more confident than we ought that our work of reading is constructive. Perhaps "demolishing the self" might be one substitutable phrase. Or "reconfiguring." Or "unsettling." These last do not have the grand and invitational ring that seems appropriate to an introductory course in the humanities. Harold Bloom's assertion that reading deeply in the canon can have no other consequence than to teach us "the proper use" of our solitude has less appeal than the more aesthetically optimistic varieties of the same idea that we saw in the introduction to this book, but it provides a useful check when we feel inclined to make too great a claim for the work of English departments or when we become too invested in the practical ramifications of whatever it is we hope to stimulate by intense aesthetic experience.[8]

"Building" remains a useful word, however, because it conveys the notion, to which even Bloom might assent, that there is some kind of developmental process at play in a person who reads a number of demanding and complex works. Something changes; some things give way and are replaced by others. By "things" we mean, presumably, beliefs, or values, or emotions. Perhaps a better phrase than "building a self" might be "growing a self"—not in the sense that the self is a seed, and we watch it become what it was always meant to be, but rather that through reading, the self might simply become larger, that it might absorb more—and more complex notions—of life and living. One is reminded of Elaine Scarry's thesis that beauty is generative.[9] It produces more instances of itself. And in that production, the self is intimately involved.

In encounters with great works (and even to write that last phrase causes a hesitation today: Should greatness be qualified by quotation marks? If we neglect the quotation marks, do we reveal our lack of irony? Do we show no indication of awareness?), beauty itself is produced, and part of what is beautiful is the self in relation to the work. As Wendy Steiner reminds us, beauty itself exists nowhere, but rather vibrates along a spectrum between subject and object, never stable, never wholly "in" or "of" something.[10] As to what the self might actually be and why it is or should be regarded as an obviously good thing to build or expand it, we venture that consciousness seems preferable, all things considered, to a state of oblivion and that knowledge of all kinds, including knowledge about the inner life of ourselves and other human beings, strikes us as more desirable than its alternative.

When we speak about "building the self" in the context of a literary education, therefore, we are referring to the self as something that develops over time and through contact with selves other than our own. Perhaps other terms than "self" might also do better, though the obvious contenders have their own problems: The nineteenth-century notion of "character" might have been a substitute, had it not fallen into disuse in postimperial postmodernity, and the less stodgy term "taste" seems somehow too flimsy to justify the laboring after it (taste, after all, has always been merely acquired; character, at least, used to be built). "Building a self" has for some academic ears pleasingly puritan overtones, inferring a hewing and a making, a transformation that brings to mind John Donne's smithy of a God in the workshop more than it does the taking up of a Wildean mask in the salon. Recall that Professor Tayler did not merely promise a better brand of cocktail conversation as the consequence of taking his course.

But ultimately it is not possible to answer in any satisfactory way the question of what, in the course of teaching and reading great works of literature, it is that we actually build—what a self might be, or what we should term the changes or adjustments or simple turning on of certain light switches that can occur as a result of reading. Perhaps one can only rely on a gut feeling, an intuition, that Denby's teacher was right and that his term for what happens is sufficient. Literature courses can offer the student a chance to build a self.

In the end, theories about the purpose of a liberal arts education come down to such statements of faith. But the belief that an experience of beauty is an integral part of the experience of literature, and thus an important part of building the self, does not inevitably or always run counter to the practices of theory that are also, after all, themselves expressions of belief. There is no way to be done with arguments about canons and ideologies and whose interests have been shortchanged in canon formation, but such arguments are extraordinarily useful in helping to define what we care most about; they also remind us of the great store of works that continue to exist whether they are taught or not. Arguments about canon formation also return us with unfailing regularity to the question, who decides what shall be taught? And, just as important, is the question of what will go untaught.

A teacher may once have loved a work, but perhaps he or she now feels that love inappropriate or hard to justify. In a tortured essay about, among other things, the rift between her younger reading self and the sophisticated theorist she has since become, Pamela Caughie writes that while she once loved D. H. Lawrence, she could not possibly teach his works to her own students given what she now knows. This is a first-class example of what we might term "hoarding beauty." In this case the hoarding is practiced by a teacher who has herself experienced the aesthetic power of a work but now withholds it from her students because of the work's disturbing, problematic, or wrongheaded ideas.

Lawrence, according to Caughie, is amazingly beautiful, but he can no longer be taught by any respectable theorist. It's not entirely clear from the somewhat elegiac tone of the essay whether she regrets this or considers Lawrence a necessary sacrifice on the altar of political correctness. What is clear is that she is hoarding not only the work but also her passion for it—a passion that would surely contribute in important ways to the complexity and necessity of teaching difficult authors such as Lawrence.[11]

Why and how a student might love a work—love being a complicated thing that does not necessarily connote unqualified approval—rarely figures into our thinking about how we might teach a work. Passion itself is peculiarly absent from student discussions about their responses to literature. One reason for this may be that teachers themselves don't always seem passionate. The very fact that "she really cares about her subject!" is a comment that students think unusual enough to be worth making in their evaluations of a class should tip us off to a dearth of passion in teaching. There are obvious and admirable exceptions, of course, and perhaps (we hope) in every department. Frank Lentricchia writes memorably, if somewhat narcissistically, about closing the door to his classroom and spending the session feverishly reciting for his students. (There must be halfway measures, one would think, but Lentricchia has the passion of the convert.)

Passion need not be limited to a teacher's in-class performance. While Bloom's insistence on the solitary nature of reading does not entail a second act of inevitably wishing to share the work, he himself might be said to share beauty more than any other contemporary critic writing in English, thanks to an extraordinary level of production and eloquent, accessible prose. Denby's engaging account of his return to Columbia University to read great literature appears to be largely and refreshingly motivated by a desire to share beauty. Unfortunately, and in contrast, the kind of writing about reading produced by English professors tends to aim at a narrow, rather than wide, audience. And our teaching is too often similarly narrow. Graduate seminars, for example, are often regarded as plums precisely because many professors most enjoy speaking to students who already know what it is fashionable to think, and who are comfortable in a setting in which the supposedly "secondary" or theoretical text is elevated to a position of greater authority over the work than the students' own experience of it.

The subject of hoarding beauty—of withholding our knowledge of or passion for a work—also raises once again that tricky issue of what primary, or literary, texts are chosen for those graduate seminars. In our own institution, when it comes time to take qualifying exams, students must often scramble to read the novels and poems that constitute the best-known literature of their chosen field but that have been pushed aside in favor of more obscure works. Professors have hoarded their own canonical knowledge in favor of teaching graduate students what is currently of scholarly interest to those professors.

Then there is the far more serious issue of selecting works for courses that introduce undergraduates to literature as a discipline. Deciding what merits inclusion in a survey course—often a student's only or last visit with some, if not all, of these books—is an impossible task. In order to make an informed decision, one must first know the possible contenders oneself, if only from one's own dimly recalled undergraduate courses. Important works are always left out because there is not enough time to read and discuss everything.

What works are important? Each syllabus necessarily reflects the preferences of its creator, but important literature does not always reflect what is most obviously relevant; nor should it necessarily be what students can relate to; nor must it be what they will, at first sitting, even like. There is a tradition of letters within which other works of literature may be understood, and in order to appreciate more fully what might be imagined in the future, our students first need to learn about that tradition.

We do not suggest that a literary education should not change over time. Some process of substitution is inevitable and even desirable. But we need to be cautious in our substitutions. Who is worthy of being a trade for Shakespeare? Is there another novel that can serve in place of *Ulysses*? If more great works appear on the scene, we simply have more to read, but it's a rare arrival that should convince us to give up *Paradise Lost* in its place.

The phrase "hoarding beauty" does not, however, refer only to the withholding of certain works from students whose only chance to read them in a scholarly environment is, for most of them, in college. (In fairness, the kind of hoarding described above really functions as a bartering system whereby one work gets switched for another. The question is whether the terms of the barter shortchange the student. The teacher presumably believes this is not the case.) A teacher may also be said to be hoarding beauty when she or he does not make time in class to address the aesthetic shape of a work being taught. This is, after all, what we as teachers are trained to do. Literature professors are generally not trained in philosophy, sociology, or history. We may have a deep interest in such disciplines and may draw in useful and exciting ways from them. But philosophers, sociologists, and historians will always do their work better than we do it, and professors of literature ought to be able to "do" literature better than anybody else.

What "doing literature" entails is showing students how a work is distinct and extraordinary and teaching them both where it came from and what has subsequently sprung from it. "Doing literature" is, by definition, opposed to hoarding because teaching *any* kind of fine and complex literature—ancient, canonical, or newly arrived—provides an occasion to share beauty, to acknowledge the powerful aesthetic experience that is a part, and a primary factor, of a work's reason for being.

The student reader may already have some sense of the work as a powerful force. As we noted earlier, we know that students are having intense aesthetic experiences, and if we do not hear much about those experiences, it may be because we are implicitly suggesting to them that such experiences are secondary to content. Or perhaps we imply by our silence that it is a given that aesthetic experiences occur but that they do not merit consideration or discussion. In any case, it is clear that students lack a formal language with which to describe their emotional response to a work of art and, importantly, with which to defend and explain it. As Emory Elliott puts it, "What do you mean when you say, 'That's a fabulous poem' or 'That's a terrific novel?'. . . . It's been too long that we haven't had such a language."[12]

The consequence of being without "such a language" for our students is too often an embarrassed refusal on their part to engage with the work at the personal level. In place of this personal engagement, they reach for an interpretive framework. This is where theory may offer itself as a means of speeding up or defining the critical response, thereby distancing the reader from the work. For example, before they read *Jane Eyre*, students might be told that they will be asked to undertake a certain kind of analysis of it. Predictably, the analytical perspective rather than the student response will direct the in-class discussion and even the reading of the work. Or perhaps, with students having been asked to read the novel or a part of it before the class, the teacher will lead discussion to focus on a variety of topics—for example, the peculiarities of the class system within which Jane makes her way as a governess; or the shaping force of colonialism; or the role of religion in the novel; or gender inequities; and so on.

Each of these lines of inquiry is valid, potentially productive, and arguably necessary for a richer understanding of the novel in its time as well as ours. What is missing from both approaches to teaching the book, however, is an acknowledgement of it as *a work of art* that affects the reader in a variety of ways. The primary reason we value *Jane Eyre*, and why it can support the myriad conversations we might opt to have about it, is that it is a work of art. This is not a particularly fashionable assertion, and what it means, exactly, is debatable. But before students are encouraged to discuss the cultural or political life of the novel, we might pause and ask them, as we might ask ourselves: What was it like to read this book? What did the language make you feel? How did it do this?

The questions are simple ones. They foreground the language of the novel and the reader's response to it. What should come first is a student's intimate engagement with the work and the opportunity to think about what that engagement was like. Formal questions—queries about *how* the work has done whatever it has done—can then follow as a matter of articulating that initial engagement. Questions about political, social, and historical issues should also follow, but not precede, discussion of one's reading, which is, after all, the initial way we know the work. And still later questions—What's valuable about this novel and why?—allow all kinds of theoretical play, including discussion of canon politics and syllabus formation.

If questions relating to form precede those tending to content, it is nonetheless almost inevitable that content will be arrived at eventually. It is our experience, however, that formal analysis gives students a much sturdier vocabulary and more specific textual examples with which to discuss the author's treatment of that content. Historical, political, and sociological questions then emerge *out of* the work, as opposed to being imposed upon it; such questions offer a variety of ways to understand the many complex levels at which a piece of writing can engage us, while what a work actually *means* may be distant as a destination, perhaps indeed never realized or even (our preference) attempted.

Figuring out what a work means is, of course, frequently the goal of undergraduates; their teachers, who share that goal less often, nonetheless may nurture a desire for meaning by proving to their students with critical acrobatics that works are rarely what they appear to be. For anxious students, the work of literary criticism is thus safer or perhaps simply more understandable when viewed as a form of translation. Figuring out what something means for them equates with turning the text into another language, always and without exception a lesser language that fits more tidily into their pockets and with which they can leave the class satisfied that they have "got it." Meaning as a single destination, or purpose, looms less large in the mind of the reader, however, when there are multiple possibilities generated by serious close reading. Close reading of this order pursues the many, often conflicting, interpretations of the generative work and avoids flattening it to make it fit any particular imposed narrative.

Close reading is a necessary component of literary criticism. Oddly, though, close reading is not something routinely or formally taught, or overtly demonstrated, so that even if students are able to identify their response to a particular arrangement of words, they may not be able to explain or defend that response by showing how it has been textually produced. Few teachers have demonstrated the powers of close reading more brilliantly than Stanley Fish, whose painstakingly slow movements through the opening lines of *Paradise Lost* have themselves achieved a kind of canonical status. It is Fish who most famously persuades us that a work of art *is* what it *does*, and without close reading we can never experience what it does, nor can we convincingly discuss it. Close reading, then, must be the first component of literary study, and teaching students how to read, as well as telling them what to read, should be the cornerstone of the job of teaching literature. In both we seem to have lost confidence and ability. To tell someone how to read may strike us as the height of arrogance, but it is only arrogance if we tell them what to feel or think about the work. In the same vein, it is a false and dangerous humility that causes us to choose a selection of works with the students' limitations, rather than their aspirations, in mind.

***

The next section of this chapter highlights some of the goals of literary study that we consider worthwhile but that have received little attention in recent years. We also hope to identify some means by which these goals might be met. Some of them, in fact, already have been identified in the previous section. One of the results of writing this book has been the realization that what we think literary study should accomplish—its point of arrival, if there could be such a thing—is actually what we think literature itself does to us anyway—the journey itself. All literature teaches us how to read it, if we are only prepared to be taught.

We offer no particular pedagogical theory, then, beyond our sense that perhaps we ought to allow literature to make its own case while we learn to listen attentively, instead of constantly telling our students to "interrogate" the work as though they know what it is they are waiting to hear. This metaphor of torturing texts is a sorry one and should remind us that subjects under interrogation generally tell what they think they are expected to say. The aim of these suggestions is to answer the question implicitly raised by Donoghue at this chapter's beginning: how do we keep the pushing world at bay and allow beauty into the classroom? With this in mind, then, we need to ask what it is that the study of literature should do in order to speed beauty's return. We have a few proposals.

The first proposal is that *the study of literature should help us to be other than what and where we are.* By this we mean that literature should assist in imaginative transformation. "Art," as Arnold Weinstein puts it, "is that other place that can become ours, those other selves we also are. The experience of art is a precious exercise in freedom, in negotiating subjectivities and lives that are not our own."[13] Whether or not we literally can or do become those other selves is irrelevant. Literature involves the imagination; it works on the imagination as the imagination works on it. Moreover, the study of literature teaches us to be other than what we are across time as well as space. Again, Weinstein: Art "is an extension of your life, a way for you to partake, as Emerson said long ago, of the commonwealth, to enter into the great bloodstream that courses through history in the form of art."[14] The study of literature teaches us how to be elsewhere; beauty is a means of transport.

Of course literature cannot really make us travel through time, through space, through race, through gender. Yet it is odd to think that one would ever have to defend the notion that the inner life is as real and as vibrant a place as the outer world. When we hear that playing the piano may affect the brain to make it more hospitable to the study of mathematics, we wonder at the resistance to the notion that literature might be transformative. What effect reading Shakespeare may have on the structure of the brain is unknown. Perhaps the transformation is very small; perhaps it has no physical component or is exceedingly temporary. But change of some kind seems likely, if only in the sense that imaginative travel into the consciousness of someone other than ourselves reminds us that our own consciousnesses are not the standard.

Murdoch argues that one of the hardest things about being human is imagining centers of consciousness independent of one's self.[15] The word she uses for this is tolerance, and she argues for the promotion of tolerance through the life of the imagination—the life, we argue here, sustained and encouraged through literary study. For Murdoch, tolerance is a prerequisite for virtuous action because it is necessary for compassion, for the kind of fellow feeling that precedes just action. But in order to have tolerance—in order, that is, to imagine oneself as anywhere other than the center of the universe—one needs humility, imagination, and something to push them to the side. We believe that beauty can be that something.

The second proposition thus emerges out of the first: *beauty both requires and helps us to move to the side.* What does this mean in the context of studying literature? It means something more than the physical act of merely moving aside from the world, as Donoghue suggests we must, in order to focus on reading. It means rather that one's ego, circumstances, personality, and so on must be made secondary in the experience of beauty. In the case of reading, that self must be demoted or checked before one can fully engage with the work.

But as we come up with that formulation, we realize quickly that it cannot be possible for the self to be fully to the side or to be put away. To shed one's identity in order to read?—it sounds like some bizarre and impossible psychiatric feat (what would be doing the reading if we were to have somehow successfully extracted the self?). A selfless reading is impossible because we are, inevitably, creatures of our own time. Our readings are contingent; no one can read with complete temporal or selfless freedom. Readers are culturebound; readers are burdened with knowledge.

And yet a profound and stubborn and oddly magical paradox remains. While we must and can only read in our time, reading, because it is an aesthetic experience, provides a means of breaking out of our stifling presentness. Perhaps it is less of a breaking out that we experience and instead a more modest perception of a glimmer of light from elsewhere. Or perhaps in reading we are made somehow less comfortable or are forced to revisit some notion or modify an attitude. This is what decentering involves, and as much as it is intensified by an aesthetic experience, putting the self aside also must occur *before* we can really get moving, as it were, before we can be taken elsewhere. The self must be relinquished to the extent that its motivation for reading cannot grow from a desire to affirm what it knows or already is. Thus we come full circle and must add a qualification to the second proposition: *In order to move to the side, we have to be taken elsewhere.*

Literature is not the only means of transport. But because of its power to decenter the self, it is a source of wonder and thus of beauty. Murdoch, who introduces this notion in "The Sovereignty of Good over Other Concepts," claims that the "most obvious thing in our surroundings which is an occasion for 'unselfing' . . . is what is popularly called 'beauty.'"[16] Scarry's term for unselfing, or decentering, is "opiated adjacency"; she writes that "[a] beautiful thing is not the only thing in the world that can make us feel adjacent; nor is it the only thing in the world that brings a state of acute pleasure. But it appears to be one of the few phenomena in the world that brings about both simultaneously: it permits us to be adjacent while also permitting us to experience extreme pleasure, thereby creating the sense that it is our own adjacency that is pleasure-bearing."[17]

We agree with Murdoch that "anything which alters consciousness in the direction of unselfishness, objectivity and realism is to be connected with virtue."[18] We think it is probable that intense aesthetic experience of any kind may alter consciousness in the ways that Murdoch describes and that through such experiences we are led toward "a progressive revelation of something which exists independently of me."[19] We believe that great literature can do this and that this apprehension of goodness outside ourselves—not created by us—is itself a good thing.

But critical practices as they are often taught in universities today don't make much occasion for altering consciousness, nor do they model humility. To be humble—that is, to be open to surprise and receptive to wonder as opposed to being forearmed and foreknowing—is to be out of step with contemporary thinking about what it means to be a sophisticated reader. Our argument is that students should not be taught to approach works with anything other than curiosity and an openness to experience. Clarity of vision—the kind of clarity needed to make judgments, defend evaluations, and choose what works one will retain for one's own personal canon—is more likely if decentering is possible. It ought to be easier to consider what a work is if one's own anxieties and neuroses are kept at bay. And to keep them from the center of one's study, to make oneself secondary—to assume adjacency—is to be humble. Humility is thus more than an attitude with which to approach the text; it is a prerequisite for clear-sightedness. "The humble man," writes Murdoch, "because he sees himself as nothing, can see other things as they are."[20]

If there is anything that ought to be the goal of literary study, surely it is this. Literary study can help us to see things as they are, not just the works themselves but also the world with which those works engage. It seems perverse to imagine an argument in defense of the opposite—that reading great

works cannot help us to see things as they are. Imagine an introductory literature course that began with that depressing assertion. Such a viewpoint, however, does exist, and it even thrives in many college classrooms, resting largely
upon a drearily relativist belief that because things are really not absolutely or
only one way or another, it is therefore misguided to try and see what a thing
"really" is, since a thing isn't really anything at all.

We would accept the first part of that belief: experience teaches us that
complexity and density in art results in, let's say, a poem being many things
and not one thing only. Indeed, we would argue that a good poem is by definition many things. If we say that we should try to see poems "as they are,"
we refer not to the act of interpretation, but rather to the ways in which we
are able to recognize that any poem is itself only and not another poem. One
can add a whole list of other possible outcomes of seeing a work as it is: being
able to assert the value or merits of the work; to see in it the very poems it
is not and thus to understand it in its literary-historical tradition; or in the
case of a recent work, to posit the potential of the poem to outlast its author's
generation—and so on. Mention of value, merit, and the projected survival
of the work through time are logically excised from the classroom conversation as soon as a teacher decides that a work cannot really be anything at all
because it is so busy being many other things that it has no intrinsic being of
its own but is a mere reflection of its reader's needs and desires.

Close and attentive reading teaches us otherwise. To deny the uniqueness
of an aesthetic experience is also to deny the inner life of the reader. No two
readings of *Mrs. Dalloway* are the same, but this doesn't mean that *Mrs. Dalloway* has no real existence worth examination. The real existence of *Mrs.
Dalloway* can be examined on the page, in class, as a close and exhilarating
experience. What *Mrs. Dalloway* is *as a work of art* can be the subject of discussion as readers see what the work does and does not do; as they discover
where history and politics and language shape all the possibilities of reading
the work; as they read, and read closely, the novel before them.

This brings us to our third proposal: *beauty demands that we pay attention.* The precursor to clearing "our minds of selfish care," as Murdoch has
it, is attentiveness. Attentiveness in reading requires that one read slowly.
Donoghue is explicit: "Aesthetic reading is the slowest reading possible."[21]
One can be open-minded, adjacent, curious, and all the rest, but if one reads
carelessly or too quickly or without an ear to the rhythm that the author is
establishing, one may as well read anything at all. Of course, one can profit-
ably apply one's reading techniques to anything at all, and the worst New
Historicism, in sharp distinction from the best, is founded upon this theory.
But we talk here of self-consciously aesthetic reading, not the reading that is

really a hunt for historical or political information or indeed for anything at all other than the sound of the words and the imagery they create in one's mind. Donoghue would presumably put this activity before our second proposition (that beauty requires and helps us to move to the side), since he claims that "reading . . . aesthetically will clear a little space in one's mind for disinterestedness."[22]

Close reading, the practice in which we focus on the language and its shapes before doing anything else, is adjacency's accomplice; as a practice it requires that we allow the work to be what it is. Fine teaching is also grounded upon close reading, but since fine teaching is not all that is required for getting tenure or being promoted, close reading may or may not be the center of classroom experience. All truly excellent scholarship, however, also begins with close reading, and any discussion of literature is always most persuasive when it starts life as textual analysis.

Our fourth proposal, therefore, is that, in the context of literary studies, *paying attention to a literary work means close reading*. If we fail to teach students how to close read and fail to perform close reading ourselves—publicly, in the classroom, aloud, in front of students as well as with them—we are not demonstrating the craft in which we have been trained and which ought to make English majors superior readers and writers of demanding works. Professors of literature ought to be able to close read better than anybody else. Before we teach students how to do research or provide them with ways of approaching a work, we should first show them *how* to read and then make them do it.

What this means in the crudest sense is that teachers of literature need to teach students how to talk about the words in front of them. Fish has noted famously (and correctly, in our view) that a work is what it does; but if students lack any formal terminology or knowledge of literary devices, how are they to describe what it does? Presumably in many cases it is a sense of feeling underequipped to discuss what a work *does* that forces many students to retreat into a helpless relativism or to refuse to evaluate the work in any way beyond the merely subjective.

In our insistence that close reading take precedence over all theorizing and hypothesis, then, are we advocating for the old New Criticism, a return to the study of literature divorced from history as it was practiced for perhaps two-thirds of the last century? Emphatically, we are not. Certainly, all effective close reading depends in vital ways upon the skills of formalism—the ability to read a work closely by looking at the work as an organic and self-contained form. But New Critics argued that everything necessary to understand a work is present to the work, and while that argument is certainly defensible, the phrase "what is necessary" strikes us as somehow lesser than the idea of what might prove useful, suggestive, or enriching as we read. Moreover, if we really believe that a work is what it does, then we are also committed to the belief that not everything that a work does can be grasped by a study of its immediate textual presence. Readers reading bring both life and change to a work. Our preference is for a reading that begins with no clear borders drawn up around the work and with no preset limitations or expectations; our ideal reading has but one golden rule: it should begin by paying close attention to what is written. What follows depends upon the reader and whatever kind of theory, political interests, historical knowledge, or biographical information he or she may pursue.

One way of thinking about this is to recall Greenblatt's observation that "[w]onder has not been alien to literary criticism, but it has been associated (if only implicitly) with formalism rather than historicism."[23] For the term "wonder," we would substitute "beauty," but we think Greenblatt is right. Further, we think the association of beauty with New Criticism and its closed, prescribed, and goal-oriented readings has been harmful. Greenblatt regrets the loss of wonder that seems to occur when New Historicism focuses on the "resonance" of a literary work or related object—what and how the artifact has come to mean during the passage of time. He writes that far from ignoring or doing away with the wonder that has led him to fine works and objects in the first place, his desire as an historicist is in fact "to extend this wonder beyond the formal boundaries of works of art, just as [he wishes] to intensify resonance within those boundaries."[24] There's no law against either, of course, but perhaps one of the most telling observations made by Greenblatt in this essay is his admission that "it is easier to pass from wonder to resonance than from resonance to wonder."[25] To put it more baldly, it is harder to experience the beauty of something if one comes to it only after it has been theorized. For that reason alone, let the beauty, or wonder, be felt first; then let us investigate how and what, exactly, its object has come to work upon us.

What this means in terms of the classroom is that *the study of form, part of close reading, should generally precede that of content.* This is our fifth proposal. We say "generally" rather than "always" precede because while it is usually the case that examination of form will lead to a richer discussion of content, it also happens that subject matter can be so overwhelming that it's difficult to keep it at bay. We would argue that an intensified focus on form in such cases can actually help students to acknowledge their immediate emotional responses to the material and to consider why they may feel conflicted about a work. But occasionally what the work seems to be "about" at first reading cannot be held at arms' length, and then presumably the force of the subject itself would lead discussion, at least until a time when readers might pause to consider how that subject is presented to them.

Many of the common arguments against formalism have already been addressed in this chapter or the one preceding it because they are in fact very close to the arguments against beauty: like beauty, formalism is held to conspire "with the totalitarian zeal of the eye, the gaze; . . . in literary criticism it is so obsessed with the autonomy of the poem that it ignores the tendency of words to sprawl beyond their formal limits; and . . . a concern for beauty of form is an elitist satisfaction, morally disgusting while people are dying of hunger and disease." But as Donoghue goes on to add, "These arguments imply a claim for art that no serious critic makes. No one claims that a great symphony makes redundant the work of dentists, doctors, physicist, biologists, or politicians. Such a symphony makes the world a better place, richer in possibility and spirit; listening to it does not make people better or worse."[26]

In this Donoghue aligns himself with Bloom; he believes that while the world is better off for its great works, readers are not necessarily better off for having read them. Scarry's position is more provocative, as we saw earlier, in that she posits a relationship between beauty and justice—a direct bond between the aesthetic and the moral good. In Scarry's world, the individual will likely be improved by contact with great art. Beauty, she insists, does a person good by sensitizing him or her to the world outside.

This is a profoundly difficult belief to defend, in large part because it is so easy to imagine two other things that might occur as a result of an encounter with beauty. First, if one believes that beauty can change someone, why might it not be for the worse? Second, if beauty really teaches us sensitivity and inspires us to move outward toward compassion, how are we to account for the gruesome image of cruelty at work in the midst of beauty? One imagines a torturer who listens to arias or recites poetry as he works, a situation where there seems to be a complete disconnect between what the torturer experiences aesthetically and what he is still able to perform. This would be the beauty as distraction or anesthesia argument—and the torturer is an instance of the evil aesthete, the true decadent.

These are serious problems for anyone who defends beauty, and they are even more serious for a person who wants to claim that beauty has moral utility—that it does us good and is good for us. The two questions posed here raise important issues that need to be acknowledged and explored. Perhaps such questions are not wholly answerable, but our argument in this book is that it is time for us to take up such vast and unanswerable questions again. We should have a greater confidence in the extraordinary possibilities of art, and we should be prepared to make extraordinary claims on its behalf as well as to defend the significance of our responses to it. We echo Simon Jarvis when he attacks "the widespread assumption that the difficulties associated with such aporetic categories as nature, subjectivity, beauty, goodness and truth can be overcome simply by suppressing, avoiding, or junking those categories—or by subjecting them to 'ideology-critique,' that is to say, to ideology."[27] We should not avoid beauty because it is difficult, because the questions it raises make us uncomfortable, or because our answers fall short of a complete accounting.

With regard to the first question, whether a great work of literature could make someone worse rather than better, there are all kinds of ways to go. One could argue that a corrupting work (think of Dorian Gray's yellow book) could not in fact be a great work at all and that greatness by definition does not corrupt but rather instructs its reader in the workings of corruption or of the corrupt mind. Alternatively, one could argue that a great work on an evil topic might make its reader less good and that if literature has the power to change us, it can surely change us for worse as well as for better. A third argument might hold that literature changes nobody for better or for worse. That last position, with all due respect to Bloom and Donoghue, seems weakest of all in that it doesn't ring true to experience and seems merely to offer a safe haven for those who would rather not tackle all the problematic ramifications of arguing for either of the first two positions.

The second question—the one that holds before us the cruel man whose love of fine music appears not to have taught him compassion at all—must also be addressed. Scarry does not fully acknowledge the darker side of beauty, but war movies express it to disturbing effect, from the Valkyries music as a soundtrack to bombs falling on Vietnamese villages (*Apocalypse Now*) to the technical delights of classical piano accompanying the massacre of Jews in the Warsaw ghetto (*Schindler's List*).

Do images of beauty in the company and service of evil wholly undermine any claims we might make on beauty's behalf for goodness? It would be foolish to ignore this question, though perhaps even more foolish to believe that one could answer it in any satisfactory way. The relationship between beauty and evil is surely as complex as that between beauty and goodness; the complexity need not scare us away from the consideration of either. One of the problems for Scarry's argument is that human beings are, as Murdoch puts it, "admittedly specialised creatures where morality is concerned and merit in one area does not seem to guarantee merit in another. The good artist is not necessarily wise at home, and the concentration camp guard can be a kindly father."[28] We can thrill to the music while we drop the bombs; play the piano and shoot families; and go home afterwards as dutiful children to aging parents.[29]

In the course of teaching the undergraduate seminar on beauty out of which this book grew, we have frequently discussed these issues, both in class and out of it, one of us usually admonishing the other that, after all, these are extreme examples, and their very extremity lessens the importance of dealing with them. Most people, this same one of us says, are not opera-loving torturers or Nazis. Most people, she adds, are in fact fairly normal, and their lives and sometimes behaviors are improved by profound aesthetic experiences. Most people bring to beauty a sensibility that has the potential to be shaped and turned outward by its encounters.

Some, presumably, do not. In such cases, there is a chance that beauty may be entirely overlooked or, worse, that it may, as its critics charge, be used as an anesthetic, numbing rather than sensitizing a person to the world beyond. But there is also always a chance that it may open the person to other worlds and thus inspire the imagination to compassion. Beauty, as we argued earlier, isn't a stable property; if we agree that it vibrates somewhere in the space that exists between the perceiver and the object, then we can surely also agree that what a person brings to beauty is likely to have some bearing on what the consequence of that encounter might be. If most people are normal and even good, it seems plausible that there is a potential for an increase in goodness.[30]

This is a view of beauty and the world that is, obviously, optimistic. It is radical rather than cautious. It holds that beauty might, in fact, *do* something—imaginably bad but more probably good. It is a view that grants a space for beauty to be grand in its consequences rather than limited in its effects. It is also a view that depends upon common sense (always a red flag to the ideologue); it depends, that is, upon a feeling borne out by personal experience. It is, also obviously, a view of beauty that owes something to reception theory: a kind of reader-response version of the aesthetic that admits history into its purview and that holds that beauty is as changeable as it is transcendent. What we, the authors of this book, have come, somewhat wearily, to call the "Nazi/Mozart problem" is much harder to resolve if one believes in beauty as an absolute, existing independently of human beings. If such were the case, it would be beauty that fails to convert the torturer to goodness; beauty, because it inspires him to both cruelty and deafness, would even be the facilitator of his evil. Our position is rather that the torturer brings his evil to beauty; that he is what he is despite, not because of, his aesthetic passions; that it is he who fails to live up to the beauty he enjoys; that he misses some part of its call to wider fellow feeling.[31] "Even great art," as Iris Murdoch writes, cannot guarantee the quality of its consumer's consciousness. . . . [Sometimes it may be] properly experienced and even a shallow experience of what is great can have its effect. . . . good art . . . affords us a pure delight in the independent existence of what is excellent. Both in its genesis and its enjoyment it is a thing totally opposed to selfish obsession. It invigorates our best faculties and . . . inspires love in the highest part of the soul. It is able to do this partly by virtue of something which it shares with nature: a perfection of form which invites unpossessive contemplation and resists absorption into the selfish dream life of the consciousness.[32]

By "properly experienced" we take Murdoch to mean that when we engage with art under the best circumstances, we are in Scarry's state of adjacency, which allows us to enjoy the art without regard to our own selves or desires. So it follows that it is in the spirit of "unpossessive contemplation" that we should teach reading, if we are to teach at all, because a certain degree of humility is called for in teaching, and the shallowness of experience that Murdoch describes is as likely to be true of the teacher as the student. But the sense that it is teaching itself, and not just art, that "invigorates our best faculties" and "inspires love in the highest part of the soul" should also hold true for the teacher.

This brings us to our final proposal: *teaching has to do with love*. The desire to teach should be the desire to share beauty. It should not be a desire to make someone think in a particular way; teachers should not work toward a uniformity of response, nor should they insist exclusively upon a certain method of reading. Making a space for beauty involves acknowledging and exploring the distinctions and connections between art and life, not pretending both are the same. The relationship between art and life is forged in part by the emotional response—the love—that we have for a work of art, and students should be permitted to acknowledge that response and should be given the words to describe it. Moreover, the aesthetic experience that is the experience of beauty can open up views of the world that alter and challenge rather than merely reinforce what is already known. According to Weinstein, "the experience of art yields a view of human reality as something networked, crisscrossed with ties and bonds, quite at odds with the individuated world we take to be real." Weinstein reveals his true colors as an aesthetic optimist by adding that "art constitutes a personal as well as a cultural gift that is far more practical, useful, than had been suspected."[33] Even Greenblatt, historicist par excellence, admits to the limits of historicizing and to the necessary priority of aesthetic wonder itself:

That's the sense of resonance: that you're in a whole world in which something that's happening here is also resonating with something quite far away, something going on in the north of England, something going on in London, something going on outside of this orbit entirely. But it only works as an imaginative apprehension . . . if you also stay in touch with the wonder that's brought you to this thing in the first place. The stakes here are not ultimately about recreating a lost world, but about recreating that world in relation to the thing that takes your breath away. And if you lose that sense of wonder, if it's only about historical recreation, it has a slightly musty quality of original-instrument stuff. What I wanted to do [by writing a biography of Shakespeare] was to get that sense of being in touch with this lost world while holding onto what draws readers and audiences there in the first place.[34]

Holding onto what draws us there in the first place: that ought to be the primary responsibility of the teacher.

CHAPTER 4

"Beauty Anyhow":
Reading Virginia Woolf in Vermont

And somehow or other, the windows being open, and the book held so that
it rested upon a background of escallonia hedges and distant blue, instead
of being a book it seemed as if what I read was laid upon the landscape not
printed, bound, or sewn up, but somehow the product of trees and fields and
the hot summer sky, like the air which swam, on fine mornings, round the
outline of things.

—Virginia Woolf, "Reading"

This interchange between reading and living can be tricky.
—Hermione Lee, *Virginia Woolf*

I am reading *Mrs. Dalloway* with seventeen students in a barn in Vermont.
It's a hot afternoon, and there's a fan chugging away noisily and ineffectu-
ally in the window. Outside the sky is a deep and startling navy blue. As
always, I'm wondering whether we should go outdoors and sit in a meadow,
lie on our backs and examine the outline of the mountains that cradle us,
watch the leaves of the silver birches shift in the wind like daubs of paint in an
Impressionist painting. If we lie on our backs and watch the mountains while
we talk about Virginia Woolf, will our discussion of Mrs. Dalloway's love of
beauty be more memorable, perhaps more insightful? Will an experience of
beauty in nature help us to articulate the beauty of the novel?

As always, I decide that our surroundings will be distracting—the real
mountains will win out over the literary roses; the black flies will interrupt

our concentration—and so we remain indoors. We are stuck at the point in the work where Mrs. Dalloway is confused between the Albanians and the Armenians but has a sense that her love of flowers helps them in some way:

> [Richard] was already halfway to the House of Commons, to his Armenians, his Albanians, having settled her on the sofa, looking at his roses. And people would say, "Clarissa Dalloway is spoilt." She cared much more for her roses than for the Armenians. Hunted out of existence, maimed, frozen, the victims of cruelty and injustice (she had heard Richard say so over and over again)— no, she could feel nothing for the Albanians, or was it the Armenians? but she loved her roses (didn't that help the Armenians?)—the only flowers she could bear to see cut.[1]

Usually, at this point in my experience of reading the novel in a classroom, someone is offended by this sheltered, upper-middle-class woman who fusses with floral decoration and glosses over the enormity of human suffering in so trivial and inexact a manner. There is something repellent in Clarissa's confusion, in the narcissism with which she substitutes a taste for beauty for unpleasant fact. How might it be that a love of roses can transform itself into help for the Armenians (Albanians)? What does Clarissa's love of beauty have to do with anything beyond itself? And, if it doesn't, what can it possibly be worth?

We are stuck at this point in the barn because we cannot bear to give Mrs. Dalloway over to those who see her as the disconnected, brittle, tinkling hostess of Woolf's overly precious imagination. There is something in the novel, this group of readers is arguing, that supports Clarissa in her peculiar, vague, inarticulate notion of connection with the Armenians. We are trying to claim that we do not have to give her up. But in our efforts to support this claim, we are just as vague as she is. What are we trying to hold on to in our struggle with this passage, I wonder, other than our sense that Clarissa Dalloway is more than utterly trivial? Why do we feel that Woolf offers something more here than a merely parodic instance of aestheticism in bad taste? Does Woolf herself actually need defending from the same charges? The questions from the seminar grow outward from our observation of Mrs. Dalloway's passing intuition to a wider acknowledgement of a range of related questions: How does beauty itself function in this work? What does it do in Woolf's work generally? Does it in fact do anything at all? "Must it?" a student asks.

Whatever else beauty may do in Woolf, surely in this novel it functions most vitally as a lifeline through the work, which begins with Mrs. Dalloway saying that she will "buy the flowers herself." One could argue that beauty plots the novel and provides it with its impetus forward and backward through time as well as up and down through space. By this I mean that the pleasure we take in the text as a result of what it does to us makes us feel that we are experiencing beauty. Like Emily Dickinson, who claimed to recognize poetry by means of its physical effects on her ("If I read a book and it makes my whole body so cold no fire can ever warm me, I know *that* is poetry"[2]), we know Woolf's prose is beautiful in our experience of it, and the experience is as kinetic as it is somatic—that is, it changes, it evolves, and it is as organic and as mobile in its development as it is possible for language to be.

Mulling these things over, we turn back to the extraordinary first page of the novel and examine how the ghost narrative of the day at Bourton emerges, rising up through the narrative of London as the birdlike Mrs. Dalloway moves up and simultaneously downward ("What a lark! What a plunge!") into the past and down her front steps into the sunlight of a June day. The words echo almost at once like brief aural memories: as she goes out of her door, in a temporal parallel she bursts open the French windows of her youth and plunges into the past of the garden. The London morning is "fresh as if issued to children on a beach," and soon comes that echo and the reader's own creative experience of textual memory as the Bourton air is also recalled, in the next paragraph, as "fresh," "calm," "like the flap of a wave; the kiss of a wave."

As the echoes fall on each other like leaves (or waves), out of the metaphor of the morning as a gift to children the narratives of the two different mornings grow, joined at the root. Clarissa is eighteen, at Bourton, "looking at the flowers," with everything in motion except her own perceiving self—the smoke "winding," the "rooks rising, falling," and she "standing and looking"—and Clarissa is also fifty-two, a woman in London who goes out to buy flowers. The craft of the paragraph is beautiful, and the beauty created by such moments in the novel is simultaneously its plot line, differently dressed. The story itself—what happens—is no less and no more than the slide, echo, and shift of the language that creates a sense of place for the reader, a place temporally as well as geographically created out of our aesthetic response.

The philosophical problem of beauty as a subject in *Mrs. Dalloway*, that is to say the question raised by Mrs. Dalloway as to whether a love of beauty might affect the wider world, is sometimes, and perhaps appropriately, eclipsed by the experience of the book itself. *Mrs. Dalloway* is a profoundly beautiful work. Beauty serves as its plot because it is what keeps us going; it is the structural and thematic web on which the rest of the text suspends itself. It is the beauty in the work that takes us from one point to innumerable others or rather from one experience to another. It is thus the experience of beauty that creates the world of the novel for the reader, the series of pleasurable recognitions that a reader may have that "life is like that." But beauty in this novel is also more than a web, a structure supporting other things; it is something dynamic, a series of directions or impulses that moves us in innumerable mnemonic directions. This is its purpose; this is what it does. The beauty of the prose is in fact both practical and necessary.

But what are we meant to do with the pleasures of its experience? In order for the beauty of the prose to move us, literally, through the text, to make us turn the pages, it must affect us in some way. Thus we are returned to Mrs. Dalloway's question: "[S]he loved her roses (didn't that help the Armenians?)." It is from that parenthetical aside (the love comes first, as fact; its consequences must follow, as conjecture) that we begin to grow our own questions. Is it possible, we wonder, to describe the ways that the beauty of this novel might affect *us*? And how might we evaluate them? Might we judge the value of this work according to what its beauty is able to accomplish? Does the book excite us to certain kinds of behaviors? And what kind of behaviors would those be? We go back to the beginning of the book again. Reading together, we arrive with Clarissa at Mulberry's, the florists:

> There were flowers: delphiniums, sweet peas, bunches of lilac; and carnations, masses of carnations. There were roses; there were irises. . . . And then, opening her eyes, how fresh like frilled linen clean from a laundry laid in wicker trays the roses looked; and dark and prim the red carnations, holding their heads up; and all the sweet peas spreading in their bowls, tinged violet, snow white, pale—as if it were the evening and girls in muslin frocks came out to pick sweet peas and roses after the superb summer's day, with its almost blue-black sky, its delphiniums, its carnations, its arum lilies was over; and it was the moment between six and seven when every flower—roses, carnations, irises, lilac—glows; white, violet, red, deep orange; every flower seems to burn by itself, softly, purely in the misty beds; and how she loved the grey-white moths spinning in and out, over the cherry pie, over the evening primroses![3]

Sitting in the Vermont barn, we note a few things that at first reading had passed us by: for example, after the sweet peas in their bowls are described in increasingly imprecise and suggestive terms—"tinged violet, snow white [What's that, exactly? Is snow warm or cold as a color? Pinkish? Bluish?], pale"—there is a dash, followed by a more lavish display of names and colors. These blooms are the flowers of simile, not of realism, and if we look closely at the text, we see that the sweet peas and roses of the summer's evening are not those of the flower shop at all. It is the echo of their names that moves us from the flowers as things to the flowers of association and, ultimately, memory.

As the images emerge, the flowers carry us toward a memory that, at first generalized in its appeal to the eye, seems to grow ever more precise: we move to a time (evening), to a particular time of evening (dusk), to a particular sentiment (love of the moths), to a specific place (Bourton). The beauty of the flowers that are for sale more than thirty years later in London (roses, irises, carnations, and sweet peas) takes Clarissa away, transports her to another summer's day with a "blue-black sky" and thereby to other, *first* imagined and *then* remembered, flowers. Thus from her pleasure in the flowers, she moves from a simile ("as if it were the evening") to a more precise location in the past, with a peculiar temporal tension generated by the phrase "every flower seems to burn by itself" and the recollection of a particular, intense, and mnemonically distinct feeling: "how she loved the grey-white moths . . . !"

What is it that makes this passage so beautiful? There is simplicity and there is stasis—flowers lying in trays—that lead color by color on a dynamic trajectory into imagination and from there to memory. There is thus present the same tension that so marks the cubist painting, in which the precise location of the figure (someone mentions Marcel Duchamp's *Nude Descending a Staircase*) cannot be determined; so kinetic is the work, yet at every point where the eye may rest, there is calm and stillness, an absence of motion, a purity of angles and design.

The reader can also observe the generative property that Elaine Scarry identifies as one of beauty's essential components: the beautiful thing replicates itself through imitation, through reproduction, or, as here, through leading to other related experiences of beauty. Clarissa looks at flowers; the flowers move her to imaginative musing and from there to memory, with yet more flowers created in her mind—a poignant bouquet recalling not just the loss of moments and the passage of time but also the complexity of relations between memory and desire and their incarnation here as art.

The passage is obviously visual in its emphasis. Its appeal is first to the eye: we have color and shape before we have association and memory. In this it is consistent with much of Woolf's work, profoundly shaped by a life spent among painters and critics of the visual arts. Roger Fry's influence on Woolf has been well documented, as has the extraordinarily significant and lifelong aesthetic presence of Vanessa Bell, so to think about the formal properties of Woolf's experimental writing—its refusal of conventional chronology, its dynamism, its color—is almost inevitably to think of that writing in the context of the history of art. It is also to recall the derivation of the term "aesthetics" itself, from the verb "to perceive." Woolf's prose seems to aim at aesthetic purity in that its effort is toward the closest perception possible. Indeed, like Lily Briscoe's persistent "But this is what I see; this is what I see,"[4] it is almost painfully insistent on the primacy of subjective experience, the importance of the effort to convey in images "the exact shapes my brain holds."[5]

But there's also a satisfying *aural* richness in the incantatory array at Miss Pym's flower shop that is not fully accounted for by its referents. We don't actually need to know what a delphinium looks like in order to take pleasure in the sound of its name. We don't have to know what all the flowers are any more than we need a lexicon of fruit to be enchanted by the splendor of the lists in "Goblin Market." The beauty of Christina Rossetti's poem, however, comes definitively attached to a moral: beauty seduces Lizzie and Laura, and it must be resisted and overcome in favor of human relations. Beauty in that poem is a snare and a temptation, something that lures readers off the path of salvation. In Woolf's novel, by contrast, beauty doesn't seem to be particularly dangerous, although passages such as the one in the flower shop are probably the primary cause of Woolf's rejection over the years by critics who seem to have had the same misgivings that some of the students in the barn are experiencing: Isn't this depiction of beauty supposed to *do* something? Should it not improve the work on some level, be purposive, instructive, in service to some larger idea? If it doesn't yield anything other than a temporary and private pleasure, if its only purpose is to propel us through the novel, then perhaps the charges of brittleness, parochialism, and self-absorption leveled at Clarissa Dalloway can be extended to her creator (as indeed they are).

It's worth noting that critics have largely ignored the aesthetic charge of Woolf's work in favor of an overemphasis on the feminism of her oeuvre. I say overemphasis because it's not for her politics that Woolf's work deserves its place in the canon. Her defenders would have a much stronger case to make if they focused instead on the glories, as Woolf might say, of the prose itself. It's the odd, jangling, jarring, always fresh *language* of the novels, the extraordinary formal shape of the essays, that makes their prose art and assures their longevity and value rather than the feminism expressed in some of them. But at the same time, the beauty of Woolf's work gives rise to questions more easily posed than answered and more comfortably ignored altogether. It is also the case that some of the questions lead us on impossible and ultimately frustrating quests. We are wrestling with one such question right now, because we are back to our problem with the Albanians and the Armenians.

***

Does or doesn't Clarissa's love of roses somehow help them? Pamela Caughie does not exactly attempt to answer the question, but in an article entitled "How Do We Keep Desire from Passing with Beauty?" she examines its reiteration in a number of critical works. She finds the question of whether or not loving the roses helps the Armenians "taken seriously, perhaps for the first time in Woolf criticism" in 1977 by Lee Edwards, whose conclusion to this difficult issue argues that "we damn ourselves if, in constructing a view of the world we deny a connection between politics and feelings . . . and so create a politics lacking both beauty and joy."[6]

Edwards's response seems to anticipate those students in the barn today, anxious to save not just Clarissa but Woolf herself from the embarrassingly bad taste of being socially oblivious. Even if it's only Clarissa that needs to be saved (assuming that Woolf does not share her protagonist's convictions regarding beauty and is merely showing how shallow Clarissa is), the mental gymnastics involved in that defense result in unacceptably vague conclusions. "Somehow," a student says, the Armenians are to be helped by a beauty loosed upon the world that will shame us all into a more equitable social order. But how?

The conversation in the barn inevitably turns, as indeed does Caughie's article, to Scarry's arguments on beauty, which we have already read together for the class. Caughie is no doubt right in her guess that Scarry would like to "answer Mrs. Dalloway's question in the affirmative—yes, Clarissa, your admiration of roses does help the Armenians," because one of Scarry's arguments in *On Beauty and Being Just* is that "the love of beauty increases one's desire for social justice."[7] Since all of us in the barn today are teachers, we have a particular interest in the relationship between our own literary affections and the possible social consequences that such affections may have. (Teaching may in fact be the perfect career for someone who believes that such a relationship exists.) As we read the passage about Clarissa, the love of roses evolves rather swiftly into a love of beauty generally and then regroups as a discussion about a love of literature. Conversation ensues regarding the relationship between one's own passion for literature and whether or not it might actually have an effect on anything beyond itself.

As it happens, Caughie's article makes the same shift in gears. Teachers, she points out, are obviously going to find the argument attractive that in teaching their students "to appreciate the beauty of a well-turned phrase and to strive to reproduce that balance and clarity in their own writing, we help the Armenians." But Caughie's problem with the argument is that it "betrays a nostalgia for a notion of pedagogy and liberal education that . . . has passed."[8]

It is odd that Caughie does not waste her time wondering whether or not the argument, nostalgia notwithstanding, is *true*. It is also interesting that in our own discussion of this topic in the barn, out of a class of seventeen high school English teachers, not one of them finds the argument nostalgic. The argument concerning our teaching and its effect on the Armenians is no doubt of interest to us because it casts our jobs as teachers of literature in a pleasingly benign light. But whether or not that light is earned, and whether or not a particular "notion of pedagogy and literary education" has really passed, there remains the stubborn and experiential fact of beauty in Woolf's work and how it affects the reader. Caughie's essay, for all its insightfulness, ultimately distances itself from a discussion of beauty in Woolf and instead makes a detour to her own confession:

> Well, one can hardly deny that the vocabulary of beauty has not had much currency lately. When I was a graduate student in the mid 1980s, I used to raise eyebrows even then when I proclaimed *The Rainbow* by D. H. Lawrence the most beautiful novel in the English language. Today, I could no longer make such a statement, not because it would be politically incorrect, but because it would be critically irresponsible, or rather irresponsive to the social relations in which Lawrence's writing is embedded.[9]

This is a truly bizarre statement. What does Caughie really *think* about Lawrence? Who knows? Note that she does *not* say that she no longer finds *The Rainbow* beautiful. What she says is that she could "no longer make such a statement." This is not because such a statement is no longer true—that is, that she no longer finds the work beautiful. It is because to say that she still loves *The Rainbow* would be "critically irresponsible."

What is the difference between being "politically incorrect" and being "critically irresponsible"? It is not clear what Caughie means by her distinction. Instead of clarifying, she goes on to qualify her statement by adding that to love *The Rainbow*, to find it "the most beautiful novel," would be unresponsive to things outside the work.

We can of course come up with a whole heap of things that might fall under the heading "social relations in which [any author]'s writing is embedded." Do we always approve of such relations? Given the history of the world and of the humans in it, it seems likely that an author could always be found to offend someone. As a rule it would seem a bad idea to allow external realities—"social relations"—to have boundless sway over our evaluation of a work. We would lose a lot of good works that way. Looking at another work by Lawrence, the short story "The Woman Who Rode Away," Caughie admits to a "certain beauty" that might even be "radically decentering in that the narrative attempts to extend the beauty and truth of the native cosmology to Western culture as an antidote to its crass materialism." But, she asks, "Where do the values expressed in the narrative come from? Who would want to endorse Lawrence's vision of cosmic unity and sexual harmony? Where does the responsibility lie for such a vision?"[10] These are all fine questions to be asking, but neither the questions nor the answers have much to do with whether it is worth our time to read Lawrence.

Caughie puts the cart before the horse, the values of the work above the primary experience of reading it. It's interesting that she doesn't choose *The Rainbow* as her example of the problem with Lawrence. Perhaps that's because, as she once thought and possibly still privately believes, *The Rainbow* is indeed a fine and, yes, beautiful book. "The Woman Who Rode Away" is nowhere near as good, and part of the reason for its weakness is the crudeness to which Caughie rightly objects, the degree to which Lawrence's own views permeate the text to its detriment. Iris Murdoch has an excellent phrase for this: where a writer is at his or her most intrusive, whether with politics or sexual boorishness, or when he or she is noticeably on a soapbox, she describes the effect as "the fumes of personality." Murdoch actually singles out Lawrence, whose "literary presence . . . is too bossy,"[11] and she finds him to be especially pungent.

It's arguable that Caughie is really objecting to the fumes of Lawrence. "The Woman Who Rode Away" is not especially beautiful because it's too full of fumes—Lawrence's presence, not just his style, is all over it. We object to the fumes, and Caughie says that she objects to the values, but the consequences are the same—we both find the work diminished. This is where we part company with Caughie: we don't subsequently deem Lawrence to be *always* unworthy because *sometimes* he is clumsy or offensive, or because his values don't reflect our own, or because he intrudes in irritating ways in certain of his works. Sometimes—*The Rainbow* is a good example—Lawrence's work is free from the fumes of his personality, and we, too, are free to judge it without feeling overburdened by the "social relations" it represents.

Instead of answering Clarissa's question, Caughie's essay, like the literary criticism of the past two decades that she describes, sidesteps it entirely. In part, as Caughie argues, this is because "there is no simple relation between art and social justice or between theory and politics." Indeed, as she points out, "the belief that we must find a causal link . . . leads to . . . ugly charges."[12] As evidence of this, she spends some time evaluating Martha Nussbaum's harsh analysis of Judith Butler's famously obscure prose, in which Nussbaum criticizes Butler's complexity. To be precise: "Nussbaum says Butler's bad writing collaborates with evil."[13]

Nussbaum arrives at this analysis, Caughie claims, because her reasoning is Cartesian at base: "the notion that difficulty means interference with communication, a failure to clarify one's meaning, is a Cartesian reading of opaqueness."[14] Nussbaum is worse than mistaken about Butler, therefore; she is, according to Caughie, out of date in her assumptions that language has to do with communication. The notion that there might be a connection or a relationship between an aesthetic emotion and a social action is itself faulty in that it reflects a commitment to "the classic contract," the contract "between word and world"[15] that no longer holds up.

What seems to be absent here, however (and necessarily absent for the logic of Caughie's essay to stand), is a sense of how written language that is intentionally obscure would serve in a world where ideas really matter. If it is ever imperative that we understand Butler—a matter, let us say, of life and death—then perhaps she will feel compelled to write more clearly. Of course, in the aesthetic realm to which Butler's writing belongs, language has multiple roles—it may be ambiguous, suggestive, productively obscure. Clarissa's intuition about her love of roses belongs to this aesthetic world. Its appeal to a sense of connectivity (something having to do with something else) is one to which Caughie cannot fully respond because to do so would be to fall into Nussbaum's trap of assuming some kind of contractual relationship between word and thing. More simply, and more problematically, Clarissa's question is a moral one, and it invites a moral judgment.

Clarissa's intuition that something has to do with another thing may be clouded and short on specifics and logic, but that doesn't mean it is without merit. The difficulty lies in establishing what that relation might be and whether it is consistent enough to warrant its use as a defense against doing away with beauty. Caughie's attentions, however, are finally not with Clarissa or with beauty at all, but with the question she finds to be more pressing: "who controls representation?" Or, as John Berger puts it, "What matters now is who uses that language for what purpose."[16]

The "now" of Berger's statement is 1973. As English professors, we find the more interesting question, both then and now, to be the one that Clarissa comes close to posing—What do the roses have to do with the Armenians? But of course, it depends upon what we think "matters" most —on what, exactly, our interest is. To people whose primary interest is free speech or censorship or whose task is to chart power relations and to address social inequities, Berger's statement regarding language is accurate. If the reader's motivations are really best met by graphing power, then "who uses . . . language for what purpose" is what matters most in *Mrs. Dalloway* or in any other novel.

The problem is, however, that Woolf's novels are not really the best or most productive sites on which to be pursuing social activism. Good novels defy goal-oriented readings, just as they make unsatisfactory graphs, statistics, manifestos for social change. When Caughie puts questions of beauty to the side to state that "what matters now" are questions to do with social control, she leaves an extraordinary number of readers behind—readers for whom beauty still matters; readers for whom reading has little or nothing to do with policing society; readers for whom *The Rainbow* continues to be a beautiful book, one of Lawrence's best.

Novels often invite the kind of difficult questions that Clarissa herself brushes up against. What is the relationship between art and the world, between an aesthetic experience and a moral impulse? What might make it possible for a love of roses to transform itself into help for the Armenians? Never mind that these questions are ultimately unanswerable in the sense that there is no final point of arrival with which all readers will feel satisfaction. It is the business of art to keep us engaged with complex issues, and it is not necessary that the issues be new. It is in fact likely that many of the issues we encounter in our aesthetic experiences are deeply familiar to us. We don't give up on questions because they've been asked before. Yet Caughie suggests that our interest in beauty has "passed," to be replaced with the notion of desire. "Beauty," she argues, "is an imposed notion of what is pleasing or sublime; desire is dynamic, something that happens between subjects."[17] This seems rather an old-fashioned view of beauty, and it is hard to imagine that such a view has much currency now, if it ever did. What is to be gained by arguing that beauty is conceptually distinct from its perceiving subjects? That it is absolute, imposed, inherited, objective? Who believes nowadays that such a notion of beauty even exists?

As far back as 1914, Woolf's brother-in-law Clive Bell argued that "[a]ny system of aesthetics which pretends to be based on some objective truth is so palpably ridiculous as not to be worth discussing."[18] From the Bloomsbury perspective, "[t]he significance of 'significant form' lies finally in the eye of the beholder."[19] Wendy Steiner's more recent but equally subjective description of the workings of beauty—of beauty as a function—certainly seems closer to the mark than Caughie's:

> We often say that something or someone is beautiful . . . when what we mean is that they have value *for us*. . . . Even when we use the term in a purely artistic context, a beautiful object is something we value, and we value it because it touches our dearest concerns. In our gratitude toward what moves us so, we attribute to it the *property* of beauty, but what we are actually experiencing is a special *relation* between it and ourselves. We discover it as valuable, meaningful, pleasurable, *to us*.[20]

When Caughie argues that "[b]eauty originates in representation; it is the image that mediates our desires," she neglects an entire category of natural objects; or perhaps she means that our pleasure in the beautiful is always mediated by some more powerful image to which our aesthetic sense is sadly victim and that our pleasures are necessarily shaped for us, whether we know it or not, by those who "control representation."[21]

This is quite a depressing view of the world, but outside of totalitarian regimes, it's fortunately not one that people's life experience really confirms. Beauty, like all aesthetic experience, is beyond state control and certainly beyond the control of those who might wish to instruct us either for it or against it; it might in fact accurately be termed out of control. No one can force you to find a symphony beautiful, to like the effect of green on yellow, or to be more moved by Alfred Tennyson than by Thomas Hardy. Beauty isn't prescribed and it can't be forced; it merely happens to us, often unexpectedly, and sometimes against our will.[22] If art is, as Murdoch so memorably put it, "close dangerous play with unconscious forces," then beauty is one of those forces.[23] To argue that something so basic to human existence has "passed" from our discussion of literature—has been done away with, or deconstructed, or replaced with something else more in keeping with how we now prefer to do things ("displaced by the notion of desire" is Caughie's version)—seems futile, like outlawing joy or grief. Beauty *is*; and to declare it over or no longer appropriate or meaningful as a term of description or as a subject for discussion in literature is laughably at odds with the vast lot of shared human experience.

This is probably the most damaging aspect of Caughie's argument: it doesn't speak to or for most people, and thus it can be used as yet another example of the ways in which academia speaks increasingly only to and for itself. When Caughie concludes her essay by identifying the "real conflict" now going on in the humanities, she suggests that distinctions "between those who appreciate beauty and those who oppose it, or between those whose moral integrity is evident in their clear prose and those who write badly and thus collaborate with evil" are not as serious in their implications. Of course, Caughie is intentionally ironic in her polarizations. Few people are really opponents of beauty. But plenty of academics have made it part of their business to neglect beauty's role in their teaching and scholarly lives. Similarly, the claim that obscure writing indicates a collaboration "with evil" *is* far-fetched, but it is also true that producing prose intelligible to only a tiny percent of persons raises serious ethical questions about the purposes of scholarship, questions that seem at least as significant to the moral well-being of our professional and personal lives as the question of "who controls representation."

***

We are still in the barn. It is hotter than ever, and now a deerfly has made its way into the room. The question of beauty is still before us, but it seems to have produced not exactly copies of itself, but rather variations on its own theme. Now beside the issue of the relationship between the roses and the Armenians is the more generally stated problem: What does Clarissa's love of beauty have to do with anything beyond itself? And what can it possibly be worth? The majority of the class appears to want to argue that beauty has a function in the novel that embodies the question raised by Clarissa; that is to say, there is a strong bias emerging in favor of beauty *doing* something.

We return to the novel, this time to the passage in which Peter Walsh is on his way to Clarissa's party. The passage begins with a question: "he was about to have an experience. But what?"

> Beauty anyhow. Not the crude beauty of the eye. It was not beauty pure and simple—Bedford Place leading into Russell Square. It was straightness and emptiness of course; the symmetry of a corridor; but it was also windows lit up, a piano, a gramophone sounding; a sense of pleasure-making hidden, but now and again emerging when, through the uncurtained window, the window left open, one saw parties sitting over tables, young people slowly circling, conversations between men and women, maids idly looking out (a strange comment theirs, when work was done), stockings drying on top ledges, a parrot, a few plants. Absorbing, mysterious, of infinite richness, this life. And in the large square where the cabs shot and swerved so quick, there were loitering couples, dallying, embracing, shrunk up under the shower of a tree; that was moving; so silent, so absorbed, that one passed, discreetly, timidly, as if in the presence of some sacred ceremony to interrupt which would have been impious. That was interesting. And so on into the flare and glare.[24]

To be accurate, the passage doesn't really start there at all. It starts some half-dozen pages earlier, when the narrative shifts into Peter's consciousness; nor does it end until he walks into the illuminated doorway of Clarissa's party. But a number of the students pick out these very lines, perhaps because the paragraph seems both to pose a question and to promise an answer, or perhaps because there is a sense of conclusion as well as of continuity at the end. Most likely we also pick it out because, in addition to being explicitly about beauty, it appeals to the reader rhythmically as well as visually. Mary Ann Caws writes persuasively about the stylistic shifts that authors make in order to emphasize certain passages (she calls this "framing");[25] but here there is no formal shift, no movement to, for example, the overtly theatrical, no play with tenses. What sets this passage apart is its sense of aesthetic containment, arrived at through its introduction ("Beauty anyhow"), its understated conclusion ("That was interesting"),[26] and its final conflation of the specific with the universal (Peter's walk "into the flare and glare" with our own mortal paths).

Most obviously, of course, the prose has formal qualities that (again) reify its subject. We look at the way in which Peter first attempts to summarize what is about to happen and then qualifies it with "Not . . . not . . . —" and we note that Woolf's dash offers the typological equivalent of "Bedford Place leading in to Russell Square." Beauty as Peter imagines he will see it, or as he is seeing it (the language of the text allows for no temporal or psychological distinction), is beauty overheard, beauty overseen; it is not arranged for his perusal, but rather it is found, incidental, as he wanders by. It is happenstance—the "uncurtained window, the window left open"—that allows for this beauty, which is both intimate and synecdochical, hinting at something beyond itself.

What is beautiful for Peter here is only incomplete, suggested. Yet the fragments are sufficient.[27] It is the moment of perception and understanding Henry James writes of in "The Art of Fiction," when he describes how a brief glimpse of something may be transformed into art. For James, as for Fry, "if experience consists of impressions, it may be said that impressions *are* experience."[28] This is surely as much the case with Woolf, and with Peter Walsh, as it was with James and with Walter Pater before him.[29] Impressions, the sensory fragments that cling to us like pollen or smoke as we pass by, are the starting places for stories; something may come of them; they may take us anywhere.

For Denis Donoghue, this passage from Woolf's novel illustrates the idea that "[w]hen you pay attention to a particular value [in this case, beauty], it seems to extend its purview, so that in the end nothing seems to be beyond its reach."[30] Woolf, he says, "lets Peter Walsh enjoy the privilege of beauty, such that no other value is allowed to take over the occasion. For the time being, Peter is an aesthete."[31] Donoghue is right that Peter's aestheticism may be only temporary, and it is interesting that it is at odds with the kind of couch-ridden immobility with which the more traditional aesthete of literary history is associated (Peter's aesthetic experience grows from walking). Nor does it suggest a limitation of outlook, the kind of claustrophobia we experience, say, with the oppressively gorgeous interiors of *Dorian Gray*. Whether or not Peter's (Pater's?) aesthetic sensibility is responsible for his unhappiness, for the sense of frustration and loss he experiences on Clarissa's sofa, is hard to say. In this passage, however, he seems to be driven forward rather than stultified by his sense of beauty, which comes to him through the endless unfinished narrative threads of a visible world. He is peaceful, calmed, curious, interested, detached. He is, one might say, in the perfect frame of mind for an aesthetic experience. He has his own pain, his private sorrow, but it is put to the side; he himself is decentered while his imagination and perceptual powers are in full play. Beauty is, again, a means of transportation—in this case, it literally gets Peter to the party. Its effect is practical, both for the character who moves through London and for the reader who is similarly propelled through the novel. But its effect is also pleasurable; the walk is transformed into a series of delicate epiphanies, and reading of the walk, we take pleasure in the nod of recognition: yes, life is like that. There is a correspondence—a truthfulness—that brings its own peculiar satisfaction.

What is the nature of this satisfaction? Why should it be pleasant, or even moving, to note the correspondences between our own private experience and the language of a novel or poem?

This is where beauty is at its most powerful and most paradoxical, for while we may be thrown by its strangeness, we may at the same time be thrilled by its familiarity. This familiarity comes to us as a sense that, as Scott Russell Sanders puts it, this is "how things *ought* to be."[32] It is a conflation of desire (that things should be like this); happiness (that in this moment they are); and recognition (of impermanence—either our own or of the moment, object, or experience). Caughie is right to suggest that beauty has to do with desire. Part of the satisfaction we feel when we find a line of prose, for example, that seems beautiful because it is true grows from a sense of desire for the order or harmony expressed in the line; the line is somehow in tune with how we think things should be, or it matches up in some way with what we sense to be the case or wish were the case.

As for the question, "what is it worth if it doesn't do anything?" one might propose the answer that ultimately beauty's worth comes from its fundamental affirmation of human experience, an affirmation that is both optimistic and social. While on the one hand, our experience of beauty is necessarily solitary and private (we use our own senses, our *own* memories and desires), in reading beauty we are also engaging in a profoundly social act that sets us against solitude. By agreeing to the text's implicit proposal ("Isn't life like this?") with our own involuntary response ("Yes! This is how life really is!"), we forge bonds with other imaginations, other readers, other minds. Not only does the novel in our hands seems larger but also the shared world itself expands.

Thus while critical emphasis on the subjective nature of the experience of beauty is vitally important, it is also worth underscoring that beauty in literature, like beauty in any form, can lead to *common ground* and illuminating *public* exchange. Ask a classroom of students to identify the passages in any novel that they found most beautiful, and there will be a good deal of agreement on what prose most arrested them. There will also be surprises and enough variety of response to remind one of the subjective basis of aesthetic judgment. And on some occasions one may also be persuaded of the errors of one's previous oversight.[33]

Here's one such example: In my many readings of *Mrs. Dalloway*, I had never paid as much attention to Septimus Smith's perceptual world as I did to that of Clarissa or of Peter. But during the course of picking out and examining passages of extreme beauty for the class that now finds us fixated on Clarissa, many of my students said that they were drawn to two passages involving Septimus, and their insistence upon both the beauty of these passages and their significance to the novel led me to look at them more closely. In the first of these passages, the war-damaged veteran is struggling to emerge from a hallucination or dream. Like one drowning, Septimus tries to pull himself out of a cacophony of nightmare and back into the London daylight:

> He had only to open his eyes; but a weight was on them; a fear. He strained; he pushed; he looked; he saw Regent's Park before him. Long streamers of sunlight fawned at his feet. The trees waved, brandished. We welcome, the world seemed to say; we accept; we create. Beauty, the world seemed to say. And as if to prove it (scientifically) wherever he looked at the houses, at the railings, at the antelopes stretching over the palings, beauty sprang instantly. To watch a leaf quivering in the rush of air was an exquisite joy. Up in the sky swallows swooping, swerving, flinging themselves in and out, round and round, yet always with perfect control as if elastics held them; and the flies rising and falling; and the sun spotting now this leaf, now that, in mockery, dazzling it with soft gold in pure good temper; and now and again some chime (it might be a motor horn) tinkling divinely on the grass stalks—all of this, calm and reasonable as it was, made out of ordinary things as it was, was the truth now; beauty, that was the truth now. Beauty was everywhere.[34]

When we read through this passage as a class, after observing the overt references to beauty—that it is the focus of Septimus's consciousness and that for him it has urgent but inexplicable importance—we note the way in which this passage has an economy of reference that links it intimately with other scenes, including those of Clarissa and of Peter. There are consistencies, such as a continual sense of movement evoked by verb forms; echoes and repetitions, lending lyricism and a peculiar sense of instant déjà vu even within one paragraph; metaphors of water that recall the imaginary children on the beach of the novel's first page as well as Clarissa's plunge into the currents of her past. These are shared elements across the novel, both stylistic and substantial. The chime that tinkles "divinely" may be the ripple effect of Big Ben that marks Clarissa's day and reminds us that the same sun, the same sounds, that accompany her are also those that accompany Septimus. Even the word "brandished" to describe the trees recalls us to Clarissa's vision of "brandishing of silver flashing—plumes" as she sits on her sofa with Peter.[35] The passage, we see on a slow reading, is knit into the novel, recalling us to other parts, both forward and back.

Our focus on how the passage works on us imaginatively, aesthetically, and emotionally—based on our assumption that what it *does* is what it *is*—leads us in this way to an extraordinary experience of the work opening up. What at first had seemed a discrete passage now enlarges what has gone before. It thus comes as no surprise that the very elements that students found in the first passage are now also found by them to be present in the second, which comes later in the book when Septimus is at home (and as Elizabeth Dalloway is boarding the Westminster omnibus):

> Going and coming, beckoning, signaling, so the light and shadow which now made the wall grey, now the bananas bright yellow, now made the Strand grey, now made the omnibuses bright yellow, seemed to Septimus Warren Smith lying on the sofa in the sitting-room; watching the watery gold glow and fade with the astonishing sensibility of some live creature on the roses, on the wallpaper. Outside the trees dragged their leaves like nets through the depths of the air; the sound of water was in the room and through the waves came the voices of birds singing. Every power poured its treasures on his head, and his hand lay there on the back of the sofa, as he had seen his hand lie when he was bathing, floating, on the top of the waves, while far away on shore he heard dogs barking and barking far away. Fear no more, says the heart in the body; fear no more.
>
> He was not afraid. At every moment Nature signified by some laughing hint like that gold spot which went round the wall—there, there, there—her determination to show, by brandishing her plumes, shaking her tresses, flinging her mantle this way and that, beautifully, always beautifully, and standing close up to breathe through her hollowed hands Shakespeare's words, her meaning.[36]

Again we find the kinetic verbs; the shifting light; the changing objects according to that impressionistic light, as though we are with Elizabeth on top of the bus as well as here with Septimus. Again we discover the element of water in which trees drag their leaves "like nets" and through which the voices of birds are heard. Again Nature is "brandishing her plumes," and again Clarissa's moment on the sofa is recalled by shared association and even by the simple presence of the word "sofa." Similarly, the words "there, there, there," gesture as much to Clarissa's pats on Peter's knee following his tears as they do to the anxious, emphatic direction of Septimus's consciousness as it follows the sunbeam on the wall. There are more obvious links with Clarissa, such as Septimus's echo of a fragment from *Cymbeline* spotted earlier that morning by Clarissa in the window of Hatchards. And there is the shadow play of the war, with the image of a disconnected body part ("his hand lay there . . . as he had seen his hand lie . . . ").

Reading the passages together in this way, aloud, makes us more sensitive to the economy of vocabulary in this novel, a parsimoniousness that generates a sense of echo, or of resonance, as though Woolf had set herself the task of writing with a particular number of words that might be used in various ways. And interestingly, what we seem as a group of readers to find most arresting are those very places where the language is most economically used, places, that is, where the prose moves us imagistically, or rhythmically, or through simple repetition of vocabulary, to other parts of the text and where we glimpse or sense a tension between extraordinary formal symphonic complexity and the pleasure afforded us by the simplest of things: in the second passage, a circle of light moving on wallpaper. We give this pleasure, as well as the complexity in which it plays a part, the name of beauty. But what, to repeat the question, is all this beauty worth if it doesn't do anything?

It is not possible to say what beauty in Woolf is worth, though it is possible to try to describe what it does. For those who do not find Woolf's prose especially beautiful, its function in the quoted passages is presumably ineffective, for without a sense of the beauty there can be no sense of correspondence, no apprehension of harmony or alignment of the self with the language on the page. For this reason alone—the profoundly *personal* nature of response, the fact that there is no guarantee of beauty—there can be no one statement regarding its utility in Woolf. Each instance of literary beauty is always specific to itself and its reader, and it is not generalizable.

But why then should one teach it? And if beauty is fully dependent, how *could* one teach it? Moreover, doesn't beauty just come at the reader regardless? Doesn't talking about it perhaps even spoil it? Shouldn't literary beauty be just the incidental occurrence of Peter Walsh's experience—the thing that happens to us as we make our way through *Mrs. Dalloway* on our way to somewhere else (perhaps a degree in English)?

In Chapter 3 we proposed various ways in which beauty might be restored to a classroom discussion of literature. But it is obvious that one cannot teach a person to see beauty where she or he cannot see it. What a teacher *can* do is discover what it is about a work that moves readers and then bring those passages forward for shared scrutiny. The emotions that beauty may arouse can be usefully compared and often found, in fact, to be very similar. A history of beauty, like any effort to describe it, would necessarily be a history or an account of response. We might ask our students: What is it that we agree upon? Where do our notions of beauty in language converge—and where do they part ways? Why does this word or phrase or series of phrases affect us to such a degree?

Yet while these questions address *how* one might teach beauty, they do not, we realize, answer the question regarding *why* one should. Why talk about beauty? Why teach it?

One answer is the kinds of conversations that seem to ensue. Without a doubt, the most memorable classes we've been part of have involved students passionately and with great technical skill persuading other students of the beauty of their favorite passages and thus expanding, for all of us, and forever, the limits of the work itself. After the discussions in the barn concerning Clarissa, the flowers, Peter's walk through London, and Septimus's trees, it's hard to imagine what a classroom session on this particular book would be like if one were to ignore the beauty of the work. Our focus on beauty in *Mrs. Dalloway*, both as a complex subject in the book and as a way of making our way through it—its formal beauty—has caused us to give considerable weight to the personal responses generated by the novel. In this way, our discussion has been wide-ranging and spontaneous, with a good deal of variation. At the same time, we have found peculiar and even unsettling common ground, and we have been influenced in our responses by authoritative and well-defended close readings.

There is undoubtedly a tension between those two strains of the discussion, between the intensely personal nature of the response and the intellectual consideration of the work's formal negotiations. That tension would likely dissipate if we were to ignore the beauty of the prose. We would have a more coherent and probably more uniform response to the work because to allow discussion of beauty is also to acknowledge the real life of the work as uncontrollable, even dangerous. By "real life," I mean aesthetic life; I do not refer to the accuracy with which Woolf portrays London in 1923, or Richard's political work, or Miss Kilman's mackintosh, or anything else that might be grist for the New Historicist mill. These are undeniably part of the material life of the novel and of the world inhabited by its characters. But they are *primarily* of interest to us because Woolf writes about them in a novel. Their life is contingent upon their author's perceptual faculties, and as such, their power over us is magical before it is anything else at all. To ignore this is to make the novel smaller, safer, and lesser than it is.

Furthermore, to overlook beauty in our literary studies generally is to overlook the fact that, according to at least one romantic school of thought, literature is by its nature organic, and the greatness of any literary work lies in its potential for growth, reevaluation, rethinking, and rereading. Beauty, to recall Stendhal, is a promise; it is forward looking; it is just out of our grasp; it brings with it the possibility for change. It is in this sense that beauty makes literature—in our case, *Mrs. Dalloway*—larger. To acknowledge the power of beauty within the work is to acknowledge that the work itself is really out of our control, not of our own solitary making. To acknowledge the beauty of it is to recognize that the work is larger than we are and cannot ever be fully accounted for.

To acknowledge beauty is, inevitably, to admit that beauty does in fact do something. It doesn't have to—that's to say, it doesn't have either a *prescribed* or a *specific* job—but it has an effect; it has ramifications of one kind or another. Its results are always unpredictable. Clarissa Dalloway's vague notion that beauty somehow helps the world reflects a therapeutic notion of beauty that cannot hold up to scrutiny. At the same time, one of the results of both the subject of beauty and beauty as a formal device in Woolf's work for the readers of this class in that stiflingly hot barn has been to turn our attention to the ethical issues concerning the relationship (or lack thereof) between beauty and social responsibility. These are issues latent to our situation in Vermont as readers in a summer school of English, pleasantly remote from Donoghue's "pushing world." It is late summer, 2003. The *New York Times* lies on the library table for us to look at if we choose, but often we do not choose. We choose to read Virginia Woolf or Robert Frost and to absorb the mountain views from our Adirondack chairs. And part of the pleasure that we feel in our reading, indeed, seems to come from our sense that, as readers, we are in the right place. We have made—or there has been made for us—a generous space for beauty. Where else ought we to be?

The question is not entirely fatuous. Elsewhere I have taken nineteenth-century writer T. F. Goodall to task for his determination that "beauty consists in appropriateness; the right thing in the right place is the beautiful thing. Truth is beauty."[37] Yet for all its rigid and classbound inferences (in Goodall's case he was referring to the peasants on the Norfolk broads as much as to the marigolds in the fields), the dictum is thought-provoking in its assertion that the location of a person or thing, with regard to other persons or things, is fully relevant to its beauty. In Thomas Hardy we see the same kind of sensitivity to place in his depiction of Wessex as well as in his play with scale. Hardy, moreover, reminds us that the right place is as much an accident of time as of geography: as in Woolf's work, the small moments of a day may be capacious and rich with psychological incident, while deep time—the grandness of geological history—may be concertinaed into a second of insight. Tess Durbeyfield stands over her dying horse under the cold stars; Stephen Smith hangs from the cliff and stares into the eye of the troglodyte fossil.[38] The beauty of such moments depends on accidents of time and space that bring humans into momentary collision with their environments. We might call this the beauty of juxtaposition.

In Hardy's work the juxtaposition is beautiful to us as readers because of the irony and pathos that lend the scene additional resonance. We can enjoy the beauty of the moment even if the subjects themselves are hardly in the state of detachment necessary to experience their lives as aesthetic. But in our own extraliterary lives, we may take pleasure in juxtaposition—the sunbeam on the wallpaper; the cloud over the omnibus—and find our deepest happiness on occasion in our sense that "the right thing" is in "the right place," which may, perhaps, and if only for a moment, include ourselves.

***

Sanders has written that something that seems beautiful to us is so because

> it gives us a glimpse of the underlying order of things. The swirl of a galaxy and the swirl of a gown resemble one another not merely by accident, but because they follow the grain of the universe. That grain runs through our own depths. What we find beautiful accords with our most profound sense of how things *ought* to be. Ordinarily, we live in a tension between our perceptions and our desires. When we encounter beauty, that tension vanishes, and outward and inward images agree.[39]

It is the "*ought* to be" that most strikes me about this account, its reminder that beauty is always at a remove, associated as much or more with loss and longing as with possession and contentment. The *ought* reminds us of one reason for the melancholy we often associate with the beautiful, a melancholy that Woolf records as powerfully as Hardy;[40] in our lives it may arise from the temporality of any beautiful experience and the implied certainty of our own end. Sitting in the classroom on an August afternoon we agree: Life ought to be like this; everyone ought to be able to experience this; summer ought to go on forever.

Yet in that same classroom I am not quite bold enough to claim, as perhaps Sanders would, that *Mrs. Dalloway* seems especially beautiful to us because it follows "the grain of the universe," nor am I fully convinced that in thus following the grain, beautiful things necessarily resemble each other. The Green Mountains of Vermont seem very far from "the swing, tramp, and trudge," the "triumph and the jingle" of Woolf's London on a June morning in 1923. What seems likely to me, however, is that our *responses* to what is beautiful (in Sanders's case, images from the Hubbell space telescope and photographs of his daughter's wedding; in our case, Woolf's novel and the meadows and mountains among which we read it) have a family resemblance. Surely it is the similarity of the emotions we feel in response to these things that causes us to suppose that the things in themselves have some relation.[41]

Sanders's suggestion that in beauty we may find a "glimpse of the underlying order of things" is nonetheless profoundly important. Notwithstanding his own despair at modernity and its many ailments, Sanders here shows his true colors as an aesthetic optimist, and in this we would join him. To state some kind of belief in an "underlying order of things" is to turn one's back on all those who have taught us and continue to teach us the meaningless chaos of the world. For students these days it is often to risk ridicule; for professors, the charge of naïveté or, worse, religious fundamentalism. And yet our relationship to the "underlying order of things" should not be so easily dismissed. It is our very intuition, or desire, or lack, or love of order that draws us to formal, rather than exclusively to natural, aesthetic experiences. In later life we gravitate toward certain works of art either because they offer us something we have come to wish were so or because they give us something we feel to be the case. If we are good existentialists, even of the postmodern variety, we must surely assent to the proposition that we might choose to believe in an underlying order because it corresponds with our experience of the world. Sanders's experience, like that of many of my students, is that there is a correspondence between human beings and the world in which they live. Literature offers instances of that correspondence; so does nature:

> A screech owl calls, a comet streaks the night sky, a story moves unerringly to a close, a child lays an arrowhead in the palm of my hand, a welder installs a pair of railings on our front steps, my daughter smiles at me through her bridal veil, and I feel for a moment at peace, in place, content. I sense in those momentary encounters a harmony between myself and whatever I behold. The word that seems to fit most exactly this feeling of resonance, this sympathetic vibration between inside and outside, is *beauty*.[42]

The order intuited here by Sanders is expressed musically: there is harmony, resonance, vibration; "impulses from the world," he writes earlier in the same piece, "stir a responsive chord." Woolf herself reaches for the musical metaphor when, in *To the Lighthouse*, she writes of the perceptual effort involved in synthesizing all late-summer sounds into some kind of harmony:

> And now as if the cleaning and the scrubbing and the scything and the mowing had drowned it there rose that half-heard melody, that intermittent music which the ear half catches but lets fall; a bark, a bleat; irregular, intermittent,

yet somehow related; the hum of an insect, the tremor of cut grass, dissevered yet somehow belonging; the jar of a dorbeetle, the squeak of a wheel, loud, low, but mysteriously related; which the ear strains to bring together and is always on the verge of harmonising, but they are never quite heard, never fully harmonised, and at last, in the evening, one after another the sounds die out, and the harmony falters, and silence falls.[43]

Woolf's imaginative ear never quite manages to bring the disparate sounds into full union, yet the sounds remain "somehow related . . . somehow belonging." Part of the beauty of this conception surely lies in the use of the word "somehow," with its human mix of doubtful assertion and frustrated desire. This *ought* to be the case; this *is* the case. Either way, night falls. The sounds "die out."

***

It is late summer for us also, and we are still in the barn, and we are still thinking about *Mrs. Dalloway*. But we are also thinking about events in other parts of the world. Can the beauty of this novel cause us, in E. M. Forster's words, to "only connect" with what is going on elsewhere? Or are we, like Clarissa Dalloway, embarrassingly deluded in our vague sense that the aesthetic experiences of this novel, and of this summer, will somehow be for the good? The question that has emerged out of our reading of Woolf's novel has ultimately turned out to be the question implicitly present to our own situation as readers set apart from the world: *what is the relationship between our experience of literary beauty and the world beyond that experience?* Like Woolf in the epigraph to this chapter, like Clarissa Dalloway, "somehow or another . . . it seem[s] as if what [we] read was laid upon the landscape . . . somehow the product of trees and fields and the hot summer sky."[44] But truthfully, we are no closer to an answer that will always serve. We are here, now, reading *Mrs. Dalloway* in Vermont, our thoughts and questions shaped and tempered by the pleasures of precisely that experience and no other.

And thus perhaps our failure is in itself an answer. Far from being able to use this novel as some kind of literary template for a theory of beauty, after our close and shared readings, we find its emotional consequence to be both contingent and specific; our experience of it is fully related to what we as a class of different thinkers and readers and teachers have brought to it. Thinking about beauty in *Mrs. Dalloway* has seemed to force a consideration of place, time, and specificity. Our responses to Woolf's prose are nuanced and unexpected, but the one observable fact—the thing (to subvert Fry's reading of Impressionism) that is the same at two in the afternoon and at five—is that these responses vary as much at different points in our own lives and circumstances as they do from person to person. Accident has its place in our reading, and a line of prose is often tempered for us by the unexpected juxtaposition of self and place, perhaps bumping up against our circumstance or our personal history. One's interpretation of those juxtapositions, both in and out of the text, is extraordinarily personal and fully contingent on one's philosophy, politics, and religion.

And yet in reading, and in talking about our reading, we find that we can share our responses to those moments of beauty publicly in ways that *expand* our own readings rather than merely substitute for them. As we reread a work, we may find comfort in what is familiar, but we may also find ourselves surprised by a beauty previously unseen—by what we had not noticed or by what we had previously not found beautiful. We are alerted to something different and new, by what has, perhaps, always been there but has been brought into relief by our own change in circumstances, life, or location. And it is surely because beauty is not predictable that it *is* a way in which we are alerted to things.

There exists no definable relationship between our experience of literary beauty and the world; between the mountains and the book; between the world beyond the mountains and the internal world of the imagination. In Woolf's *To the Lighthouse* it is an act of conscious will that allows us to hear the music of the disparate parts of the landscape; or, if we are Lily Briscoe, to conceive of the picture as a whole; or, if we are Mrs. Ramsay, to bring the individuals around a dinner table together. In each case, the experience of beauty is merely a step on the way toward unity. Rose's flower arrangement; the delicacy of the candlelight reflected in the glass panes of the windows so that they reflect the outside world "waterily"—these are aesthetic objects or moments necessary to the shift of consciousness involved in creating a whole from unrelated parts. Yet it is through the beauty of such moments that the whole is achieved; and as Woolf writes in that novel, and as our shared experience of reading *Mrs. Dalloway* affirms, it is not beauty alone but rather the "looking together [which] united them."[45]

CHAPTER 5

Beauty and Balance: James Merrill on Santorini

"He has his own pain, his private sorrow, but it is put to the side; he himself is decentered while his imagination and perceptual powers are in full play." In our last chapter, we described Peter Walsh in Woolf's *Mrs. Dalloway* in this way, as his consort with beauty liberates him into a less narcissistic, more lucid, more alive emotional and perceptual realm. When beauty returns to the classroom as an explicit object of study, this complex process of "unselfing" for the sake of ethical clarity and for a sense of reconciliation to the truths of human life is often the focus of discussion. And nowhere is that process more intricately described than in great literature.

University teachers of beauty do two things, principally, in front of the classroom: they lead students in a close analysis of imaginative works that disclose and animate aesthetic experience, and they themselves—teachers of beauty—model, in their way of teaching, their own dynamic, contingent, valuable grasping at aesthetic experience. To walk students through a text like *Mrs. Dalloway*, or like James Merrill's long poem "Santorini: Stopping the Leak," which this chapter will analyze, is to disclose one's own stake in aesthetic experience; it is to display an evolved and evolving ethical sensibility that has learned from engaging in beauty the primary importance of striving for a certain shaky but nonetheless serviceable *balance* in life.[1]

William Arrowsmith is trying to get at this particular classroom reality when he writes that

The humanities are largely Dionysiac or Titanic; they cannot be wholly grasped by the intellect; they must be suffered, felt, seen. This inexpressible turmoil of our animal emotional life is an experience of other chaos matched by our own chaos. We see the form and order not as pure and abstract but as something emerged from chaos, something which has suffered into being. The humanities are always caught up in the actual chaos of living, and they also emerge from that chaos. If they touch us at all, they touch us totally, for they speak to what we are too.[2]

Paying attention to a literary work, as we said in the last chapter, means close reading. And the sort of close reading that prompts an experience of the beautiful (rather than prompting a recitation, for instance, of the political) is essentially about form. It is about intuiting, through attentiveness as much to a poem's shape as to its content, the artist's aesthetic gesture of coherence-creation and ultimately his or her poem's generation in readers of an "unselfing" moral response. The powerful poem has the same capacity as other beautiful objects to rivet the attention, to put the self to the side, to take you somewhere else, to convince you of the teeming vitality of existence, to draw you toward love through the experience of woundedness—generally all of the attributes of the beautiful that we have just considered. And the powerful teacher of beauty has the same capacity, as Arrowsmith suggests, to rivet students to the supreme human business of emerging from suffering and chaos into realized humanity.

The particular promise of happiness a poet like Merrill expresses in "Santorini" epitomizes the defense of beauty as an experience and a pedagogy that we are urging in this book. Always contingent, always suffered into being, it is nonetheless at its heart a conviction of inner and outer balance that enables further, intensified existence. Beauty at its best is no passive luxuriating. Rather, beauty embodied in brilliant art and intense responsiveness is the outcome of a challenging process of ordering and overcoming chaos. It amounts to a complex moral and intellectual activity that involves an initial confrontation with a seemingly disintegrated world and then a succeeding intuition of an underlying integration.

The most powerful art yields the hard-earned gratification of a world re-formed through our own powers of patient, autonomous construction. "Beauty," writes Theodor Adorno, "is . . . a curative sickness. It arrests life, and therefore its decay."[3] Moreover, in arresting and employing our attention in selfless and restorative ways, art and morality, "with certain provisos," writes Iris Murdoch, are "one."[4]

One can follow this movement out from beauty to morality in "Santorini: Stopping the Leak." Its speaker self-consciously cultivates solitude in order, as Adorno suggests, to arrest life long enough to effect a "cure." And as a powerful aesthetic object, Merrill's poem clearly aims to arrest life for its reader with the same clarifying, curative end in mind.

Merrill's poem explores the affinities between Santorini, the volcanic Greek island whose beauty repeatedly recreates itself after, and out of, catastrophic eruptions, and all human beings as they similarly struggle to resist—even as they derive beauty from—catastrophe. The poem presents the extended meditation of a middle-aged man who, having recently evaded personal disaster (he has just completed radiation treatments for a skin cancer that is now, he hopes, "extinct"), turns to celebrate his survival with a trip to the most renowned of the Cyclades Islands. Once on Santorini, he discovers in the island's fragile but reliable form of survival a form of survival founded on a willingness to be autonomous, vulnerable, and therefore periodically destroyed; an exemplar for our own efforts to retain a sense of physical, spiritual, and aesthetic integrity. Like many of Merrill's best poems, "Santorini" is essentially a sort of moral argument, a stroll around various existential stances in the world, and an affirmation, finally, of one particular stance above all others.

Merrill's poem is transparently autobiographical, its first-person voice very much the poet's own as he ponders the best ways to thrive as an artist and a man amid the "late settings" (the title of the 1985 Merrill collection in which the poem originally appeared) of the poet's advancing age (he died in 1995, ten years after the poem appeared).[5] Bringing to an end his long years of regular residence in Greece (a country whose embrace of much of the ugliness of modernity has disillusioned him) and suffering a dry spell in his erotic life, Merrill expresses the same sense of being "islanded" by his encroaching years evoked by Virginia Woolf's Clarissa Dalloway, and any number of other aging fictive and poetic voices, as if to suggest that the adage "No man is an island" is less and less true as one becomes quieter, more reflective, and more inward-looking with time. Youth, Merrill suggests in "Santorini," is an unselfconscious condition of world-assimilation in which one's boundaries are infinitely and excitingly flexible; age, on the other hand, is a condition that, as the poet writes, "[knows] its limits."[6]

Age knows the limit of physical mortality in a way youth does not; but, just as importantly, age recognizes the importance of remaining "oblivious" to this very knowledge in order not to withdraw altogether into the islanded self. The stroller on Santorini, in this instance, knows the "limits" of islands, since to be on an island like Santorini is to know the limits of shorelines in a very literal way. But one ought to prefer, Merrill suggests, oblivion to those reminders of our physical termination. Indeed, Merrill's advance in this poem over many other aesthetic renderings of age involves this heroic determination to retain the fresh ecstatic world-adoration that he had when young, for this is the only way he can remain a poet in and of the world.

Catastrophic endings, though strategically evaded, nonetheless have a crucial role to play in this exercise of self-renewal. In another, much earlier poem, "The Thousand and Second Night," Merrill includes a quotation from Germaine Nahman in which she writes that, as one ages, "calamities (tumor and apoplexy no less than flood and volcano) may at last be hailed as positive reassurances, perverse if you like, of life in the old girl yet."[7] Similarly, the British philosopher Gillian Rose, in her memoir, *Love's Work*, writes,

> A crisis of illness, bereavement, separation, natural disaster, could be the opportunity to make contact with deeper levels of the terrors of the soul, to loose and to bind, to bind and to loose. A soul which is not bound is as mad as one with cemented boundaries. To grow in love-ability is to accept the boundaries of oneself and others, while remaining vulnerable, woundable, around the bounds. Acknowledgement of conditionality is the only unconditionality of human love.[8]

Thus, even if, as the poet ages, "the worst keeps dawning" on him (as Merrill writes in another late poem, "The Inner Room"), he must accept this trauma and breakage as a kind of necessary precondition of the reanimation of weakening life. One way of "braving the elements"—the title of another Merrill collection—of human existence is to take the breakage in one's hands and fashion something new and beautiful out of it, to discover amid wreckage the hidden poem.

It is, in short, the complex business of keeping intact and afloat, remaining precariously composed and balanced in life, walking upright on the hot volcanic sand of Santorini despite the cancer that has manifested itself in the poet's foot and made walking difficult, that Merrill explores with his characteristic philosophical subtlety and stylistic beauty in this poem. Perhaps because the reality of increasing disability in this "late" poem makes the stakes in the game of survival increasingly high, its clash of emotional depth and glittering surfaces creates the most powerful lyrical utterance in Merrill's repertoire. Merrill's excavation of the metaphor of the volcanic island, expressive for him not merely of autonomous integrity but of the intricate vulnerability of that integrity, is patient, resolute, and skillful; he delves into a much-used image and emerges with a wholly new created artifact.

In particular, Merrill discovers on the island of Santorini the crucial necessity in life of a stance I would call not so much *ecstasy* as (continuing to employ the Greek terminology appropriate to Merrill's choice of Greece as a second spiritual and actual home throughout his life) *isostasy*. Isostasy is the condition of being subjected to equal pressure from every side, yet maintaining one's balance within that pressure. Its geological meaning involves the general equilibrium in the earth's crust, maintained by a yielding flow of rock material beneath the surface, under gravitative stress. The concept of isostasy, related to that of equipoise, seems to capture best what Merrill has in mind as the ideal stance of the realized man and poet: such a person strives for a particular form of grace under pressure and learns that the way to attain this is not through a rigid self-enclosure, but on the contrary through a strategic yielding to the pull of mortality.

The exceptionally beautiful island of Santorini exemplifies this stance of isostasy because it remains totally vulnerable to natural forces—not merely its volcanic depths but, just as importantly, the fierce radiance of the Aegean sun—and reveals that it is precisely that vulnerability, that yielding, that assures its survival. Isolated, small, lying in endless reflective waters, the island is fully open to the radiance of the sun scorching its white chapels and dry vineyards. That radiance is both creative and destructive, producing at once the wine and olives of the island and a parched land and people wholly dependent upon imported water. Santorini puts in relief the lesson that you cannot have the radiance without the burning, that the process of healing and regeneration is at one with the process of undoing. Placing this complex spiritual education upon the island of Santorini allows Merrill to isolate its stages and witness its most dramatic effects.

It is not really Santorini's postcard beauty, but rather the island's weird mix of the gorgeous and the morbid that sets the scene for the poet's attempt to come to terms with the fact that, despite a lifetime of successful efforts toward regeneration, his physical and creative vitality is finally beginning to "leak" away. Although Santorini's fiery exoticism has inspired the poet to "stop" the leaking of his vitality in a kind of cauterization, he understands that, like the island's volcano, his own "multiplex"—the small island of cancer on the larger island of his body—is merely dormant. Just as Santorini's usually quiet, solid, and beautiful volcano lulls people into a sense of safety, so each of us is a sort of island whose integrity, while intact, lulls us into forgetfulness of lurking disintegration. It is this condition of forgetfulness that Merrill's poem wants most to explore. "Santorini" expresses the poet's conviction that the best way to live with the knowledge of the leaking away of life is through the cultivation of "an oblivion / That [knows] its limits,"[9] which is to say (as Merrill writes in another poem, "Prose of Departures") through the cultivation of a "form of conscious evasion."[10] Thus one critic writes of Merrill that, for him, learning is a "process of absorption, forgetting, and reminiscence."[11]

Islands are particularly useful symbolic forms for this conveyance of the notion that even as we live our lives fully, with this complex sort of oblivion, we need to remain conscious of limits—our imperfection, life's imperfection, life's brevity. In his poem "To Marguerite—Continued," Matthew Arnold writes that "islands feel the enclasping flow" of water around them, "[a]nd then their endless bounds they know."[12] On volcanic islands, moreover, one lives within sight of past and imminent catastrophic limits to the integrity of one's world. Indeed, one is aware that even the present seeming solidity of the volcano is an illusion—lava may continually leak from its cone, and, just under the surface, fires rage.

Yet volcanic islands like Santorini are also energizingly beautiful to us, with their black sand, white domed villages, and smoky calderas. Their very ability to resolidify into habitable, shapely earth is a profound affirmation of human as well as aesthetic regeneration, as Merrill suggests in another poem, "Island in the Works." Despite "untold blue / subversions," despite the "depth-wish" of waves, the reemergent volcanic island "construes" itself anew, its soil "first arid, hard, / Soon root fast, ramifying, / Always more fruitful."[13] "I'm surfacing, I'm home!" the island exults at the end of the poem. "Open the atlas. Here: / This dot, securely netted / Under the starry dome."[14] That dot is both the island in the sea or in the pages of the atlas, and the final period of the completed poem, which confirms the successful—though always shaky—resolution of the poet's efforts at formed expressivity. Merrill recognizes in this paradox the power of aesthetic form itself: poetic art is both culture's harsh reminder of limits and, in its beauty and integrity, its source of solace. Thus when the poet performs, toward the end of "Santorini," a "grave dance" over the fragile surface of island Earth, he is really performing his own poem, a classically beautiful, restrained, but intricately musical, act of *gravitas*.

Merrill, like another American poet, Donald Justice, and like American expatriate painter Cy Twombly, is essentially a classicist in form and content. For him the solidification of language into the fundamentals of poetic form is the same act of cultural and personal restoration that the island of Santorini, reclaimed after every eruption by its inhabitants, and, more modestly, repainted every year, affirms. "Santorini" is a highly worked poem whose brilliant and exact end rhymes and shapely stanzas affirm the primary value of shining new light into the sort of highly formal poetry that has been obscured by modern, open form. For the poet, islands express most powerfully of all natural objects the compulsion to restructure, to impose and reimpose established, embellished form on an entropic world.

Furthermore, islands allow poets to assume a particular stance, a stance of high relief, as they plant themselves upon a dynamic and beautiful assertion of identity. One of Merrill's strongest influences, W. H. Auden, addresses an island directly in his poem, "On This Island":

> Stand stable here
> And silent be,
> That through the channels of the ear
> May wander like a river
> The swaying sound of the sea.[15]

For Auden, as for the Yeats of "The Lake Isle of Innisfree," islands have to do with stopping things, with interrupting the overwhelming flow of the sea and making landfall. In the powerful silence they create, a space and distance for contemplation of the world is created within the poet. The fluid channels within his ear will only here be able to pick up a sense of the enormity of the world. Like Wallace Stevens's jar in Tennessee, islands make the surrounding sea rise up to meet them, and they thereby define a world. Going to an island means in this context stopping the leakage of vitality, of shapeliness, by, ironically, stopping the processes of life itself; the "unsponsored, free" solitude of the island (the phrase is from Stevens's "Sunday Morning," which concludes with an image of modern secular life as islanded) offers the outer silence that allows the world to stop and the poet to regenerate. Rudyard Kipling captured this quality of islands when he wrote in his 1902 poem, "Broken Men": "God bless the thoughtful islands / Where never warrants come."[16] Yet Santorini's poet never forgets that, despite their seeming "warrantless" existence, islands may be devastatingly susceptible to outside forces. (Recall the fate of the island of Montserrat after a recent volcanic eruption, in which ash entombed it in a matter of hours.)

One of the reasons Merrill's poem is so important is that, at a time when people tend to fear autonomy and refuse to acknowledge limits, "Santorini" is a powerful reminder of the imperishable and enabling truths of being human. Its ancient sources and lush language lend the poem a seductive grace, a persuasive genuineness, as it argues for the classical verities of aesthetic shapeliness, emotional clarity, and personal endurance.

Although Merrill's poem evokes both classical and modern dance, its fundamental movement actually involves what the poet characterizes as a "stroll" through the "worst"—that is, a sort of ramble through thoughts and images of impending mortality. His plantar wart has left his foot "sore," but he and a companion, Nelly, walk much of the mountainous length of Santorini anyway, in a kind of defiance of his weakened condition and in a haze of delight with the "magnificent" beauty of the island. The point is "less to ignore / The worst than stroll through it by evening light."[17] In the hands of Merrill, Santorini becomes a stroll garden, where one contemplates at once the serenity and the precariousness of the world, a dual reality nicely suggested by Merrill's use of the phrase "evening light."

The time is dusk, and the brilliant light of the island is now evening out, just as the passionate intensity of the poet's highly lit life is beginning to diminish. The light is "evening," but it is nonetheless still light, and the play upon degrees and kinds of radiance in this poem by one of the world's most heliotropic poets (only Blake makes more of the sun than Merrill) will deepen throughout "Santorini." The very first stanza, recalling the "lethal x / Rays" targeted on the "isolated" island of the poet's foot cancer, establishes the poem's central and abiding idea: the radiance of the world is at once lethal and healing, a life force to which we must be receptive if we are to thrive, despite our knowledge (lightly buried under a saving oblivion) of its dangers.[18]

In his magisterial work, *The Changing Light at Sandover*, Merrill had already clearly stated this idea. The deity of the poem, called "God B," the poet writes,

> . . . USES HIS ATOMIC
> POWER AS BOTH BENEVOLENT (SUN) & CHASTISING (BOMBS)
> USES IT AS HIS ONE AGENT TO CREATE & DESTROY.[19]

Atomic bombs are only the most dramatic evidence of cataclysmic radiant energy. More importantly, Merrill writes in the next stanza of "Santorini," the sun itself, especially upon the vulnerable, utterly receptive island of Santorini, can be both brilliant and burning: "Inches overhead," he notes, gazing at the sky, "a blue that burns, / That all but blackens—heaven as a flue?— / Against this white that all but calcifies."[20] So intense is the September sunlight (note the autumnal month) on the island that it transforms it into a kind of cauldron from which heaven draws the smoke created not only by the caldera but also by the steady scorching of the island's white houses, houses that lie "unmelted on the crest" of the island's high cliff "like snow."[21]

Yet this disintegrative scorching that produces a radiant earthly heat can, again, be seen as a version of aesthetic creation itself. Just as Santorini's main village lies "unmelted on [a] crest like snow," so the artist survives precariously, perched on the edge of a boiling abyss, deriving beauty precisely out of that hot and risky inclination. Despite the terror, fragility, and brevity of life (Santorini's "cliff-coagulations . . . regress / To null mist at a blow from the moon mallet," the poet writes, evoking the random "blows" of destruction in human lives), all—but particularly the artist—are compelled to "hold steady." By holding steady (the phrase can be understood literally here as the instruction one receives from medical personnel when being x-rayed) and being, the poet later writes, "light of soul," the poet "let[s] go" of things, lets rush up into the celestial flue the warming poetry that a cold and bare heaven needs. In return for this warmth, heaven will beam down vitalizing radiance.[22]

This relationship of mutual radiance is beautifully expressed in another poem of Merrill's, "Little Fanfare for Felix Magowan." Essentially a modest occasional poem on the birth of a relative's child, "Felix Magowan" addresses the infant, telling him that "the sun is a great friend," but in its intrinsic violence it "cannot change." The child is not the sun's child, but the child of "earth" and "time," which will, mercifully, "blot [the sun] out" in a "lifelong eclipse" and allow growth. Yet the "black pupil rimmed with rays" that the child's eye makes is a kind of miniature sun in itself (Merrill keeps in play puns on "sun" and "son" throughout the verse). It is

> Contracted to its task—
> That of revealing by obscuring
> The sunlike friend behind it.
> Unseen by you, may he shine back always
> From what you see, from others.

Again, every human being incorporates a sunlike radiance, a spiritual heat and light, which shines forth to the world with life-giving energy. It is precisely that energy that Merrill, himself moving toward the end of life, is attempting to preserve in "Santorini."[23]

Both the volcanic island and the poet, then, represent heat conductors. Both constantly absorb the energy of the sun, and, on the island and in the poet, lies nothing less than the potential to reanimate the world through the alchemical transformation of cold into hot. Like Prospero in another autumnal island drama, the poet in Merrill's rendering is a magician of the elements who transforms a dead world into a living one. The poem, as in Percy Bysshe Shelley's famous image of the fading coal,[24] is the cooling "solid" object of beauty that remains after the fire of inspiration has dimmed.

Like Prospero, too, Merrill recognizes that only in an act of renunciation, of letting go, of being light of soul, can the poet lessen the pressures of reality sufficiently to thrive and recreate in his way. The idea here is that within each human island lies a volcano, a source of anxiety and despair whose pressure can build perilously. Malcolm Lowry, author of the great modernist novel *Under the Volcano*, whose story is set in the shadow of Mexico's two great volcanoes, writes of these psychic pressures in this way:

> Why were there volcanic eruptions? People pretended not to know. Because, they might suggest tentatively, under the rocks beneath the surface of the

earth, steam, its pressure constantly rising, was generated; because the rocks and the water, decomposing, formed gases, which combined with the molten material from below; because the watery rocks near the surface were unable to restrain the growing complex of pressures, and the whole mass exploded.[25]

Merrill's poem can be understood as an effort to escape the fate of Lowry's hero, Geoffrey Firman (whose name has echoes of "fire"): psychic collapse under the pressures of personal guilt and a world veering toward destruction (the novel was written on the verge of the Second World War; much of Merrill's work explores the specter of nuclear annihilation). Like Arnold (author also of "Empedocles on Etna"), Lowry figured spiritual collapse and death as a fall into a volcano, as the inability to bear the rising heat of the world.

But Merrill has a far more positive rendering of the force of volcanic islands than Lowry. Disintegrative pressures, which produce breaks, are in fact what we need; without the experience of rupture, we are unable to contrive new forms and ways of being. In an essay titled "Elementary Bravery: The Unity of James Merrill's Poetry," David Lehman first cites two pertinent lines from Yeats's poem, "Crazy Jane Talks with the Bishop": "For nothing can be sole or whole / That has not been rent." He then goes on to argue that for Merrill as well, "fragmentation . . . precedes or accompanies unity."[26] While for Arnold, for example, the condition of being an island figures the condition of wistful and yearning separation from other people, a sense of having been hopelessly and painfully fragmented—"For surely once, they feel, we were / Parts of a single continent!"—for Merrill, an acceptance of the reality of this fragmentation is a necessary precondition for movement and growth. Lowry, like Arnold, expresses in his novel an all-or-nothing demand for reunification:

Ah, who would have thought of it then as other than a single integrated rock? But granted it had been split, was there no way before total disintegration should set in of at least saving the severed halves? There was no way. The violence of the fire which split the rock apart had also incited the destruction of each separate rock, cancelling the power that might have held them unities. Oh, but why—by some fanciful geological thaumaturgy, couldn't the pieces be welded together again![27]

Resisting at all times the seduction of such grand syntheses, such permanent symbiotic unions, Merrill celebrates contingency and the rewards of radiant earthly clarity.

"Santorini: Stopping the Leak" divides itself into five stages that track the poet's slow progress from "terminal" to "creative" radiance. Seeking to put behind him his recent radiation treatments, he revels in the very different sort of radiance Santorini sheds. He has hesitated to visit the island because, knowing that "it would be—is—magnificent," he would have preferred a "companion." But he is alone, occasionally befriended only by Nelly, an island resident. Yet despite his physical and emotional shakiness—

> Brushes? These five of mine with nothingness
> Threatening forever to unmake
> The living form [radiation] sees through in a trice

—he reminds himself that the fundamental imperative is to "hold steady." Holding steady means not merely remaining medically stable but, as an artist ("I've prepared my palette"), focusing his own radiant vision on the brilliantly arrested formal beauty of the island in order to "paint" it.[28]

The second section of the poem moves from the poet's and the island's current stability to the unimaginably cataclysmic origin of present-day Santorini:

> Innermost chaos understood at first
> As Gaia's long-pent-up emotions crippling
> Her sun-thrilled body, spun to the great Lyre;
> Pent up, but all too soon unleashed—outburst
> Savage enough to bury in its fire
> The pendant charms she wore, palace and stripling,
> A molten afterbirth . . .[29]

Merrill here recalls the spectacular eruption of Santorini's ancient volcano, probably one of the most violent eruptions ever, with massive destructive breadth. In that immense drowning, both civilization and nature ("palace and stripling") were seemingly permanently demolished; yet, gradually, a "molten afterbirth" manifested itself, in which the poet imagines the human soul, clinging to "its own fusing senses," having eventually "crawl[ed] at last / Away unshriveled by the holocaust. . . ."[30]

The slow rebirth of Santorini from annihilation reveals, astonishingly, three islands now in place of the original one—as if to suggest that destruction may ultimately turn out to be generative. And now the fiery Empedocles, "Leaper headlong into that primal scene," has been replaced by the tourist, gazing into the "[r]im of that old disaster"—a phrase strongly reminiscent of Wallace Stevens's "Sunday Morning"—and the main island, with its views onto the magnificent caldera, is famous as a site of unsurpassed natural beauty, as if nature, once destroyed, reforms itself with yet greater splendor.

Still, an "eerie radiation" remains in the air of the island, famous also "for its vampires":

> Clearly, as the gods decline,
> An eerie radiation fills the air
> And eats their armor. The Byzantine Empire's
> Avian-angelic iridescence
> Shrank to black flitterings in the lymph of peasants.[31]

The grandeur of that early mythic world, with its pantheon of deities shedding Apollonian clarity, has in fact, Merrill suggests, been lost forever, replaced by a darkly malign internal force, a kind of perverse absorption of that original radiant outburst, which gradually erodes our humanity. In these final lines of the poem's second section, the poet obliquely recalls his own diseased and vulnerable body, the blood cells losing their immunities.

Like the poet, Nelly is also a wounded being; deaf, she too is coping with encroaching age, and she still mourns the sudden death of a beloved twin brother years ago from a lightning strike (another "random blow from the moon mallet"). Lightning is felt as yet another form of radiance here, a blinding electrical "flicker" both sublime and deadly. Yet, feeling uneasy at this reminder of life's fragility, the poet reminds himself that he's unlikely very soon to lose his own life; rather, he's in the process of losing "an ingrown guest" on his foot, and—more disturbingly—Greece itself:

> Corrupted whites and blues,
> Taverns torn down for banks, the personnel
> Grown fat and mulish, marbles clogged with soot . . .
> Things just aren't what they were—no more am I,
> No more is Nelly. The good word's goodbye[32]

Merrill now introduces another crucial theme in "Santorini": in order to survive with a full life, one must be willing to let certain things go. Again, Merrill renders this idea of strategic renunciation in terms of classical values—the value of graceful lightness, of willing restraint, of a certain stoical acceptance of loss—even when a resoundingly significant aspect of life (in his case, Merrill's love of Greece) is at issue. Goodbye is sometimes a very good word, signaling an ability to cut one's losses and move on to something new.

The following section of the poem enlarges this theme of willing renunciation as the poet, reminding himself of the imperative to "be light, light-footed, light of soul / Quick to let go," jumps forward in time to his home in Athens, where he decides to "leave the bulk behind" and go back to his primary home in Connecticut. Let the "killing rays" of the sun burn away his life in that city—he'll leave behind his bed, his pictures, his records, and his books, so that they can live "yet more life" in the hands of others.[33]

The seeming clarity and ease of this tossing off is immediately undermined by the poet's "long, flowing fits / Of seeing" during a nap that he takes in his soon-to-be-abandoned Athens home. Here, the perils of "psychic incontinence," a condition to which artists are particularly susceptible, manifest themselves. For much as he would like to bid a neat goodbye to a threateningly inchoate past, he cannot; his own convoluted mental reality will assert itself despite his efforts at orderly progress. In dreams, the poet loses his sense of stabilized identity; his sympathetic aesthetic energy now generates one vignette after another, each

> . . . churning down the optic sluice,
> Faces young, old, . . .
> . . . all random, ravenous images
>
> Avid for inwardness . . .
> . . .
> The warm spate bears me on, helpless, unable
> Either to sink or swim . . .

In this Rilkean invocation of inwardness, the poet feels the horror of drowning in the viscous contingency, the thingness, of the world.[34]

But this sense of being compelled by any and every thing in the world to "imagine" it, to assimilate it into the poet's inwardness and thereby save it from death by shaping it into permanent aesthetic form, now transmutes into a related fear of being overcome by the cancer that has emerged on the poet's foot. Psychic incontinence somehow also initiates a sort of cellular incontinence, in which the unchecked growth of cancer will overwhelm the poet physically. Throwing off the bed-sheets, the poet now directly confronts his terror at the prospect of his own mortality:

> Sobbing for air
> I hobble to the mirror, wordlessly
> Frame this petition to its oval, where
> Behind a twitching human curtain smiles
> Those revels' Queen, in easy ownership,
> Sated, my vigor coloring her lip.[35]

Like Santorini's blood-draining vampire, the poet's cancerous muse has always parasitically lived off of his "vigor," but she is now, in the poet's latter days, taking more and more dominion over him. He prays to that powerful malignancy for the continued survival of his "snowflake-singular" identity, his particular poetic self, despite the ultimately unstoppable force of dissolution.

After this outburst of anguish, the poet returns us to the island of Santorini, to a calmer setting where he can work out in full consciousness, in full sunlight, the forms of his endurance. Santorini is indeed an "oblivion / that knows its limits," and from Santorini he will learn to know his own. The island's "symbiosis with the molten genie" is "imbecile"—in the sense of weak—but precisely because the island displays and acknowledges its weakness, it can survive its own meanings. In a passage of surpassing delicacy, Merrill evokes that gorgeous fragility: "I hear the ferrous, feather-light diluvian / Lava clink at a knife-tap from our guide."[36] "We must be light!" the poet again affirms. We must also "attain the double / Site of our last excursion: Prophet Elias' / Radar-crowned monastery."[37] The effort to attain this saving double vision, a fearless apprehension of death and life, will be the burden of the rest of the poem as the poet continues his stroll through the worst on Santorini. In a dark underground classroom, hidden for centuries from Turkish rulers, the poet, himself now one of many "Small pupils widening" (again, as in "Felix Magowan," the reference is both to the widening of the pupil of the eye in darkness and to the expansion of knowledge), comes to understand the way in which language, even in the austere and risky conditions of that classroom, has always seemed able to "resurrect / Sibyl and scribe's illuminated leaves." [38]

High above the hidden classroom stand the radar towers—a jarring modern "crown" for this ancient and reticent setting. And this, too, is part of the double vision the poet must attain: an acceptance of yet another debased and threatening form of radiation in the world, an acceptance, finally, of the ugliness of modernity itself even as the classical vision remains compelling and generative for him. Spiritual and profane radiance meet atop this cliff in Santorini, and the poet must learn to assimilate both.

Nelly and the poet, in the final three stanzas of the poem, now put the monastery behind them and go off in search of "the precinct of Apollo of the Herds." Here the poem will attain its radiant apogee in the realm of the god of sunlight, poetry, prophecy, and music, all of which will come together on the island in the measured, harmonious, and balanced order of art. On this open field, in solitude, the poet discovers a "heavenly forge," another fiery setting, but this one benign, in which the language of art, the heated word of the poet, is

> Snapped up by North Wind, bellowed to recycle
> The bare, thyme-tousled world we'd stumbled on,
> Its highbrow wholly given to the Sun
> Who beamingly returned the gift.[39]

Here, Shelley's entreaty to the west wind to vitalize and broadcast his poetic voice[40] is answered in a resounding affirmative by the forces of nature, which the poet's "bellow"—here, his expansive, musical lungs, which make an instrument of the air—transforms into expressive beauty and order, thus "recycling" the world.

Merrill's classicism emerges most clearly now. This is a world recycled (there is probably a pun on "Cyclades" here; the poet has "renamed" the island, just as the monks in the buried monastery continually reanimated the Greek language during years of its suppression), not made radically new and different. The world has been both bare and chaotic ("thyme-tousled" has obvious echoes of "time"); the poet's creative power lends it the meaning and temporal order it had lost. This is really the heart of Merrill's aesthetic and spiritual cosmology. Take the risk of exposure to clarity, to sunlight, and you will be rewarded in the following way: the radiance you, in turn, create under the inspiration of solar light will return sunward and be received gratefully by the sun, who will, in turn, in an endless dialogue, return light.

But that "bellow" has also meant to suggest, more prosaically, the poet with his camera (the bellow is an expansible feature of some cameras) as he produces a final version of radiance—the light-explosion of photography. He notices that a hole has "burnt through [his] film—by one-split-second glance!" of the sun. "I drew a breath. So much for radiance."[41] He has allowed his film to be exposed to the sunlight for only an instant, but that has been enough, so overwhelmingly powerful is that force. Once again, Merrill reminds us, radiance is as destructive as it is creative; and this haunting by destructive radiance will appear in his later, somewhat frightening poem set in Japan, "Prose of Departure," in which the visiting poet, feeling physically ill and full of anxiety about the health of various sick friends, writes,

> The prevailing light in this "Hiroshima" of trivial symptoms and empty forebodings is neither sunrise nor moonglow but rays that promptly undo whatever enters their path. They strip the garden to clawed sand. They whip the modern hotel room back into fatal shape: the proportions and elisions of centuries. In their haste to photograph Truth they eat through a blue-and-white cotton robe, barely pausing to burn its pattern onto the body shocked alert. . . . [42]

This is the wholly dark vision of stark and killing radiance, a body utterly exposed to deadly radiation, a world unredeemed, untransfigured, and unsoftened, by the tactical and tactful evasions of art.

Nonetheless, having reminded us what awaits him, the poet, on Santorini, concludes with a celebratory dance:

> Here, finally, music that would take Satie
> Twenty-five hundred years to reinvent
> Put naked immaturity through paces
> Of a grave dance—as if catastrophe
> Could long be lulled by slim waists and shy faces.
> Our "worst" in part lived through, part imminent,
> We made on sore feet, and by then *were* made
> For a black beach, a tavern in the shade.[43]

Merrill's extensive poetic search for equipoise concludes here, with a grave dance that reconnects the poet to the ancient ground of life; he has put himself through the paces in order to discover the enduring stance of vital existence. And the music that animates that posture is the perpetual music of serenity, sensuality, community, and vulnerability that the Greeks knew as the gynophores and that Erik Satie would reinvent centuries later. Nothing has changed; the dance of culture is as it has always been, a complex tensional act in which silence, stark truth, and morbidity are put off, lulled for a time, by the evasive grandeur of aesthetic form.

The slow, close reading a formally complex poem like "Santorini" demands is a difficult discipline, one that calls upon teachers to model in their teaching a patient, deliberative, and withholding form of discussion and lecture. By "withholding," I mean that they must, to the extent possible, allow the poem, and the poem alone—not the personality and beliefs of the professor or the students—to hold center stage, to compel everyone's attention; they must resist the temptation to anticipate the poem's meanings.

A politically minded, content-based professor might be inclined to jump to the one clearly political allusion in the poem: the reference to underground classrooms, where Greek scribes protected their language from Turkish rulers. But in terms of the poem's underlying form, this overt history of conflict is not particularly important, since "Santorini," as a beautiful poem about a beautiful island, achieves a far more complex dialectic and a moral and spiritual, rather than political, dialectic at that. The poet's extensive musings about Santorini move him and the reader toward a personal stability within existential instability, an inner assurance of solidity amid an outwardly unsolid world. These are the aesthetic uses of solitude.

A political reader is liable to be unconcerned with the slow, musing, philosophical feel of this poem. He or she is more likely to light on the poet's assurance that despite centuries of repression, the Greeks have always been able to "resurrect / Sibyl and scribe's illuminated leaves" and find it naïve and indifferent to the bloody reality of national struggle. If the main thing you are looking for in a poem, or any piece of writing, is clarity toward an immediate praxis, then Merrill's pensive, arcane, and highly wrought work will look reactionary and quietist, his complaints about "mulish" contemporary Greece elitist.

Truth to Merrill's poem, though, involves a willing entry into his philosophical and aesthetic consciousness and, to some extent, a suspension of your own. Indeed, "willing" isn't quite the word. For the aesthetically responsive reader, entry is virtually unavoidable, as the power of the beautiful object compels your attention. "But great writing—great writing forces you to submit to its vision," argues Zadie Smith.[44] When we read "Santorini," we are caught by the powerful beauty of the language and form of a poem that features a speaker himself caught up in the powerful beauty of an island; we are riveted by the intensity of his exemplary capacity for aesthetic response. Merrill is our guide through Santorini—what he has loved, he knows others will love—and his invigorated poetics draws us on an irresistible spiritual quest.

Yet there's no easy salvation here, no sentimental reassurance. The larger context of this poem is a sick, aging man rather pathetically hoping for rejuvenation on the island. The sort of triumph we feel at the end of a beautiful meditation on the aesthetic like this one is the triumph of the contingent self, the self that has made it through to a rich subjectivity and a strong individuality, even as it is inescapably brought, at the end of the day, to a "black beach." That dark limit to consciousness, the catastrophe that lurks behind and indeed paradoxically *generated* the spectacular beauty of Santorini, is always there; and in that generally disregarded but ever peripherally alive disaster lies the "politics" of the aesthetic, to which we will turn in the next chapter.

CHAPTER 6

Beauty After 9/11: Don DeLillo in New York

Two months after the September 11 attacks, Don DeLillo—Brooklyn-born, dyed-in-the-wool New Yorker, chronicler of postmodern American life in that city and elsewhere—wrote an essay titled "In the Ruins of the Future" on the subject of the terror events.[1] In that essay, this grieving and traumatized New Yorker described the desperation of his nephew and his nephew's family as they saved themselves from the ash and toxic air of the World Trade Center site, only blocks from their apartment. But he framed this personal account with a larger set of arguments about what the attack meant and what the novelist might be able to offer us in the wake of such an event.

DeLillo wrote that the "high gloss of our modernity" in America drew the fury of the attackers—the "thrust of our technology," "the power of American culture to penetrate every wall, home, life and mind." "Technology is our fate, our truth. It is what we mean when we call ourselves the only superpower on the planet. . . . But whatever great skeins of technology lie ahead, ever more complex . . . the future has yielded, for now, to medieval experience, to the old slow furies of cut-throat religion." Because the terrorists believe that technology "brings death to their customs and beliefs," they will use that technology—our planes—as "a thing that kills." The terrorists, he wrote, "want to bring back the past." They literally want to kill modernity and all it implies. They have, as DeLillo's title suggests, "ruined" the future—a particularly American future—and we must now begin rebuilding that future from the ruins.

But what does "our modernity" imply exactly? What does it mean to be a modern American? DeLillo reminds us that the American tradition is, of course, one of "free expression and [a] justice [system with] provisions for the rights of the accused." He reminds us that we are "rich, privileged, and strong." People around the world admire, envy, and hate us for these things, and maybe a lot of them have a right to resent our arrogance and the long arm of our geopolitical power. But, says DeLillo, "there is no logic in [the] apocalypse" that was 9/11: "They have gone beyond the bounds of passionate payback. This is heaven and hell, a sense of armed martyrdom as the surpassing drama of human existence." This is, in other words, a madness, a fanaticism so hate-filled and violent as to be beyond our comprehension.

Yet if it is incomprehensible, it is not, DeLillo suggests, omnipotent. Although the terrorists have temporarily seized the "narrative" of the world, "it is left to us to create the counternarrative." All of DeLillo's novels can be seen as attempting that—to write the counternarrative to terror of all sorts. And it is a counternarrative that features prominently the redemptive possibilities of beauty. Few artists have made the artist himself or herself as important, as culturally central, as DeLillo has, and he has made the artist important because the artist is one of the few cultural figures who can help us transcend the fear, cynicism, and withdrawal that accompany life in a traumatizing and unreal environment by seducing us into the selflessness that will calm our fear and quicken our empathy.

Faced with destruction and catastrophe, we must begin to recuperate what we can out of it, make it not so much meaningful as emotionally acceptable, something we can get beyond in order to build a sane and legitimate cultural and personal narrative. Here is another novelist, Martin Amis, writing also about 9/11:

> A novel is politely known as a work of the imagination; and the imagination, that day, was of course fully commandeered, and to no purpose. Whenever that sense of heavy incredulity seems about to dissipate, I still find, an emergent detail will eagerly replenish it: the 'pink mist' in the air, caused by the explosion of the falling bodies; the fact that the second plane, on impact, was traveling at nearly 600 mph, a speed that would bring it to the point of disintegration. (What was it like to be a passenger on that plane? What was it like to see it coming towards you?)[2]

These are the horrors, the immediate and unassimilable details of the unspeakable event. We can only focus on the small things—the particular lives and deaths, the objects saved, the sounds of voices on cell phones. And this is where the novelist comes in, for the artist is the person who selects, who ferrets out the pivotal details, the deeply telling phrase or musical series or gesture that will allow us the only sort of access we can tolerate into enormity.

We go to the artist for an ordering of events, for a subtle unfolding of possible, plausible meanings that will help us attain some balance.

Richard Rorty writes that "[w]hat you share with other people [is] an ability to sympathize with the pain of others."[3] What the literary artist possesses is much more than this this: the ability to "imagine the moment," as DeLillo writes, "desperately."[4] Writing in the 1950s about the "end of ideology," Henry David Aiken saw this fundamental imperative of the serious writer equally clearly in his own topical terms:

> I can assent to the proposition that on the first day of an atomic war every major city in the United States would be destroyed, without in the least *realizing*, in human terms, what the statement really means. . . . I must somehow try symbolically to live through the horror and the agony of such a calamity . . . it is essential that I find a way of thinking and talking about the fact which will make me realize from a practical, and even, if you please, from a metaphysical point of view, what it comes to. For most of us, this can be done only through the artificial linguistic devices, known to every reader of fiction and of poetry, which enable us to perform "in imagination," as we say, those symbolic actions in which alone the 'reality' of *literary* art exists.[5]

Aiken is describing the quest for the authentic voice, meaningful form, and felt reality that underlies all of DeLillo's work.

Teachers of beauty in the university classroom both perform and analyze the shaping human imagination as it takes chaos and pain and gives it fragile, restorative, aesthetic form. This means that the pedagogy of beauty, while never crudely therapeutic, has as an implicit aim the regeneration of hope—what Rorty has in mind when he talks about inspiration—through the demonstration of the power of aesthetic consciousness.

***

In the immediate aftermath of 9/11, some New Yorkers fled upstate, to the Catskill and Adirondack mountains, and to the Hudson Valley. A few bought homes and started new lives there, too horrified to return to the city. For years I've had a summer house in the Catskills, and after the attacks the place took on a new character.

It was still beautiful in the old ways: The August night sky outside the house was spectacular. A bright moon left the rim of the mountains, and the blue clouds over them, visible. The house stands alone on a hill. There are no neighbors and few lights. The large canopy above it glimmers with airliners and satellites and Perseids. Below, when the sun is out, there are high-forested hills and a green valley, mainly trees, with some fields. Behind the hills is a Catskill range. After months of summer heat in Washington, D.C., the cold air feels like a freak of nature, an instance of forgetting what August is supposed to be.

A maze of paths is sculpted out of the wildflower field in front of the house. You walk the field and see birds and snakes and spider webs in the stands of flowers. Butterflies settle on the rim of your hat. The noise is incessant: birdsong, crickets, the wind in the pines, farm machinery. When you walk the dirt road at the bottom of the field, you can hear frogs squawk along the ponds. When you walk the path from the house to its pond, you carry a pair of scissors to snip overgrowth as you go. There's a small, neglected cabin overlooking the pond.

The business of leisurely business here is pleasant: we're always vaguely doing something useful as we wander about—pulling reeds out of the pond, collecting twigs, resettling stones. But in the larger sense, we do little to alter the life of the house, outside or in. A new chaise for the deck, a white chest of drawers, a few perennials—these are the measures we take with the place. Nature keeps it beautiful.

Our main business is being here, watching the weather write the book of the world, as Donald Hall, who lives on a farm in New Hampshire, puts it. Watching the world leaf through its chapters. Of course, poetry—the sort of thing Hall writes—makes nothing happen, as Auden puts it; but by that he suggested that nothing was, in fact, a something. Poetry suspends the distracting business of quotidian life and draws a special attentiveness out of us: it makes the "nothing" of a quietly subterranean world "happen."

More broadly, our many experiences of beauty over a lifetime, built and natural, educate us in the varieties of order that may exist in the world. Natural beauty displays the earth in a state of fitness, things being what they are supposed to be. Ethically, this sense of how things should be implies a corresponding sense of what things look like when they are wrong, and it also implies an impulse to right them. Out of this tutored sense of natural fitness may come, among other things, a heightened environmental awareness.

The fabricated regularities of a beautiful poem, play, novel, or symphony constitute a kind of reassurance for us: Despite the disorder of the social world, despite our own fragility, look what we can do. We can create entire gorgeous worlds—Yoknapatawpha, Dublin—that in their own terms contain and display a satisfying as well as clarifying structural integrity.

Yet in the summer after 9/11, the tranquil natural beauty of the New York mountains felt different to me. It felt like something to which one fled in fear. I found, under these circumstances, DeLillo's aesthetic consciousness more valuable than ever, since it intuits not merely our drive toward life and beauty but also the terrorist's drive toward death. And this is another "balance" that the pedagogy of beauty should express in the classroom. It should be clear to our students, as we have said before, that life is a battle and that the beautiful life always emerges out of a struggle to overcome the anonymity, conformity, fanaticism, and cruelty that comprise what's ugliest in us. It is all the more important, then, that novelists like DeLillo give imaginative life to what sustains us and that teachers express somehow in their self-presentation and in their focus upon the beautiful artwork, the dynamic, imperiled nature of the effort toward beauty.

I've thought a lot about the therapeutic beauties of places like the Catskill house, "aside from a pushing world," since the attacks. Indeed, I worried, in the weeks just after, that the vastly creative beauty of New York City, what DeLillo calls the city's "daily sweeping taken-for-granted greatness,"[6] would seriously diminish. Yet if an understandable impulse after that atrocity involved a sense of helplessness and an impulse to retreat, most New Yorkers demonstrated their resistance by remaining, and by, among other things, flocking to inspiring concerts and plays—powerful aesthetic creations that worked to strengthen their faith in benign human agency and a benign future. A New Yorker in DeLillo's latest novel, *Falling Man* (2007), comments in the immediate aftermath of September 11 that "People read poems. People I know, they read poetry to ease the shock and pain, give them a kind of space, something beautiful in language . . . to bring comfort or composure."[7]

New Yorkers flocked to performances of Mozart and Shakespeare in the days following the attack because, on the simplest level, they wanted to be reminded that beauty, not only ugliness, existed in the world. More profoundly, they wanted the strongest possible reassertion of our architectural gifts as makers and not destroyers of worlds. The most beautiful art discloses the mysterious affinity between human consciousness and the physical matter of the world, the way in which we inexhaustibly come to the world both loving its quiet regular life (as Mrs. Dalloway loves a city whose familiar routines she struggles to recover in the aftermath of war) and loving to make or experience formal echoes of that regularity.

Not that artworks passively reiterate the natural orderings we see around us; on the contrary, we expect our art to be, as Iris Murdoch wrote, dangerous play with powerful forces. We expect it to convey the arbitrary, violent, and senseless thing human experience can be. We want the twisted and edgy effect of Gustav Mahler's music, for example, because we want our art to be adequate to the distortions and uncertainties of our times. The strongest artists offer us, as Leonard Bernstein, Roger Scruton and Dmitri Tymoczko agree, intensely controlled passion; they stitch raw enigma to patterned cloth.

We also expect our artwork to express the existential sadness all human beings experience. As we argued earlier in this book, beauty is always associated with loss and longing, the melancholy we often associate with what is beautiful speaking to our own mortality. The self-sufficient, quiet beauty of my setting—a house high on a hill with a view of valleys and farms and the Catskill mountains—shows me a world that keeps on going without me, whose life long predated and will long postdate mine.

***

This sense of a world whose life persists beyond and in some sense above one, and the question of what sort of experience one is to have with such a place, is strongly marked in DeLillo's beauty-obsessed novel, *The Names*. The high house that haunts James Axton, the novel's main character, is that great icon of beauty, the Acropolis in Athens. Axton's changing relationship to its stunning order and endurance allows DeLillo to set in motion important reflections on beauty and its relation to ethics and politics—specifically, American politics.

Axton, an American engaged in vague U.S. government contract work in Greece, begins the novel in a condition of active evasion—moral and emotional evasion of his personal misery and literal evasion of the Acropolis. Despite its dominance over the city, Axton refuses to visit it. From the outset of the story, he makes a sharp distinction between tolerable modern Athens, "imperfect, blaring," and the intolerable "beauty, dignity, order, proportion" of that "somber rock," where "so much converges."[8]

Yet in the penultimate scene of the novel, Axton does finally climb the hill to the Acropolis, and he perceives once he gets there that it "was not a thing to study but to feel. It wasn't aloof, rational, timeless, pure. . . . It wasn't a relic species of dead Greece, but part of the living city below it." Indeed, a "human feeling" emerges from the stone: "I found a cry for pity. . . . [an] open cry, this voice we know as our own."[9]

The ultimate value of beautiful objects and sounds, DeLillo suggests, resides in their power to express at once the peculiar individuality of each of us as well as the human truths we share, the voice we know as our collective voice. All of his novels feature aesthetic epiphanies, when characters encounter what Bill Gray, the novelist at the center of DeLillo's novel *Mao II*, calls "the uninventable poetry, inside the pain, of what people say." Gray (who has himself retreated from New York City to the woods upstate in an effort to unblock his writing) has in mind a sentence a cab driver said to him years ago: "I was born under the old tutelage the earlier the better."[10] Gray tells himself he must remember this sentence (and he does—it flows through his mind as he is dying), for it represents a form of beauty that issues from the contingencies of a particular life and is thus an obscure but gratifying emblem of the achievement of individuality, precisely the achievement Alexander Nehamas sees as the reward of a lifelong receptivity to beauty.[11]

The late social theorist Gillian Rose called this uninventable poetry the "rhetoric of virtue, virtue alive to the negative, [which is] discernable in the pathos of syntax, where eternity shines through violence, where transcendence percolates immanence."[12] We are drawn powerfully to this individualized and vulnerable rhetoric, for it discloses truly and beautifully the complex reality of wounded yet persistent being.

The return of beauty to literary studies means, in part, attuning students to the close reading that the pathos of syntax demands. Like Gray, Rose, and other students of beauty, our university students should be able to discern, in their social and aesthetic experiences, this complex form of human utterance. But *The Names* makes clear precisely how difficult it is to attain the selflessness, emotional receptivity, attentiveness, and even courage to pick up these emanations. Indeed, DeLillo seems to agree with a number of political writers that Americans in particular have a hard time hearing the pathos of syntax. I want now to suggest why this is.

In a 2002 opinion column in the *New York Times*, Thomas Friedman wrote that Americans lack a sense of geopolitical reality and that this lack represents their greatest vulnerability as they enter into their own history of terror. Citing elements of our national character familiar from as far back as Alexis de Tocqueville, Friedman worries that our provinciality, naïveté, openness, optimism, pragmatic rationalism, and intellectual superficiality will render us defenseless as the brutal actuality of hatred against us begins to hit. "We are going to have to adapt," he concludes.[13] Todd Gitlin worries similarly about "the perils of American ignorance, our fantasy life of pure and unappreciated goodness," the American "combination of stupefaction and arrogance" that has produced a "flabby, self-satisfied democracy."[14]

The Names represents, among other things, an extended examination of this contemporary American mentality. Axton ultimately decides that his fundamental mistake has indeed been a kind of stupefaction, a "failure to concentrate, to occupy a serious center."[15] He is, for instance, largely clueless about the facts of the world around him. He doesn't even know that he works for the CIA. His evasion of these and other truths throughout the novel is also an evasion of beauty: he refuses to visit the Acropolis because he feels obscurely inadequate to a confrontation with it. The entire novel can be read as Axton's slow movement up the steps of the Acropolis, a metaphor for DeLillo of an American education in attentiveness to the truth through attentiveness to beauty.

Despite his willed evasions, Axton is not really surprised when a shadowy figure tries to kill an American friend of his. "I thought I sometimes detected in people who had lost property or fled, most frequently in Americans, some mild surprise that it hadn't happened sooner, that the men with the six-day beards hadn't come much earlier to burn them out . . . for the crimes of drinking whiskey, making money, jogging in shiny suits along the boulevards at dusk. Wasn't there a sense, we Americans felt, in which we had it coming?" America, Axton explains to his ex-wife, "is the world's living myth. There's no sense of wrong when you kill an American or blame America for some local disaster. This is our function, to be character types, to embody recurring themes that people can use to comfort themselves, justify themselves and so on. . . . People expect us to absorb the impact of their grievances."[16]

Axton's insistence upon diverting his attention from the implications of these and other truths is one way of living defensively in a world whose horrors, if truly admitted into awareness, would, we fear, overwhelm and paralyze us. Beauty, however, turns out to be one of the few tolerable ways in which we can approach these truths.

Axton's nonresponsive sensibility is generally shared among the cynical émigré Americans he knows in Greece. The novel describes a series of places and sounds to which these Americans cannot, or will not, respond. DeLillo divides the work into place-chapters—The Island, The Mountain, The Desert, The Prairie—and these arid locations act as symbolic backdrops for the real story of *The Names*: the effort of one American to break through his evasion of the tragic reality of human life.

Axton's own name suggests the exertion required to disrupt what one character, Owen Brademas, calls the "self-referring world." Brademas, an archeologist, tells Axton that "for thousands of years [the world] was our escape, was our refuge. Men hid from themselves in the world. We hid from God or death. The world was where we lived, the self was where we went mad and died. But now the world has made a self of its own. Why, how, never mind. What happens to us now that the world has a self? How do we say the simplest thing without falling into a trap?"[17] Any language we might want to bring to an understanding has already been co-opted and corrupted by the world; the world, Brademas argues, anticipates, trivializes, and commodifies any authentic utterance we might try to make. The novel's ongoing inquiry into the conditions of meaning and authenticity in a postmodern setting makes *The Names* as much a spiritual as a political work as it traces the various desperate and distorted efforts of serious people to live in a socially and psychologically real world.

While *White Noise* is by far the most popular, most taught, and most discussed of DeLillo's novels—the Modern Language Association has recently issued a "Teaching Guide" to the novel—*The Names* is much less read, taught, and discussed.[18] It is perceived as among the most difficult of DeLillo's novels: philosophically dense, confusing in its shifting locales and characters, and even "colder" in narrative disposition than DeLillo's other glacially detached narratives (DeLillo's work, writes Vincent Passaro, "is without even a trace of the usual autobiographical resonances"[19]). And yet I would argue that *The Names* is the most metaphysically serious and realized of DeLillo's novels. It does not obscure his ideas through irony, as *White Noise* does; rather, it is a totally serious presentation of DeLillo's deepest ideas about life, the self, virtue, justice, death—and, of course, beauty.

Because it is a blatantly and ambitiously philosophical novel, *The Names* does indeed challenge any reader who seeks its meaning. "Making things difficult for the reader," DeLillo has said in an interview, "is less an attack on the reader than it is on the age and its facile knowledge-market. The writer is driven by his conviction that some truths aren't arrived at so easily, that life is still full of mystery, that it might be better for you, Dear Reader, if you went back to the Living section of your newspaper, because this is the dying section and you don't really want to be here."[20]

In this remark, DeLillo touches on a number of themes crucial to his worldview. First, the self-referring world automatically issues false knowledge—call it "false rhetoric." Second, DeLillo is an anti-Nietzschean in regard to art. He disagrees that we have art in order not to perish of the truth. On the contrary, as DeLillo says elsewhere, "there is a set of balances and rhythms to a novel that we can't experience in real life. So I think there is a sense in which fiction can rescue history from confusion."[21] DeLillo has commented that he thinks it was the assassination of John F. Kennedy that made him a writer, a desire to create a sort of order out of the "confusion and psychic chaos and the sense of randomness that ensued from that moment in Dallas."[22] For all art's efforts, life is and remains, DeLillo insists, a mystery. Yet the strongest art, he also believes, can make us attentive enough to hear emanations of its underlying truths.

To pick up a DeLillo novel is to turn to "the dying section," not the living section. Like all serious artists, DeLillo will turn our attention to final things, to a life shaped by retrospective, even morbid, thoughts about itself. Much of the narrative energy of *The Names* is deployed in the direction of a certain form of what one might call "cultural mourning." But these same bleak truths, as André Comte-Sponville writes, "can also make us live—that is what classics and classicists called beauty."[23]

DeLillo's metaphysics narrate a series of ascending steps toward a kind of transcendent knowledge. He can be thought of as a more generous Flannery O'Connor, affording his heroes greater spiritual clarity and accomplishment than she ever did hers. Bill Gray, Bucky Wunderlick of his early novel, *Great Jones Street*, James Axton—these are brilliant and perceptive characters able both to feel the degeneration of the postmodern world into malign silence or idiotic noise and to withdraw from that world in search of buried articulations of humanity. Their adventures are essentially a series of illuminating encounters with false and illegitimate attempts to regain expressive purity. As soon as they recognize and reject false rhetoric as such, these characters are able to move closer to true.

This sort of plot trajectory is, in its bare outlines, indistinguishable from that of DeLillo's most important influence, James Joyce, in *A Portrait of the Artist as a Young Man*. Intellectual and spiritual clarity also comes about in that novel after a series of repudiations. In Joyce, a swanlike girl wading in the ocean prompts Dedalus's definitive moment of truth and beauty; DeLillo typically creates for his heroes similar moments of beauty-generated epiphanic disclosure.

Among DeLillo's characters, Bucky Wunderlick, the rock and roll megastar of *Great Jones Street*, most explicitly embodies the initial gesture of selflessness, the radical paring down of everything stupefying, for the sake of openness to beauty. Wunderlick's sonic medium is rock music, which reflects and conveys the restless, scattered semiconsciousness that a culture of speed, noise, and image fosters. Even among classical music listeners in this culture, Edward Said writes, a larger "lack of continuity, concentration and knowledge . . . has made real musical attention more or less impossible." Said describes the "continuous noise pollution all around . . . a constant 'backgroundization' of music, from supermarket and elevator music, to commercial advertising, to the ceaseless hum of unattended, usually unacknowledged habitual sound" that accounts for this gradual inability to separate out meaningful utterance.[24] Rock music at once competes with and conspires in the cultural repudiation of complexity and "voice"—its shriek drowns out lesser sounds even as the nullity of much of it glamorizes a social reality in which emotionally phobic people like Axton can dissolve their anxieties about love, work, and the meaning of life, in what Scruton describes as a "soup of amplified overtones" whose enveloping insistence seems to express some transcendent truth.[25]

The conveyor of that truth in DeLillo's novel—the rock star—becomes under these circumstances not a performer, but an icon, whipping his followers into a destructive frenzy. Wunderlick is a Jim Morrison / Syd Barrett / Kurt Cobain figure (though DeLillo created Wunderlick many years before Cobain's rise and fall became a transient national myth) who, suddenly terrified by the seemingly murderous urges he has brought to the surface in his violent audiences and by his own murderous instincts toward himself and his fans, withdraws from the world to live in a derelict, anonymous apartment in New York City: "Toward the end of the final tour it became apparent that our audience wanted more than music, more even than its own reduplicated noise. It's possible the culture had reached its limit, a point of severe tension. There was less sense of simple visceral abandon at our concerts during these last weeks. . . . Our followers, in their isolation, were not concerned with precedent now. They were free of old saints and martyrs, but fearfully so, left with their own unlabeled flesh."[26] This condition of frightening encasement in one's own "unlabeled flesh" is the very opposite of the liberating "unselfing" Murdoch isolates as part of the experience of the beautiful.

Wunderlick's crowds depend on him to "validate their emotions" of inchoate "passion and wrath." And for a time Wunderlick likes the pose of sadistic nihilist. The novel includes transcripts from interviews in which he says, "Screaming's essential to our sound now. The whole thing is nature processed through instruments and sound controls. . . . We make noise. We make it louder than anybody else and also better. . . . You have to crush people's heads. . . . What I'd really like to do is I'd like to injure people with my sound. Maybe actually kill some of them."[27] They seem to be asking for it.

"Music is the final hypnotic," one of his fans tells him. "Music puts me just so out of everything. I get taken beyond every reference that indicates who I am or how I behave. Just so out of it. Music is dangerous in so many ways. It's the most dangerous thing in the world."[28] Wunderlick's girlfriend confides in him that she wants only "the brute electricity of that sound. To make the men who made it. To keep moving. To forget everything. To *be* the sound." Wunderlick ponders this: "She wanted to exist as music does, nowhere, beyond the maps of language."[29] This, he perceives, is self-annihilation, not unselfing.

Wunderlick comes to fear the killing pressure of "unlabeled flesh" against him, flesh that demands in its unbearable isolation (so different, for instance, from James Merrill's aesthetic self-islanding) new saints and martyrs, a new sort of community that the singer must construct for it. The culture of annihilating noise has, as the novel opens, "reached its limit" for Wunderlick: "The music didn't mean the same thing," he tells his girlfriend. "I used to absolutely disappear in that sound. But then it ended. What do you do when something ends? I thought it best to go away." His girlfriend responds, "If everything's getting ugly the only thing you can do is try to teach yourself it's beautiful. . . . Eventually maybe it is."[30]

But Wunderlick fails to convince himself that his music represents anything other than a lethal embodiment of a desublimated culture. Alone in his room, he decides to undergo a spiritual retreat into silence and into mindfulness of the suffering world around him on the streets of the city. Rather like Nathaniel West's Miss Lonelyhearts, Wunderlick inaugurates a dangerous ascent toward moral awareness and emotional response as the novel builds toward its frightening climax, when members of a drug cult inject him with a substance that removes the faculty of speech. Yet this injection only literalizes the established metaphorical truth of Wunderlick's life, in which he has moved from the speechlessness of annihilating public sound to the speechlessness of spiritual extremity.

"Having no words for the things around me," the mute Wunderlick notes as he wanders the derelict quarters of New York City, he has become "unreasonably happy . . . thinking of myself as a kind of living chant." His "withdrawal to that unimprinted level where all sound is silken and nothing erodes in the mad weather of language" enables a sort of rebirth in him, so that when the faculty of speech eventually reemerges, he is ready to consider reentering the world as "voiced."[31]

DeLillo's novel is a curious modern allegory of the journey from noise to silence to voice, an ultimately hopeful account of a culture's rearticulation of itself. Both *Great Jones Street* and *The Names* in fact are intricate considerations of the nature of our culture's screaming muteness (the better-known DeLillo title is resonant here: *White Noise*) and the kinds of desperate actions to which serious people are driven in an effort to recover their voices. The decades-long muteness of another artist, the blocked and secluded Bill Gray (*Mao II*), heroically breaks when Gray risks his life—loses his life—in an effort to save a fellow writer held hostage in Lebanon.

How do we navigate between pointless, shrieking noise and traumatized silence to discover voice? For DeLillo, the accomplishment of voice begins with the perception of suffering in the world. Here is Wunderlick at the end of the novel, sounding like a combination of West and Henry Miller:

Pigeons and meningitis. Chocolate and mouse droppings. Licorice and roach hairs. Vermin on the bus we took uptown. I wondered how long I'd choose to dwell in these middle ages of plague and usury, living among traceless men and women, those whose only peace was in shouting ever more loudly. Nothing tempted them more than voicelessness. But they shouted. Transient population of thunderers and hags. They dragged through wet streets speaking in languages older than the stones of cities buried in the sand. Beds and bedbugs. Men and lice. Gonococcus curling in the lap of love.[32]

Just as Wunderlick has begun to listen to the open cries of his living stone city, so Axton will eventually be willing to listen to the Acropolis, having overcome his self-protective temptation to cushion himself from the sound of humanity. Both novels have essentially tracked elaborate moral ventures toward the ability to hear and then articulate, in a mode of lamentation, the pathos of syntax.

But what is it, more precisely, that questing listeners in Don DeLillo need to learn? They must first, it seems, understand why, as Wunderlick says, living defensively is the central theme of our age. They must clarify the basis of their own—always temporary—defensive withdrawal from the world. In the cases of Wunderlick and Gray, two brilliant writers are blocked because they feel horrifyingly appropriated by a violent and uncomprehending audience. Both withdraw. And both, having understood that what most terrifies them is the sense of having lost their individuality, their autonomy, in the artist-murdering chaos of the crowd, return to the world morally enlightened and endowed with a kind of courage.

***

In presenting the novels of Don DeLillo to our students, we should stress, among other things, the way he champions the social and political aspect of receptivity to beauty. Through art, he believes, we most powerfully hear the rhetoric of the world's grief. False rhetoric promises an end to what Rose describes as "the anxiety and ambivalence inherent in power and knowledge."[33] And if being an American is, as Michael Wood calls it, "a condition of the soul tied to a habit of the possession of power," then how much more urgent it is for Americans to maintain this anxiety about not only their personal power but also their global power.[34] How much more important it is for Americans to resist the false rhetoric of their "pure and unappreciated goodness," as Gitlin writes.[35]

For DeLillo—whether it expresses itself through fanatic Pentecostal Christians, the followers of the Reverend Moon, terrorist leaders and their followers, or Wunderlick's audience—false rhetoric always assures you that you are the pure and saved child of God, that you are happy now and do not suffer. DeLillo's characters, writes Passaro, "live with an unsettling awareness of a world we prefer to ignore."[36] "Hell is the place we don't know we're in," says an archeologist in *The Names*. "Is hell a lack of awareness?"[37]

The virtuous rhetoric of DeLillo is a humanized Blakean soundscape in which, as he writes in *The Names*, "language is the deepest being"[38] and conversation the privileged social mode, since it is in conversation that this dynamic of exchange for the sake of the liberation of the syntax of pathos can take place. "Every conversation," Axton thinks as he listens to the buzz at a Greek café,

> is a shared narrative, a thing that surges forward, too dense to allow space for the unspoken, the sterile. The talk is unconditional, the participants drawn in completely.
>
> This is a way of speaking that takes such pure joy in its own openness and ardor that we begin to feel these people are discussing language itself. What pleasure in the simplest greeting. It's as though one friend says to another, "How good it is to say How are you?" The other replying, "When I answer I am well and how are you, what I really mean is that I'm delighted to have a chance to say these familiar things—they bridge the lonely distances."[39]

While white noise represents the distracting, numbing, ambient roar postmodern American culture generates to drown out self-generated, shared discourse, authentic conversation marks the survival of shared humanity.

DeLillo's work is rife with instances of inauthentic cultural noises and images. Recently, for instance, his short story "Baader Meinhof" features a much-discussed, major New York exhibition of the works of Gerhard Richter, among them his series of large photographic portraits of members of the Baader-Meinhof gang.[40] With this story, DeLillo extends his interest in discriminating between authentic, redemptive art and self-referring, white noise art. Like Andy Warhol, whose "execution series" is featured in *Mao II*, Richter represents a pseudoartist, able to represent only in a bland and passive way the terror in the world. In his story, DeLillo implicitly echoes what many critics of the Richter exhibit have said, that this sort of art displays what Rose calls "the nihilism of disowned emotions."[41] Jed Perl describes Richter's Baader-Meinhof series as "impassively ironic . . . witheringly calculated." He calls Richter "a phony Kafka" whose "radical chic" seems to believe that "deadness is a form of hipness."[42]

Like Kafka, DeLillo inhabits the dying section, but not in order to numbly display morbidity; rather, he creates books that, in a famous statement of Kafka's, mean to serve as "the axe for the frozen sea inside us."[43] Axton's name and the many explorers with pickaxes and other such equipment in *The Names* literalize this aesthetic imperative to bring the dead city, the dead soul, back to a kind of life.

Having begun to experience the compassion for the suffering of others and oneself that Wunderlick feels when he is sympathetically mesmerized, for instance, by a brain-damaged boy, and having begun to recognize one's implication in a world of power and knowledge, we can, DeLillo suggests, aim for the highest step in this spiritual progress: a return of the soul to the city, where we can act on behalf of justice. Rose describes this progress in terms of the act of mourning: "Mourning draws on transcendent but representable justice, which makes the suffering of immediate experience visible and speakable. When completed, mourning returns the soul to the city, renewed and reinvigorated for participation, ready to take on the difficulties and injustices of the existing city. The mourner returns to negotiate and challenge the changing inner and outer boundaries of the soul and of the city; she returns to their perennial anxiety. . . . [One must bring] a soul . . . to wail at those walls."[44]

Most of the characters in *The Names* inhabit the abstract, evasive realms of the air or the underground—they fly about doing their obscure multinational business, or they sit in the dirt to perform their fanatic epigraphy. It is Axton's triumph that he finds a way to exist in the modern/ancient city, receptive to the perennial human cry within it.

And that way is the way of beauty. Axton's triumph takes part in something like what Albert Camus had in mind in the conclusion of his essay "Helen's Exile":

It is by acknowledging our ignorance, refusing to be fanatics, recognizing the world's limits and man's, through the faces of those we love, in short, by means of beauty—this is how we may rejoin the Greeks. In a way, the meaning of tomorrow's history is not what people think. It is in the struggle between creation and the inquisition. Whatever the price artists will have to pay for their empty hands, we can hope for their victory. Once again, the philosophy of darkness will dissolve above the dazzling sea. Oh, noonday thought, the Trojan war is fought far from the battleground! Once again, the terrible walls of the modern city fall, to deliver Helen's beauty, "its soul serene as the untroubled waves."[45]

Again, one is reminded of Merrill's "After Greece," in which the poet comes to a realization that, while "I want / Essentials: salt, wine, olive, the light," there are no essentials. There are simply the contingencies of his particular life and his human impulse to sympathize with the particularities of others. If we hear in those particularities, in those city walls, and in the speech of the taxi driver in *Mao II*, not merely DeLillo's uninventable poetry and Camus' ancient beauty, but also Wordsworth's "still, sad music of humanity, / Not harsh nor grating, though of ample power / To chasten and subdue,"[46] this is because we are hearing all along in DeLillo the voice of romanticism, subdued and chastened for a contemporary world, for an America suddenly tutored in the ways of catastrophe.

DeLillo ends his essay with a lyrical celebration of the New York that was, is, and will be, "the daily sweeping taken-for-granted greatness of New York," in which "all language, ritual, belief, and opinion" is accommodated.[47] It is that multilingual, rich human environment that DeLillo's novels attempt to build—now, perhaps, to rebuild. At his best, with all the "prescient terrors of his fiction," as Passaro calls them,[48] DeLillo shows us, in Rose's words, "the difficulty of thinking in the wake of disaster, without generating any fantasy of mending the world."[49] Novels like *The Names* are one powerful way of "replying to power and beating back our fear," as DeLillo elsewhere has put it, "by extending the pitch of consciousness and human possibility."[50]

CHAPTER 7

Beauty's Return

In the face of such strong expression of our human need for beauty in uncertain times, is it a coincidence that beauty appears to be on its way back? While Wendy Steiner is surely right to suggest that Venus was, for much of the twentieth century, "in exile," there is plenty of evidence to suggest that beauty is once more, and increasingly, part of ongoing conversations in classrooms among students. As we noted earlier, the nature of aesthetic experience and its implications for the central acts in literary criticism of appreciation, judgment, and evaluation, have always been of great interest to students, but for several decades that interest was demoted in terms of its relevance to the study of literature. Our argument thus far has been that that demotion was not only negligent of the actual reading experience of vast numbers of students but also significantly detrimental to the well-being and integrity of English literature as a discipline and to those persons who make their living by it. It is therefore heartening that, in tandem with the more public nature of conversation about beauty, a significant number of scholarly works on the subject have been published in the last decade or so; and the very fact that such works originate from a range of disciplines—philosophy as well as art history, biology as well as literature—suggests that the consequences of a disregard for the importance of beauty have been felt as a wider impoverishment than perhaps we previously recognized.

It is beyond the scope of this book (and, to be frank, our abilities as informed readers of English literature, rather than, say, philosophy, history, or biology)[1] to assess the particular merits of all of these works, notwithstanding our predisposition to treat their efforts kindly. Of course, a counter to our enthusiasm at what appears to be a turn in the tide might be the observation that a marked increase in books on beauty signifies only that more bad books are being produced. To that we say only: let the reader decide. Moreover, it should be noted of this recent academic attention that while each author has deemed beauty a sufficiently valuable topic to devote an entire work to it, that is perhaps the only thing one can say with confidence that unites these works. But that is precisely what one would wish—the resurgence of a varied and vigorous debate about the value as well as the nature of the aesthetic; a polyphonic discourse in which only the subject of the argument itself might indicate what in the broadest possible terms may be considered valuable. That recent works on beauty implicitly consider their subject vital in the purest sense of that word is sufficient.

In this chapter, then, rather than exhaustively documenting every last related argument that has appeared in recent years or merely choosing among preferred approaches, we want to give a sense of some of the variety of works that have led us to believe in the return of beauty. This is not, therefore, a "top ten" list of works, but rather a selective consideration of some of the purposes, projects, and themes taken up by the growing number of authors in recent years who are united, but frequently united only, as noted, by their sense that beauty matters.

***

It's hard to say who first noticed that beauty had somehow gone missing from the classroom and when exactly the alarm went up. What kind of time had elapsed in the interim? Our initial suspicion was that beauty had been done away with as an academically respectable subject for debate sometime between our high school and graduate school years. It was during the 1970s and '80s, we thought—perhaps especially the 1970s, which seemed, in music, at least, to have been a particularly low and dishonorable decade—but our theory was not borne out. The sense that beauty was in retreat seems to have been present well before the arrival of disco. In *The Meaning of Beauty* (1950), Eric Newton finds himself "goaded into writing" by the question "familiar enough in discussions on contemporary art, 'Why have so many modern artists abandoned the search for beauty?'"[2]

Newton's book speaks more to the complexities of the issues evoked and less to the external pressures that might have contributed to them, and his immediate focus is on the production of art rather than the experience of it; nonetheless, he observes, in the years immediately following the Second World War, a dropping away of academic as well as practical interest in beauty. Whether for reasons of good taste (the perceived extravagance, perhaps, of aesthetic questions following an historical period of exceptional and widespread suffering) or because other questions were simply more compelling, beauty is, according to Newton, a subject for "doomed philosophers."[3]

"Stock answers" to Newton's question concerning the abandonment of the search for beauty include first, the observation that the creation of beauty itself "is *not* the artist's principal task," and second, the theory that "[o]ur sense of beauty is so capable of development and expansion that it is dangerous to use the word as though it had an absolute value."[4] Those two answers have continued to be useful in arguments against beauty, or at least against readers who might go looking for it as a hoped-for part of their encounter with an artwork. Since, however, our aim here is to give some of the arguments for beauty—or at least to indicate some of the questions once again being posed regarding beauty—we will discount the stock answers immediately.

Regarding the first: Creation of beauty may well not be the artist's "principal task," but it is a frequent consequence of art and therefore should be taken seriously and as part of any extended discussion of the experience of art. Regarding the second: the admitted contingency of our "sense of beauty" does not necessitate the abandonment of efforts to explore it in all its various contingencies. Clive Bell, whose unpopularity in recent years has obscured his occasionally helpful and frequently stimulating contributions to this subject, begins his book *Art* (1914) by noting that any system of aesthetics that promises to found itself on objectivity is clearly absurd.[5] The starting place for any discussion of the beautiful is always subjective experience; "at the heart of any critical act is a subjective preference," as Steiner puts it some ninety years later; "the thrust of criticism is the 'I like.'"[6]

This certainly ought to be the case for works that describe an aesthetic experience centered specifically in literature, an experience that is most likely to occur while one is alone with one's "I like." It's interesting how the circumstances not only of reading but also (and by extension) of simply being alone are related. Nobody has yoked the two more elegantly than Harold Bloom, who writes, as we have already noted, that art can teach us nothing but the proper uses of our solitude.[7] This fact, as Bloom sees it, is hardly a shock, and despite the otherwise gloomy tenor of his elegy for the discipline of English literature, his statement stands as the considered appraisal of one who has spent the greater part of his life reading and whose "I like" has never, one suspects, been ignored or neglected in favor of contemporary trends.

By contrast, Frank Lentricchia's essay about his youthful passion for reading, about the solitary hours of his boyhood spent in bed with a book and the oddly debased relationships with literature that he later experienced as someone who suppressed that passion and grew up to teach only theory, has the flavor of an about-turn, a coming clean about the love that inspired him once and that he, in bad faith, neglected to pass on to his students.[8] Lentricchia's essay doesn't actually use the word "beauty," but he evokes it in the way in which we use it in this book, by indicating an intensity of aesthetic experience, pleasurable or otherwise. It should be obvious by now that we have no intention of defining beauty but rather want to consider some of the places in which beauty has been found, or rediscovered, as a subject for discussion as well as an experience in itself. What Lentricchia seems to be confessing is a secret taste for the beauty he found in literature, a taste that got him into reading in the first place, and one that he spent years both hoarding and denying.

Hoarding is, as we suggested earlier, a problem where beauty is concerned. If Elaine Scarry is right, our natural desire should be to *extend* the province of beauty; to call upon our friends to share our most recent beautiful experience; to draw or otherwise reproduce beautiful objects so that we can pass them along.[9] In light of Scarry's argument, Lentricchia's admission that he prefers not to share would be perverse, were it not the norm in academia. The generosity that Scarry imagines to be inspired by the experience of beauty is notably absent from the academic world, at least as Lentricchia describes it. The sheer pleasure of sharing that is arguably a part of the aesthetic experience itself is thus denied to many practitioners of literary criticism who not only withhold pleasure from their students but indeed, Lentricchia argues, "embark upon a course and leave their [own] happiness far behind."[10] It's interesting that Lentricchia eventually chose to reveal his secret passion for reading—to share it—and that he did so presumably at a time that guaranteed some kind of shock value (love of reading still being a perversity, as it were, and thus worthy of the gossip it inspired following its publication in the journal *Lingua Franca*). Danuta Fjellestad writes that "[w]ithin a few days, *everybody* (or so it seemed to me) was talking about the article: each casual encounter between academics, each dinner party with more than one academic at the table, each graduate seminar provided an occasion to discuss Lentricchia's essay."[11] Lentricchia's career doesn't seem to have suffered any damage, however, which suggests that the time was ripe for his confession. By the fall of 1996, when *Lingua Franca* published his piece, there was an increased openness to the idea that perhaps passion might propel art as much as politics. Lentricchia was hardly the lone radical standing up to defend the primacy of aesthetic experience in literary encounters, but he was certainly one of the better-known turncoats.

More recent and more serious inquiries into the role of beauty in literary studies have continued to situate themselves similarly in personal experience. In ways that Lentricchia doesn't acknowledge, the shift away from theory that often seems to precede the personal revelation of one's subjective encounter with a text is actually an inevitable outgrowth of reception theory, which privileges the reader in the process of "meaning making." Jane Tompkins's confession of ten years earlier,[12] lamenting the "two selves" the critic creates in order to lead the double-life of the aesthetically sensitive and the politically engaged (the reader vs. the scholar), arguably had its genesis in her own work in reception theory. Neither Tompkins nor Lentricchia takes the additional step of recognizing that there may be something of an *ethical* problem in withholding—hoarding—the personal pleasures of their textual encounters from their students. Tompkins's piece actually doesn't speak to her teaching at all, but rather to the colleagues and rivals in academia for whom she produces a kind of impersonal or pseudoscientific criticism she has come to think of as a "straitjacket."[13] Her essay is mostly about the kind of criticism she wishes she were permitted to write:

> The thing I want to say is that I've been hiding a part of myself for a long time. I've known it was there but I couldn't listen because there was no place for this person in literary criticism. The criticism I would like to write would always take off from personal experience, would always be in some way a chronicle of my hours and days.[14]

It's surely no coincidence that in finally producing such a piece of writing, Tompkins tries to convey something beautiful: "It is a beautiful day here in North Carolina . . . finally, beautiful weather. A tree outside my window just brushed by red, with one fully red leaf. (This is what I want you to see.)"[15]

Lentricchia's turn away from the straitjacket, his return to beauty, does not lead him, like Tompkins, to want to share the view; instead it leads him to a decision not to teach graduate students, who, he feels, as creatures raised at the theory trough, don't appreciate the literary pearls before them. That their appetite for theory has been shaped in large part by scholars like Lentricchia himself appears to give him a guilt that remains unaffected by any desire to show graduate students possible ways out of the theoretical mire he has helped to create. While his teaching philosophy has thus evolved into one of "do no harm," his own reading habits have also changed to protect him from the kind of criticism he once produced, criticism that asserts the moral superiority of the literary critic over "the writers that one is supposedly describing."[16]

In this, Lentricchia echoes the sentiments of Richard Rorty, whose essay "The Inspirational Value of Great Works of Literature"[17] (published in 1998 but given in lecture form before Lentricchia's article appeared) makes clear even from its title where its emphasis departs from Lentricchia's piece, which is titled the "Last Will and Testament of an Ex-Literary Critic." What exactly Lentricchia wills to the reader isn't clear. Rorty's piece, in contrast to both Tompkins's and Lentricchia's, keeps its own author out of the spotlight while it acknowledges and embodies the imperative of sharing that is fundamental to at least the teaching, if not the reading, life.

Rorty may be said to violate the rule asserted above, that one should speak whereof one knows, or at least whereof one spends one's academic life. A philosopher by trade, Rorty has, at least, a rather gratifying humility in the expression of his doubts concerning the current practices of literary departments. "Because my own disciplinary matrix is philosophy," he writes, "I cannot entirely trust my sense of what is going on in literature departments." What suspicions he has have been gleaned by "hanging around" those departments and reading what issues from them.[18] Rorty is not particularly encouraged by what he reads for some of the same reasons cited by Lentricchia. What the latter identifies as moral superiority on the part of the literary critic, Rorty defines as "knowingness," the kind of attitude adopted by theorists[19] who belong, Rorty writes,

> to what Harold Bloom calls the "School of Resentment." These people have learned from Jameson and others that they can no longer enjoy "the luxury of the old-fashioned ideological critique, the indignant moral denunciation of the other." They have also learned that hero-worship is a sign of weakness, and a temptation to elitism. So they substitute Stoic endurance for both righteous anger and social hope. They substitute knowing theorization for awe, and resentment over the failures of the past for visions of a better future.[20]

Rorty's essay returns the reader to the act of reading, which should be, he argues, an act of discovery rather than recognition. For Rorty, "If it is to have inspirational value, a work must be allowed to recontextualize much of what you previously thought you knew; it cannot, at least at first, be itself recontextualized by what you already believe."[21] There cannot be, that is to say, any preformed grid into which the work can be fit. Lentricchia says something similar in his argument that the contemporary literary critic goes to work on any given piece of writing equipped with a one-size-fits-all theory: "what is now called literary criticism is a form of Xeroxing. Tell me your theory and I'll tell you in advance what you'll say about any work of literature, especially those you haven't read."[22]

What exactly does Rorty mean by "inspirational value"? He refers the reader to Dorothy Allison's essay "Believing in Literature" for evidence of a passion wholly unreproducible by the great Xeroxing machine of theory. Allison's essay ends with a statement that has its genesis in a reading experience that, despite a certain family resemblance, differs from Bloom's in its insistence that great literature takes us not merely beyond ourselves but actually out into the world:

There is a place where we are always alone with our own mortality, where we must simply have something greater than ourselves to hold onto—God or history or politics or literature or a belief in the healing power of love, or even righteous anger. Sometimes I think they are all the same. A reason to believe, a way to take the world by the throat and insist that there is more to this life than we have ever imagined.[23]

Allison's notion is that great work challenges the imagination's boundaries to enlarge our conceptual worlds; it inspires us to "take the world by the throat." Lentricchia too argues for an aesthetic experience that both makes the known strange and forces us, as an often unexpected consequence, to see connections between ourselves and that which we might have regarded as Other: "When it's the real thing," writes Lentricchia, "literature enlarges us; strips the film of familiarity from the world; creates bonds of sympathy with all kinds, even with evil characters."[24] The experience of beauty described here, as we have already argued in the first chapters of this book, is not one of comfort or familiarity, but it is one in which imagination and the emotions contribute to a rich and often destabilizing encounter with the world beyond our selves.

The rise of cultural studies within departments of English literature has its parallel for Rorty in the rise of analytic philosophy in that each for him has come to represent the triumph of "dryness"—the kind of knowing skepticism to which Lentricchia and Bloom refer when they describe the self-assertion of the theorist above the work. Following the lead of logical positivism, according to Rorty, philosophy over the last decades has become "unromantic, and highly professional. Analytic philosophy still attracts first-rate minds, but most of these minds are busy solving problems which no nonphilosopher recognizes as problems: problems which hook up with nothing outside the discipline."[25]

At least two things are worth noting here: first, the (elsewhere acknowledged) debt to Iris Murdoch's essay "Against Dryness,"[26] and, second, Rorty's assumption that "hooking up with nothing outside" is, in fact, a problem. (It should be observed that in the last decade, almost every writer on beauty owes a debt to Murdoch, itself a rather interesting fact that demands a closer examination regarding the precise ways in which Murdoch's work appeals to the more modern and in many ways more radical aesthetics of optimism. We will return to Murdoch later in this chapter.) What does Rorty mean by his use of Murdoch's term? He sets dryness against romance, against "unprofessional prophets and demiurges," against emotion and self-creation, and, presumably, against love. (We will return to love later, too.) The dry critic views a work in a way that "gives understanding but not hope, knowledge but not self-transformation. For knowledge is a matter [for the dry critic] of putting a work in a familiar context—relating it to things already known."[27]

But why does it matter that relations with the outside world might be diminished or endangered by the pursuit of certain kinds of scholarship? After all, if Bloom is right and close study of literature doesn't actually do anything for us as a society, why should we, at least in our reading lives, care if the practical ramifications of *Paradise Lost* are indeed coterminous with its pages? What difference does it make if it "hooks up with" nothing beyond either us or itself? One of the critics whose meteoric academic career took off from his memorable reading of *Paradise Lost* now writes that there is in fact no reason to read *Paradise Lost* other than simply to read it:

> Literary interpretation, someone has recently said, has no purpose external to the arena of its practice; it is the 'constant unfolding' to ourselves 'of who we are' as practitioners. The only 'value of the conversation is the conversation itself.' That's all there is, even when we try to enlarge it by finding in it large-scale political and cultural implications. I say again, that's all there is, but it's enough for those who long ago ceased to be able to imagine themselves living any other life.[28]

If we expect Stanley Fish to produce some interesting counterargument to the notion that self-discovery is all that literary interpretation ever adds up to, we are disappointed. While the "someone" echoing Bloom goes unidentified in Fish's short essay,[29] perhaps the most depressing thing about Fish's own confession is his refusal to take up the challenge of teaching for any grander purpose than enjoying the "nice work"—the nice life—that literary criticism has given him.

The inward turn of criticism toward a culture of confession—and indeed self-absolution—is a step along the way to the return of beauty. Fish and Lentricchia are at least demonstrating the passion that fires their reading, if not their teaching, and indeed their work marks a shift in cultural sensibility that is easing the way for a return of aesthetic considerations to the study of literature; but their confessions are also warning signs of what can happen when such considerations "fail to hook up with" a life beyond our own.

Daniel O'Hara has written critically and at some length on the nature of such confessional writings in which academic stars like Lentricchia and Fish essentially walk away from the table at which they might, as prominent prac-titioners of literary criticism, be expected "to provide broadly rational and ethical grounds for literary study."[30] O'Hara's assessment of Fish is harsh. The rise of multiculturalism has been enabled, he argues, by Fish and like-minded scholars providing focus for the kind of argument that targets "self-indulgent, white male aesthetes, whom . . . society can no longer afford. Literary study, therefore, must be replaced by a more representative and responsible practice." That this kind of thing can now be said "persuasively," if egregiously, argues O'Hara, is largely due to Fish's failure, and that of his generation, to provide "a systematic defense of literature and its study."[31]

One can argue on Fish's behalf that literature requires no defense; like beauty, it needs neither army nor burglar alarm. The same is probably not the case, however, with English departments, which, at least in O'Hara's view, are in danger of disappearing entirely.[32] But Fish's greatest sin, at least as he writes about it in his confession, is not that he has failed to defend the field or make noble his profession. It is rather that *as a teacher* he has lost or turned away from the chance—the moral obligation, one might argue—to be inspirational; and it is here that he most irritates us.[33] Like Lentricchia, in his writing he stands up to reveal himself as a mere consumer rather than a reader who might teach us something about the importance of reading. He frees himself from culpability but offers in his confession no direction for the departments that have rewarded him so richly. None of this would matter were he merely talking to himself. But given the public nature of his disclaimer and the social benefits he and Lentricchia enjoy as leading critics and professors, there are, perhaps, some grounds for the more serious charge that O'Hara goes on to make: "Stanley Fish and company—and, indeed, literary study—are . . . without any general rational and moral grounds."[34] If Lentricchia thinks that literature really can't be taught, O'Hara implies, he ought to abstain from teaching it.

O'Hara's essay, despite the severity of its accusations, is in fact a positive review of Lentricchia's novel *The Edge of Night: A Confession* (1994). "The particular and immediate, the terrible beauty of contingency"[35]—this is the subject of Lentricchia's novel-memoir, "the ethical subject to be worked through."[36] O'Hara is enthusiastic about the work, and it's hard not to be similarly attracted to Lentricchia's account of his own aesthetic life: "I look for the beautiful everywhere," he writes; "I coax and stroke it when I find it stirring in front of me. . . . Art as stubborn specificity, as untheorizable peculiarity. Art"—again, the phrase is Murdoch's—"for life's sake."[37] O'Hara finds *The Edge of Night* encouraging as itself a testament to "a pervasive, if largely unexpressed, dissatisfaction with the ruling critical dogmas";[38] indeed, its very existence should be cause for examination, if not celebration, since, according to O'Hara, "[w]e are . . . at a crossroads in the profession. When a leading American critic—arguably the most famous figure of his critical generation—turns away from literary study to create a work of literature, in disgust with his profession and with a desire for discovering a freer range of vision, this phenomenon must serve as a cautionary tale, a genuine scene of instruction."[39]

Whether or not we really regard the personal transformation of the critic to be as significant as O'Hara would have it, David Lodge argues that such a phenomenon is increasingly common: "Examples could be multiplied of formerly committed partisans of Theory who have changed tack, diversified into creative writing and autobiography, rededicated themselves to teaching in encounter-group style, or left the academy altogether to become psychotherapists."[40] On Lodge's list of newly ambivalent theorists are Lentricchia and Colin MacCabe, whose revisions to his own book on James Joyce suggest some disillusionment (MacCabe writes that much of the theory originally used by him in that work "has become a paralysing orthodoxy, trumpeted by dunces"[41]). Also on the list is Frank Kermode, who, according to Lodge, "in his later publications expressed increasing dismay at the distorting effect of Theory on the appreciation and understanding of literature, especially of the past."[42]

For O'Hara, such newfound skepticism regarding the place of theory is presumably insufficient, since he seems to think that the salvation of English as a discipline necessitates a "defense of literature" requiring us "to recall clearly what literature has been and to envision specifically what it can be."[43] Rorty says something similar when he recalls Bloom's observation that these days the party of memory is the party of hope: "[Bloom's] point is that, among students of literature, it is only those who agree . . . that 'what abides was founded by poets' who are still capable of social hope. . . . [I]t is only those who still read for inspiration who are likely to be of much use in building a cooperative commonwealth."[44]

Whereas Rorty's inspirational reading leads him toward imagining a romantic utopia, however, O'Hara's dream is more modest in its reach:

> The aim should not be to dismiss canonical texts and their aesthetic analysis. Rather, it should be to equip ourselves for seeing how formal innovations and achievements in canonical and noncanonical texts compose an aesthetics of existence, a potentially exemplary *rapport à soi*, within the collective archive of culture, from which we can draw our fine inspiration and object lessons, our cautionary tales and life-profiles for emulation in our own projects of self-invention.[45]

Bloom aside, it seems that there is a practical theme emerging here: a shadow of the utilitarian; a sense not that a powerful encounter with the literary text should or must do something, but that it *might*. In Rorty, as in O'Hara, we find the stirring of what we have already identified as aesthetic optimism;

and it appears to grow out of the primary and essential experience of reading that grounds every confession.

Recalling his early love of literature, Ihab Hassan writes,

> I did not think of death when I first came to literature, nor of criticism. I thought of Beauty and Truth, and came upon them, as others have, in wayward places—attic boxes, books forgotten on a park bench, street stalls piled high with yellowing tomes. To what "interpretive community" did I then belong? Literature was my secret; it became addiction; I began to travel the "realms of gold."[46]

Hassan's confession (which includes the penitent "I have practiced criticism, and contributed my share of blatter [*sic*] to the world"[47]) is also a happy recollection of that primary and propulsive experience of reading, an experience he implicitly compares to the contemporary "resistance to literature" that we encounter in English departments.[48] If Scarry is right about the generative properties of beauty, perhaps it is the recalled beauty of those moments spent reading that years later turned Hassan outward to the world in order to consider whether or not there might not be some practical application for those moments: "I wonder if," he writes, "those instants of literary elation have some pedagogical correlative, if they prompt us to know existence with quickened gaiety and dread. Or must they remain entirely private, hermetic?"[49] While Hassan does not give any definite answer to this question, his explanation for his career choice at least points toward an aesthetic optimism grounded in the possibility of a valuable *shared* experience. "That is why I finally became a teacher of literature," he writes, "to live in the vicinity of that joy."[50]

Like all confessions, Hassan's is a markedly personal response to its subject. Even Rorty's essay, for all its focus on what might inspire us and why such inspiration should be sought out, has the flavor of intimate conversation, of sharing a truth that requires a shedding of formality and pretense. Tompkins, Fish, and Lentricchia similarly place themselves at the center of their arguments; and other, equally personal accounts of love for literature, as well as uncertainty regarding the future of literary criticism and the value of its current practices, have emerged in a variety of fields, not all of them academic.

For example, David Denby, former movie critic of *New York* magazine and now of the *New Yorker*, published a lengthy personal narrative in 1996 about his experience as a reader "sick at heart" who found a cure for his malaise by enrolling in Columbia University's core curriculum. He returned from reading Hobbes and Hegel and St. Augustine ecstatic and invigorated by the new ideas he encountered, as well as those he explored and rejected.

Denby's tome, *Great Books: My Adventures with Homer, Rousseau, Woolf, and Other Indestructible Writers of the Western World*, accomplishes much more (though admittedly with much greater effort) than the revelations of Fish and Lentricchia by offering itself as an example of how studying literature can save or at least renovate lives. Denby's book is likely to have a much more powerful impact in furthering the cause of beauty's return, and not only because it is aimed at a general, rather than narrowly academic, readership. Ultimately the book is significant because it shows somebody actually doing something as a result of reading—not somebody stopping doing something, as Lentricchia gives up on his graduate students, but somebody taking something up, albeit in this case with reading itself as both the means and the ends.

Denby's book is in large part about pleasure, and the issue it takes with the academy has mostly to do with the disappearance of pleasure from formal study. What Denby experienced at Columbia might be described in a phrase from Stephen Greenblatt's essay "Resonance and Wonder" (1990)—itself an apt title for a course in great books. In this essay, Greenblatt argues that art has the power to "stop the viewer in his tracks, to convey an arresting sense of uniqueness, to evoke an exalted attention." While Greenblatt manages, as one might expect, to historicize that sense and attention, he nevertheless accords it honor as "a distinctive achievement of our culture" and "one of its most intense pleasures."[51]

In his reading of Greenblatt's essay, Alexander Star finds America's most famous New Historicist to have thus become, in some sense, "a chastened aesthete," a role that Star finds interesting but problematic. Noting that Greenblatt "suggests that aesthetic understanding involves 'respect and admiration' for the accomplishments of others," Star wonders "whether Dante has promoted the cause of tolerance? Will a reader of Celine," he asks, "come away with a newfound respect for his fellow man?"[52]

Star's perspective seems compatible with that of Bloom, who absolves literature of any obligations other than to be good. And so before we try to tackle the rather specific question of what possible benefit could accrue from reading a work, like Dante's, that represents something bad, let's first consider the recent reappearance in the academy of its close relative: the more basic notion that literature, and indeed beauty in general, might be good for you.

***

Great books are good for you! The appeal of this argument can be spotted right away, so maybe it is best to acknowledge it at once. At some, albeit hidden, level, just about every critical theorist, every teacher of literature, and indeed most readers reading would like to believe that literature with a capital

"L" is in some way good for you. The impulse that, on occasion, makes us reach for *Anna Karenina* over—what? *People* magazine? *National Geographic?* may not always win out, but it's frequently driven in part by a vague sense that many people still have that the novel will be good for them. If that has a slightly off-putting ring to it, perhaps it's because we have come to feel that pleasure bears no relation to those phrases that lost impetus around the same time the British empire did: phrases like "it builds character" or "it expands your horizons." Those phrases don't accomplish much anymore, though we are still drawn to the ideas even if we're embarrassed by the words gesturing in their direction. But in most of us there is at least still a trace of a belief—enough to work upon us in some way—that literature ought to do us good.

To an academic, however, the more powerful appeal of the argument supporting the utility of literature (the argument that literature might *do* something rather than merely *be* whatever it is) is that it allows "professional readers"—people like themselves, who make their living by talking about literature, whether by teaching or writing or both—to feel that what they do has practical merit. Teachers (all teachers, but we are really thinking here about college professors of English) love to be told that they have changed lives. The chances are good that *they* have not, but the literature they have taught may very well have done something to an attentive student. Whether or not the literary encounter has done any *good* is quite another question to consider; but the fact remains that many of us who teach literature are predisposed to welcome the idea that intense aesthetic experience has some wider consequences than our own private emotional response.

A number of recent works appear to justify or bolster that predisposition by rendering it more respectable or, at least, by attempting to align it with less embarrassing terms, by supplying, even, a new critical vocabulary with which to argue for it. We have already mentioned Scarry's notion that beauty is generative: her claim is that beauty creates more instances of itself through our irresistible desire to share it, reproduce it, and revisit it. The two-part argument in which Scarry presents these and other thoughts about beauty has a far more ambitious reach, though it is in some ways a less passionate version of Allison's claims regarding the transformative potential of art: "what I thought literature should do . . . was simply to push people into changing their ideas about the world, and to go further, to encourage us in the work of changing the world, to making it more just and more truly human."[53]

In *On Beauty and Being Just*, Scarry seeks to draw a relationship between beauty and the idea of justice, suggesting that it is through our apprehension of the beautiful that we are sensitized to—or decentered into an awareness of—the world. In *The Scandal of Pleasure* (1995), Steiner suggests that art will make us "tolerant" and "mentally lithe."[54] Scarry's argument is more radical because her claims involve not only art but indeed all experiences of beauty. While tolerance does have a role to play in her book in its evocation through the subject of justice, the limbering up of intellectual faculties that an encounter with art might accomplish is of little apparent interest to Scarry. Notwithstanding the reference to tolerance, Steiner's position regarding the general utility of art itself is more cautious. But Scarry's book actually centers itself on the belief that beauty not only does something but does something good, so we will look at it more closely.

We have been talking so far in this book about why we believe that the return of beauty to literary study is both necessary and, as this chapter emphasizes, already underway. By "beauty" we have meant specifically an experience of pleasure in the forms of literature, an appreciation for things associated with literature or attributes of it. We have thus implicitly identified beauty as experiential, as inevitably dependent upon the perceiving (that is, reading) subject rather than independently free. But we have not dwelt on the kind of beauty touched upon earlier, in chapter one: the beauty of the ordinary and everyday world. Great works of literature may and do continually return us to and evoke or even replicate that world, and it is where they do this most powerfully that we find beauty—the beauty of recognition that yes, life is like that, or perhaps the beauty of wonder at the image a phrase may make for us. But we should note that in our discussion of beauty and literary studies (and in making that pairing the cornerstone of this book), we have implicitly *differentiated* the aesthetic from the ordinary experience and thereby suggested, as we believe, that it is both more useful and accurate to consider aesthetic response as something peculiar to the arts.

To talk about beauty as a subject in and of itself, as an untethered, nonspecific, and joyful encounter with the world, as Scarry does, is to take a rather different path and to allow into our purview things not only from the arts but also from nature. It invites, therefore, a conversation in which we must grapple with the question of whether nature can usefully be considered within the domain of aesthetics. Our belief is that it cannot, because the art object that is the focus of aesthetic study requires human intelligence, a craft, a history, and an intent, against all of which we may set nature. Art and life are distinct from each other and are judged and experienced differently. This is very far from saying that nature is not as beautiful—is not more beautiful—than anything we can find in art.

Scarry does not talk about aesthetics in her book, but by virtue of her subject matter—the importance of beauty and its relationship to fairness—aesthetics as a field of study always seems to be tangentially implicated. So it is, but only because the kind of pleasure we have from a painting of flowers and the kind of pleasure we have from a flower garden may feel, in some ways (and despite Bell),[55] similar. Scarry has no interest in differentiating between the feelings, because she is in pursuit of all kinds of beauty, beauty that can, as just noted, be found as easily in nature as in art. Beauty cannot be found on its own; Scarry argues that it must reside in things, be of them.[56] So, in her consideration of the things she finds beautiful, it is of no relevance to her argument to insist on a distinction between a flower and the painting of a flower; the distinction between those two would become meaningful and important to her only when and if someone should make the (rather peculiar) claim that because both are beautiful, both are the same, and, therefore, the flower should be examined as a work of art and judged according to the principles of art or the painting of the flower should be examined and judged according to the rules of gardening. The presence of beauty is no indication of category; beauty has no categories, though Scarry makes categories of things that are beautiful in her efforts to consider what beauty does to us.

Like Steiner (and Hassan, and Denby), Scarry notes that there has been little discussion of beauty in the humanities for the last twenty or so years. That's one of the places, we could say, that aesthetics shows itself to be a part of this discussion, and when Scarry mentions the avoidance of beauty in discussions of literature, like Denby and Hassan, she does so to suggest that some thing or things have thereby been lost. Lost to students during these years have been many opportunities and occasions to learn about what actually makes a piece of writing beautiful in the first place. And thus also lost, and lost in consequence of the first, is the sense of a connection between that beautiful writing and the world.

As Murdoch (and now Lentricchia) has written, our approach to the relationship between art and life does not have to be *either* Bloomsbury art for art's sake *or* art for any particular party line's sake. There is a middle ground. Murdoch calls it "Art for life's sake," and Scarry's goal seems to be elucidating the ways in which something we find in art—beauty—might bring us closer to something in life of which all sides of the debate might approve: Justice. To do this, Scarry must show why the political arguments against beauty are, as she puts it, incoherent.

Let's consider what those arguments are, using our own literary examples as illustrations. The first objection to beauty, writes Scarry, is that it "distracts." The first objection to beauty in the study of literature, then, is that if you're obsessing over the measure of a line or the workings of a metaphor, or if you're focusing at length on the pleasurable images in a passage by Thomas Hardy, you're not noticing that (for example) *Tess of the D'Urbervilles* is actually about

(1) a rape; (2) the rape of the working classes by the upper classes; (3) the injustice of the law against women; (4) the injustice of capital punishment; (5) the grim conditions of the laboring poor in Victorian England—and so on. As a consequence of caring about the wrong things, you are not caring about the *right* things to effect social change that will actually address those more serious wrongs depicted in the novel.

The assumption of this argument is that pleasure gleaned from the beauty of the prose is a distraction, that it is secondary, or even arbitrary, to the true meaning or goals of the work. According to this point of view, the study of beauty, says Scarry, "makes us inattentive, and therefore eventually indifferent, to the project of bringing about arrangements that are just."[57] Beauty is a seductive time-waster or, worse, a siren whose delightful music ultimately deafens us to the distressed cries of the real world.

It's hard to imagine anyone actually making this argument, although a teacher might possibly imply it by failing to encourage a student to consider how and why he or she found beauty in the novel, or by failing to initiate a discussion of craft, or by focusing entirely on content, or, more grievously, by insisting on the same arrival point regarding the meaning and importance of that novel for everyone in the class.

Scarry deals with the first objection to beauty by setting it opposite a second. The second argument that she cites against beauty "holds that when we stare at something beautiful, make it an object of sustained regard, our act is destructive to the object. . . . [T]he complaint has given rise to a generalized discrediting of the act of 'looking,' which is charged with 'reifying' the very object that appears to be the subject of admiration."[58] In other words, the problem here lies not with the thing we are looking at, but with looking itself—the objectifying gaze of the observer being the gaze of the supposedly powerful person and thus being intrusive, invasive, or an expression of superiority, aggression, or imperial or sexual prowess. A fine example of such looking might be found in James Agee's *Let Us Now Praise Famous Men*, a work in which the author wrestles agonizingly with the notion of looking and of finding beauty in what he looks at (which is extreme poverty). The complexities of the problem of looking are further compounded by the inclusion of a number of beautiful photographs of Agee's subjects by Walker Evans.

What does Scarry do with these two different arguments against beauty? Essentially, she tries to set them against each other. If the problem is that beauty makes us inattentive, she writes, then the implication is that to be attentive—to be a good watcher of the things that matter—is desirable. But if the problem is that watching is undesirable and damaging, then one cannot be a good, attentive watcher. So together, she claims, these two arguments will not stand. To counter potential criticism that there might be different kinds of looking, that while pleasure-filled perception may be bad, aversive perception—for example, outrage at injustice—can be good,[59] Scarry insists it is hard to imagine a perception that allows one to be sensitive here and deaf there. One cannot see "properly" sometimes and "improperly" at others. Scarry's position seems to be that we are either sensitive to the world or we are not, that one can't train a selective sensitivity to pick up only the sounds of things that need to be acted upon.[60]

Moreover, for Scarry the argument that the kind of looking that does not desire to change the world is bad, whereas the kind of looking that wants to change the world is good, won't hold because, she asks, how are we to know in advance what kind of thing it is that we are looking at until we look? Scarry's implication here seems to be that you have to look at the art object (or thing) *first*, and as far as possible, without preconception or interest. You must look at the object first in an effort to see (as Matthew Arnold argued) what it really is in itself and also (as Arnold did *not* argue) what it might become (or, as Oscar Wilde had it, as in itself it really is not).[61]

Scarry does not apply her theories about looking at objects to the act of teaching literature, although one might argue that teaching is really a means of getting students to look at texts. Rather, she argues that beauty—which makes us want to look long at something in the first place—can assist us "in the work of addressing injustice," and one way it does this is by "requiring of us constant perceptual acuity."[62] Beauty makes us better watchers, better gazers, she implies, because it makes us curious and hungry; we want to hear the new piece of music; we can't resist pulling the novel off the shelves. Beauty has developed our appetite for more contact with itself, which means more incidental contact with other things. Beauty therefore sensitizes us so that—and here's the bridge to the other side, the "hooking up" of literature to the world beyond—we will be more, not less, receptive to the world. We will be paying more attention, not less. Scarry puts it this way:

> The structure of perceiving beauty appears to have a two-part scaffolding: first, one's attention is involuntarily given to the beautiful person or thing; then, this quality of heightened attention is voluntarily extended out to other persons or things. It is as though beautiful things have been placed here and there throughout the world to serve as small wake-up calls to perception, spurring lapsed alertness back to its most acute level. Through its beauty, the world continually recommits us to a rigorous standard of perceptual care: if we do not search it out, it comes and finds us. The problem of lateral disregard is not, then, evidence of a weakness but of a strength: the moment we are enlisted into the first event, we have already become eligible to carry out the second.[63]

How, then, does Scarry move from beauty to justice? One way she makes the connection is by claiming a common link of both to the word and idea of "fairness." Citing John Rawls, she argues that fairness is "symmetry of everyone's relations to each other." She quotes Amartya Sen's recollection of Aristotle, that justice is "a perfect cube"; she recalls Stuart Hampshire's comment that beauty and justice share "balance and the weighing of sides."[64] She asks why it is that the scientist finds some formula "beautiful" or the physicist sees a theory as "pretty." She infers, though she does not expand upon, a relationship between truth and beauty. While not all that is true is beautiful, she writes, what is beautiful "ignites the desire for truth" within us.[65]

But why should it be that the "vocabulary of beauty," as Scarry calls it, has been in play in the fields that "aspire to have 'truth' as their object" (the examples she gives are math, physics, astrophysics, chemistry, and biochemistry) and has *not* in the humanities? Is it because we students of literature do not "aspire to have 'truth'" as our object? And if we don't, what is the object of our study? We're not talking here about surface verisimilitude or about trying to assess the extent to which language is capable of telling us the truth about the world, though there's certainly a place for that in the humanities. We're talking about some more abstract relationship that we have to each other and to the world—perhaps we could call it the truth about the human condition.

It is really no coincidence that the loss of the vocabulary of beauty has occurred at the same time that we have more or less stopped trying to understand what the truth about the human condition is or might be. There are all kinds of reasons why we have stopped pressing the question, but the most obvious one is that we don't believe in the question any more; that is, we take issue with each part of it. First, what truth? Is there one truth? Contemporary wisdom argues no. And there is no such thing as *the* human condition here. Are we talking about men or women? Africans or Europeans or Asians ? Blue collar or white collar? Homosexual, heterosexual, bisexual, transgendered? The categories proliferate.

One result of asserting that no word or work can speak to the condition of so many—that there are, indeed, many "human conditions"—has been a diminished attention to the wider world. We have invested our time instead in serving the specific needs and issues of our specific worlds. In this we have pretended to be humble but have actually displayed our arrogance, for while asserting that we "cannot speak" for anyone but our own small and selective group, we have also made ourselves deliberately deaf to all the other conditions and experiences that are out there and that might threaten to undermine or contradict our own. In the academy, certainly in the English department, speaking only for a particular group and to a particular group has meant a withdrawal into the shells of our own subdisciplines such that we cannot even talk much to each other. Overspecialization, a direct outgrowth of the idea that Truth is not the Object, prevents us from enjoying the view that an education in the humanities should afford us. Instead of standing higher and higher as we read more and more, having an ever-widening vision or understanding of the works we read and their relationship to the world and to each other, we find ourselves shrinking into a dark corner, becoming like Alice, ever smaller and smaller. And the questions that we bring to the literature we study become ever tinier, ever more minute, ever less of interest to ever fewer people.

But beauty is actually of interest to just about everyone. Everyone has a capacity to experience it; one could argue that we have a need for it. Certainly once exposed to it, we want always more. Beauty, as Scarry says, leads us to want to reproduce it, whether in our dreams, in which we revisit or reimagine the experience of beauty; in our phone calls, in which we urge others to have the experience we've just had ("go and see this movie!"); or in our reviews and essays, in which we translate beauty into words and hope that the reader, like a fax machine, can turn them back into images. We reproduce the beautiful by drawing it, photographing it, talking about it. The fact is that we always want more beauty, not less.

Another fact that springs from the first is that wanting more, we will begin to look harder for it. We will sensitize ourselves to beauty. We will pick up another CD of music; we will have eyes more receptive to painting if we have come to love a particular image, because we'll be looking for something like it elsewhere. This part of Scarry's argument, at least, is hard to refute. The generative properties of beauty seem to make us more beauty-oriented in our lives.

In itself, though, that's nothing, perhaps, other than pleasant for ourselves: beauty for beauty's sake (that would be the criticism). What Scarry claims, and what many of the other writers referenced in this chapter imply, is that beauty actually works for Murdoch's vision of "life's sake." Scarry's argument is that the forms of beauty can turn us into generally perceptive, generally receptive persons capable of empathetic acts of the imagination that allow us to move beyond our immediate shells and vicariously inhabit the world of another.

And perhaps this skill for vicarious living is a prerequisite for an intuition of justice. To be quite clear, we are *not* saying that people who don't think we should study beauty (the people who make the objections to beauty because they see it as a distraction or an objectification) do not themselves have the intuition of justice; but the fact that they *do* have an intuition of and a desire for justice may be proof that somewhere, deep down, they also have a finer sense of beauty than they are letting on. It was a love of the perfect cube that got them going; it was the sight of a butterfly's wing or a line of poetry so sharply honed that it made them wince. It was a sense of the fineness of the finer things that led them to argue for their redistribution.

Of course, beauty does not need to be redistributed, because it is self-generating. It creates itself and is in turn recreated in the eyes of its beholders. More precisely, it is generated out of the constant, and constantly variable, exchanges between subject and object. Our argument in this book has been that, as far as beauty in the realm of literary studies goes, readers need training and practice. They also need exposure to what is beautiful. Even if we cannot easily leap with Scarry from beauty to justice, we might accept the spirit of her argument when it is applied specifically to literary studies. We might agree that the self-conscious experience of beauty in literature leads us not merely to become luxuriant in beauty but additionally to learn skills useful for living in society—for fraternity, as Andreas Eshete puts it. And it is fraternity, according to this philosopher, that "underwrites liberty and equality, and hence also fraternity that underwrites liberal theories of justice."[66]

Scarry's more radical claim is that beauty keeps us in mind of that triad—liberty, equality, fraternity—and that in times of injustice, it is the presence of beauty that recalls the missing connection; it is almost as if beauty, when symmetrically weighed down, invokes justice, not merely by analogy but by restoring to us or keeping constant the sense of balance, symmetry, and harmony that is necessary to a sense of justice. It is as though beauty is the necessary condition. And it may be, if Scarry is right that "equality is the heart of beauty, that equality is pleasure-bearing, and that . . . equality is the morally highest and best feature of the world."[67]

The desire for equality grows out of our desire for beauty; this is Scarry's argument: "Folded into the uneven aesthetic surfaces of the world is a pressure toward social equality. It comes from the object's symmetry, from the corrective pressure it exerts against lateral disregard, and from its own generous availability to sensory perception."[68] It is not, then, by analogy that beauty works, but by balance, by "corrective pressure" against "lateral disregard." To the objection that we can still appreciate the need for justice without actually acting on it—that perhaps beauty readies us (but to what end?)—Scarry responds by invoking Simone Weil. What happens when we respond to beauty, she argues, is that we are decentered; removed from our own position at the center of our world.

It is at this point that Murdoch reenters the discussion. In "The Sovereignty of Good over Other Concepts," which Scarry cites here, Murdoch specifies that the most "obvious thing in our surroundings which is an occasion for 'unselfing' . . . is what is popularly called beauty."[69] Scarry's conclusion is ultimately Murdoch's, then: beauty leads us to decenter ourselves; it leads us to a sense of ourselves as lateral, no longer, as Scarry puts it, the hero or heroine of our story. "It is clear that an *ethical fairness*," she writes, "which requires 'a symmetry of everyone's relation' will be greatly assisted by an *aesthetic fairness* that creates in all participants a state of delight in their own lateralness."[70]

We are off to the side, then, and the beautiful thing, be it poem, painting, or sky, gives us balance; the beautiful thing balances us, it seems, against itself; it recalls to us, in Platonic manner, the absent higher forms of justice. What is Scarry talking about but the training of the imagination as a necessary skill toward the apprehension of justice—toward, one might more simply suggest, living in the world?

***

It is surprising how little explicit attention the role of the imagination seems to receive in those recent studies of beauty that mark both its perceived absence and its gradual return. It seems almost too obvious to note that imagination is necessary to forge a connection between aesthetic experience of the kind Scarry describes and the compassion or empathy that she sees as its consequence. George Eliot, whose most compelling characters are invested with great moral imagination (Mordecai in *Daniel Deronda* being the most striking example), is deeply interested in compassion, though her novels suggest that it is suffering, rather than beauty, that for Eliot provides compassion's most fertile source. The sensitivity or lateral regard hailed in Scarry's book appears in Eliot's fiction through a generally painful, rather than pleasurable, decentering of the self. One thinks of Dorothea Brooke lying rigid on the floor all night before she arises at dawn to look out of the window and acknowledge her connection with the rest of humanity. Countering both Scarry and Eliot are the views that beauty distracts us from suffering and may even desensitize us to it while suffering itself brutalizes its subjects. However, the more aesthetically optimistic argument, and one latent in that scene from *Middlemarch*, would be that suffering, like beauty, may also turn the self outward such that one might more easily and fully imagine the independent existence of another.

Imagining the other, affording other persons a fully developed self, is, according to Murdoch, one of the most difficult and loving acts of which humans are capable. For Murdoch it is, indeed, literature's greatest accomplishment, since without the imagination there can be no empathy: "Tolerance is connected with being able to imagine centres of reality which are remote from oneself."[71] Murdoch's view is that only very *good* literature can lead us to imagine selves unlike our own; indeed, it is one way that we can determine the merits of a work. Rather than affirming what we know, or returning us only to our selves as centers of our interest, good literature "breaks the grip of our own dull fantasy life and stirs us to the effort of true vision."[72]

While the role of the imagination is surprisingly absent from most of the recent discussions of beauty, Murdoch's traces are nonetheless everywhere and unite some of the more disparate work in surprising ways. Frederick Turner's *Beauty and the Value of Values*, for example, echoes Murdoch's insistence on the strangeness of beauty—Turner's phrase "a shiver of the strange in the experience of beauty" recalls Murdoch's assertion that art is "close dangerous play with unconscious forces."[73] The inexhaustibility of beauty for Turner means that art always has the potential to be strange: "You can never get to the bottom of something beautiful, because it always finds space inside itself for a new and surprising recapitulation of its idea that adds fresh feeling to the familiar pattern."[74] Moreover, for Turner, "the strangeness of beauty is always attended by a feeling of reminiscence and recognition."[75] It is thus ultimately connective, rather than isolating. Again, one recalls Murdoch's observation that art moves us outward and beyond ourselves.

Arnold Weinstein's study of the emotional response that is part of the literary experience insists on that outward movement: "For too long we have been encouraged to see culture as an affair of intellect, and reading as a solitary exercise. But the truth is different: literature and art are pathways of feeling, and our encounter with them is social, inscribing us in a larger community, a community composed of buried selves and loved ones, as well as the fellowship of writers over time."[76] Weinstein's study is that of the somatic life of literature: "art is . . . the human heart: the pump that keeps our body alive and the *feelings* that course through us and link us to others. Literature and art live in these two ways, as a bloodstream that connects us to the world, as a mirror for our emotions; and as a magic script that allows us both to sound our own depths and also to enter the echoing storehouse of feeling."[77] For Weinstein, as for Murdoch, the art that is great literature "reconceives our place in the world, and thereby redraws our own contours, showing us to be porous and connected. Literature and art move us into our fuller selves."[78] Ultimately the work is transportational: "*art connects.*"[79]

The temptation of much writing on beauty seems to be like Milan Kundera's or Susan Sontag's attraction to the epigram: the elegantly algebraic formulation that appears to resolve our dilemmas and contributes a sense of classicism and purity to what is a fundamentally messy project. Sure enough,

Turner begins his book with some axioms ("Beauty is nondeterministic . . . Beauty is always paradoxical . . . Beauty always opens up a new space").[80] Before the introduction is over, however, he is forced to the admission that while his initial efforts are to "set the experience of beauty squarely before us and to distinguish it from what it is not," so far we have "only a set of impressionistic descriptions of it and of its foils." Notwithstanding the stated goal of the work, which is to "develop a coherent theory of beauty, one that understands its inner dynamic and not just its outer appearance," [81] Turner's most interesting observations lie in the rather less ambitious but more passionate claims that beauty is

> central to all meaningful human life and achievement, it gives access to the objective reality of the universe, it is an independent and powerful experience in its own right, and it is culturally universal both in its general characteristics and in many details. Its absence in the family, in schools, and in public life is a direct cause of the worst of our social problems and a contributing cause of all others, and its restoration to the center of our culture will bring real improvements to the lives of all citizens.[82]

There again we find the increasingly familiar theme that attention to beauty is necessary for civic well-being. "Beauty," writes Turner, "is the guide of politics, as it is the core of morality and speculative understanding";[83] a sense of beauty is "the gentle guide both to truth and to goodness."[84]

Denis Donoghue's *Speaking of Beauty* also attends to "beauty in its social manifestations, its discursive presence."[85] Of the many works on beauty that acknowledge some of the ethical dilemmas raised by beauty's existence (the example given here is our knowledge that the Parthenon was built by slaves), Donoghue's is probably the most frank: "If there is a moral quandary here," he admits, "I can't resolve it."[86] The notion that our pleasure must be inevitably spoiled, or rather tempered or made more discreet, by its association with the "barbarism" of the culture that produced it has shifted in recent years, Donoghue argues, with the receding of the "'politicization' of literary studies;"[87] there is, he claims, a "mellowness in recent intellectual weather."[88] One sign of this is that

> "Theory" is no longer the punitive discourse it was when Michel Foucault, Jacques Derrida, Paul de Man, Stanley Fish, Fredric Jameson, and their colleagues were first engaged in it. The tone of "cultural studies" is not now as acrimonious as it has been. . . . It may be . . . that the leading figures in the culture wars have had their say and retired from the field. Some of them have taken up other issues or lost faith in their causes. But, for whatever reason,

there is more space for themes—beauty is one of them—which not long ago were held to be regressive. The word "aesthetic" is no longer a term of abuse and contempt.[89]

Donoghue, like Turner, has a series of theses regarding beauty that seem to be the result of years of rumination. The theses themselves may or may not hold up; what seems just as significant here is their authors' sense that these are vitally *important* beliefs. "Why should we regard the beauty of a beautiful thing?" Donoghue asks, and he responds with a list.[90] Answer number three, "Because it encourages a contemplative, appreciative, patient attitude in us and at least rebukes automatic recourse to appetitive desires," anticipates number four, "Because 'the appreciation of beauty in art or nature is not only (for all its difficulties) the easiest available spiritual exercise; it is also a completely adequate entry into (and not just analogy of) the good life, since it is the checking of selfishness in the interest of seeing the real.'" Donoghue then adds, "That reason is Iris Murdoch's."[91]

The checking of selfishness is a recurrent theme of much recent work on beauty, appearing in a slightly different guise elsewhere in Murdoch as the need for humility in one's encounters with art. For the most part, however, recent considerations of beauty have ignored or sidestepped the most problematic issues—those issues that arguably led to the neglect of beauty in the first place—and they have focused, like Donoghue, on the way in which "we talk about beauty."[92] Their goals are generally modest: "I cannot define beauty or the beautiful. I can point to certain details and hope you will take my word for them as manifestations of beauty categorically undefined if not indefinable. I settle for saying the little I can say, and consign the remainder to an implicative silence."[93]

Goals may, as we say, be modest. But passions are strong, and for good reason. Just as Lodge notes the late disenchantment of many theorists with their earlier work, so we observe that for many of the writers of recent works on beauty, their comments constitute life lessons. Their opinions have evolved over lifetimes; they represent the conclusions, rather than the starting points, for many of these thinkers. They are the most important things, perhaps, that these readers and critics wish to say. Maybe this is the reason for the simplicity of their arguments, for their personal tone. Maybe it is the reason they shrug off the need to either defend or prove their position. Donoghue seems to speak for many with his humility, which is matched only by his determination to speak.

That humility is, as we have suggested, the legacy of Murdoch. Likewise, Murdoch's influence reemerges in the more frequent emphasis on the utilitarian nature of beauty that seems to offer itself as an implicit defense against charges of aestheticism. Murdoch's work appeals powerfully today and provides many writers with a kind of intellectual confidence, perhaps because her questions are the most pressing and most basic questions that we know how to ask. How should we live? What is a good life? At one time, perhaps, as readers we thought that literature could help us to come up with some answers to those questions. At a later time in our careers, we were asked to put away those questions as too grand, too problematic, too impossible, too wrongheaded. (Whose life are you talking about? For which category do you presume to speak?) But those problematic and impossible questions seem to be the kinds of questions we find ourselves still asking and still wanting to ask. And in our teaching experience, they are still the questions to which our students are hoping to find answers.

In his own ruminations on the future of literary criticism, Terry Eagleton states that "[c]ultural theory as we have it promises to grapple with some fundamental problems, but on the whole fails to deliver. It has been shame faced about morality and metaphysics, embarrassed about love, biology, religion and revolution, largely silent about evil, reticent about death and suffering, dogmatic about essences, universals and foundations, and superficial about truth, objectivity and disinterestedness."[94] Eagleton has had a long and productive career as a reader, a writer, and a theorist. Like many of the works we've considered, his *After Theory* has the ring of confession as well as the flavor of a concluding statement, and it contains, certainly, a sense of disillusionment; but it also conveys a kind of gritty tenacity, a sense that there is, after all, whatever comes next. There is an "After" after theory, and perhaps theory isn't quite done yet, anyway.

Beauty certainly isn't done; indeed, as Donoghue writes, recalling Stendhal, "it seems clear that the 'tense' of beauty is the future, and that its apprehension is propelled by a politics of hope and anticipation, a surge of feeling beyond the merely given present moment."[95]

CONCLUSION

Falling Towers

Everyone in America seems to recall the weather on the morning of September 11, 2001. As I drove downtown into Washington to teach a class at our university, I heard the news of the first plane on the car radio, and I assumed it to be an accident. I also noticed, but failed to understand, a dark mass of clouds ahead of me, over the Pentagon, spreading into the blue sky. When I parked the car and walked to my office, some half-dozen blocks from the White House, I found it odd how many people on the street seemed intensely engaged with their cell phones, none of which apparently worked.

In the English department there were a few snippets of information (now I understood the smoke rising from the Pentagon), but there was no sense of what was really going on. And since no one seemed to know what the university wanted us to do, I decided to teach my class and walked across the empty quad to the classroom. No one was there; all was quiet. As it happened, we were supposed to be reading *The Waste Land* that morning, so I sat on the desk while I waited for the students to show up, and this is what I read:

> What is that sound high in the air
> Murmur of maternal lamentation
> Who are those hooded hordes swarming
> Over endless plains, stumbling in cracked earth
> Ringed by the flat horizon only
> What is the city over the mountains
> Cracks and reforms and bursts in the violet air
> Falling towers
> Jerusalem Athens Alexandria
> Vienna London
> Unreal[1]

It is impossible now for me to read T. S. Eliot's lines without seeing the image of the towers that were, as I sat reading that morning, about to fall. On that morning, not knowing what was happening, I thought instead about the maternal lamentation of the furies and, by association, about the grieving mother of Peter Walsh's dream in *Mrs. Dalloway* ("the figure of the mother whose sons have been killed in the battles of the world"[2]), and I wondered if Virginia Woolf's emotional echo of Eliot was intentional. I did not imagine, then, a new sound of lamentation "high in the air," but now I hear it in Eliot's poem, a work published seventy-nine years before that September morning. This is one of the marks of greatness in a work: it offers us a means of conceptualizing joy and grief in ways that could not, at its crafting, have been imagined. In the years after the First World War, perhaps readers of Eliot's "hooded hordes" saw in that phrase the round metal helmets of soldiers and visualized trenches running like cracks across "endless plains." Perhaps Eliot, a creature of his time, saw those too. But a few years after 2001, mention of a hood in the context of violence now summons—for this reader, at least—a photograph from Abu Ghraib. The possible images summoned by Eliot's extraordinary poem are unlimited, either by virtue of its range of reference or by the unforeseen circumstances that cause the external world to collide in unexpected ways with the internal world that is the poem.

As we move through—or across—that part of the poem I read that morning, we come across a question, only half-framed, lacking the direction of real inquiry: "What is the city over the mountains." Its lack of interrogative punctuation gives it the feeling of impotence, an impotence followed, to shocking effect, by a powerful explosion of culture and civilizations: the magical and evocative names, still unrestrained or guided by punctuation, pour like fireworks, tumble indiscriminately like bricks: "Jerusalem Athens Alexandria." In our mind's eye we see catastrophe, ancient or modern. Perhaps now, as we read, we may silently add New York to Eliot's list of cities. But we don't need to add the word that best describes the feeling, then and now, of that spectacularly beautiful morning of the falling towers, because Eliot gives it to us. He suspends the word in space, where there is no mark of closure to comfort us: "Unreal."

Of course, no one showed up in the classroom that day. After half an hour of quiet, I went back to my car and found that several hundred people suddenly wanted to travel in the same direction that I did. The sun was still shining and the morning was still fresh and new. But something horrifying was going on, and all those people who had been admiring the perfect day half an hour ago were now trying to make sense out of a confusing and incomplete new narrative. It was a beautiful day; it was an occasion of unthinkable violence. Is this what we mean when we make reference to a reconciliation of opposites—a rearrangement, perhaps, of one's world—that calls for engagement in aesthetic experience?

The answer—cautiously, and acknowledging the difficulty, perhaps impossibility, of such reconciliation, as well as the pain of rearranging one's world—is yes. Since making art is one of the things that makes us human, it affirms our dignity to engage in it. So it is with our appreciation for what is beautiful, whether we find it in art or in the natural world. Presumably the need for consolation in beauty and its affirmation of what is good in human beings was what drove the various musical performances around New York City after September 11, as well as the necessity of acknowledging what Daniel Patrick Stearns calls "the adjustment to and acceptance of a world that's forever changed."[3]

But certain kinds of consolation, particularly in the arts, are not obviously or immediately available to everyone. An appreciation for beauty in the complex workings of a piece of poetry, for example, is not innate. As Scott Russell Sanders puts it, "Anyone can take delight in a face or a flower. You need training, however, to perceive the beauty in mathematics or physics or chess, in the architecture of a tree, the design of a bird's wing, or the shiver of breath through a flute. For most of human history, that training has come from elders who taught the young how to pay attention. By paying attention we learn to savor all sorts of patterns, from quantum mechanics to patchwork quilts."[4]

Not everyone is given the chance to learn how to pay the necessary attention, and in this the universities have been unforgivably complicit. A generation of humanities professors has apparently believed that the pattern is significantly less important than the politics. We have been teaching our students, and trying to convince ourselves, that active engagement in the beautiful, and in nonpolitical, nonutilitarian thought, is morally undisciplined, self-serving, and even socially irresponsible. What we have either missed or suppressed is the fact that all people need beauty, and in our time of need we seek it out. We turn to the places where we know that we can find it: favorite books, lines of poetry, pieces of music, the comforting ritual of our daily lives. Not only do we turn to the beauty of the natural world but also, and perhaps especially urgently, we reach for the beauty made by other human beings; perhaps we even create our own. Is it merely sentimental or regressive to suggest that this quest for beauty has its own moral dimension in that it makes us, and our fellow human beings, feel better? Beauty, as Iris Murdoch says, cheers us up. In this, it is surely good, even socially responsible.

Of course, it is true to say also that beauty need not do anything. The humanities, as many have noted, "aren't for anything, at least not in the usual senses. Their use lies in the reminder that there is a certain grandeur in spec-ulative withdrawal, that there are still refuges . . . where reflection trumps activity."[5] There are indeed still such refuges, and universities ought to be chief among them. In this book we have suggested that effective teaching of literature requires the teacher to create a space for beauty that exists apart from the "pushing world"—a place, as Edward Hirsch puts it, where "silence reigns and the din of the culture—the constant buzzing noise that surrounds us—has momentarily stopped."[6] As Murdoch wrote in a letter of 1943, "I want to escape from the eternal push and rattle of time into the coolness & poise of a work of art."[7] Aesthetic reflection—with its necessary withdrawal from the world of activity, from the "eternal push and rattle"—is at its heart an attempt to capture modes of exemplary sense-making in a world that often looks senseless, a world whose narrative is always, necessarily, confusing and incomplete. Aesthetic reflection involves pursuit of the essential, though not essentialized, impulse, universal among cultures, to understand reality, to behave humanely, and to recognize oneself as subject to certain ethical imperatives.

In this book we have been struggling to reconcile what seem to be con-tradictory ideas: first, that beauty and goodness might have something to do with each other, and second, that they don't need to and shouldn't have to. Beauty, we have wanted to argue, must be free to do as it wishes; like Harold Bloom, we have wanted to avoid the slippery slope of assigning any kind of consequence or obligation to the thing that is art. We have wanted to agree with W. H. Auden that, after all, poetry makes nothing happen. But, unlike either Bloom or Auden, we have found ourselves continually nagged at by a suspicion that the experience of beauty in literature, as in life, may change us, sometimes, perhaps even mostly, for the better. James Wood suggests that the assumption that one must choose between the aesthetic and the moral is really false:

> Why should we have aesthetics *or* the moral? . . . Why not both? The aesthetic is a human product, and so it will always have a moral dimension. . . . Surely when ideas take fictive form, as they do as soon as a narrative of any serious-ness is essayed, they become indistinguishable from aesthetics? This is what an idea or an argument *is* in fiction: it has taken a form which it could not exactly have taken outside this particular fiction; it has an aesthetic shape; it has been irrevocably modified by aesthetics.[8]

That modification is surely what we look for in crisis, an adjustment of our perception, perhaps; a realignment of ourselves with any new world of fact or emotions in which we find ourselves. The remarkable poem by Adam

Zagajewski that the *New Yorker* published on its back page the week after September 11 makes its own case for beauty as it sets the tender memories of the poet against the bleak reality of his world. Adjustment or realignment is required; some kind of reconciliation between the individual and his memories is called for. But in order to achieve such reconciliation, the poem advocates a certain response. Try, it says, to praise the mutilated world:

> Remember June's long days,
> and wild strawberries, drops of rosé wine.
> The nettles that methodically overgrow
> the abandoned homesteads of exiles.
> You must praise the mutilated world.
> You watched the stylish yachts and ships;
> one of them had a long trip ahead of it,
> while salty oblivion awaited others.
> You've seen the refugees heading nowhere,
> you've heard the executioners sing joyfully.
> You should praise the mutilated world.
> Remember the moments when we were together
> in a white room and the curtain fluttered.
> Return in thought to the concert where music flared.
> You gathered acorns in the park in autumn
> and leaves eddied over the earth's scars.
> Praise the mutilated world
> and the grey feather a thrush lost,
> and the gentle light that strays and vanishes
> and returns.[9]

What is of comfort in this poem? Its tenderness? The intimacy of recalled moments of beauty set against present suffering? The nettles that will grow over abandoned homes? The disparity between executioners and scars, and the delicacy of a lost feather? The mention of a "gentle light" that, though it vanishes, will indeed return? The repetition of the word "and," evoking a safety chain and thus a possibility of continuity that can lead us into the future?

The assurance with which the poem so quietly ends seems to have spoken with extraordinary clarity to many readers. The poem made its way onto bulletin boards, refrigerators, Web sites. You can find passionate responses to it online. These responses are all different, but they are uniform in their reference to the beauty of the work and the comfort elicited by it. Does the poem cause us to cease attending to suffering or to turn away from the miseries of conflict or the horrors of unexpected violence?

Far from it. The poem itself offers, in fact, no promise of safety. It tells us that the world is mutilated. Still, the poet insists that we praise it. This is the voice of aesthetic optimism. It expresses a desire to live as we would like things to be—as they *ought* to be—at the same time that it conveys the grief of living in a world in which things are not as we would have them. In this it has precedent. As Hirsch points out, "the earliest poems seem to have been composed for ritual occasions of celebration and mourning. Thus the poetry of lamentation and the poetry of praise seem to have arisen at the same time and may always have gone hand in hand. . . . 'Only in the sphere of praise may Lamentation / walk,' Rilke declares in the eighth sonnet to Orpheus."[10] It is the very act of praise that in fact makes lamentation meaningful. It is only in elegy that we are able to give shape to what is lost and to feel as a result some kind of recuperation. For Hirsch, the elegy ritualizes grief and "thereby [makes] it more bearable. The great elegy touches the unfathomable and originates in unacceptable loss. It allows us to experience mortality. It turns loss into remembrance . . . and finds a way to deliver an inheritance."[11]

Zagajewski's poem, as elegy, does not ask us to look away. The reverse is the case, for as Alexander Nehamas says, beauty is "a call to look more attentively."[12] Readers of poetry, lovers of music, gardeners gardening—all persons who engage actively with beauty by paying close attention to it know this to be true. Yet because, in recent decades, we have misperceived the value of beauty, literary scholars have neglected the crucial work of thinking through our relationship with beautiful forms and have failed to teach our students about the way that relationship sustains and enlightens us. Who would ever enter a classroom and invite their students to consider the beauty of a work because, as Nicolas Malebranche puts it, "Attentiveness is the natural prayer of the soul"?[13] The word "soul" doesn't get much exercise in English departments any more, and neither do important philosophical concepts associated with it, such as inspiration, consolation, communality, transcendence, and love.[14] What do these have to do nowadays with the study of literature? In our public neglect of such concepts in favor of the political and the material, our answer is clear: nothing.

Of course, those literature professors who graduated from other English departments in the past thirty years or so have a reasonable defense for their neglect of matters related to the soul, since in their studies no one talked much about these things either. "Did anyone study art and aesthetics when I was in graduate school?" writes one professor:

> I was such a coward then—I never told anyone that I thought texts should be studied for their aesthetic value as well as their political or historic significance. I was afraid that if I suggested that value was not always contingent, I'd be

shipped out or something . . . [E]ngaging with aesthetics has been perceived as engaging in political quietism and in [the rejection of] relevant political issues. That's how I felt at Duke in the late 1980s—politically mushy.

Another English professor recalls the "contingency" arguments of her day, which did so much to undermine judgments of aesthetic value:

I felt I had to hide or smuggle in my humanist convictions about "what sustains people"—my faith for example in some quality of shared humanity that makes literary experience meaningful. . . . I was writing about [James] Joyce's insights into the touching human need to bury, burn, or otherwise take care of the bodies of the dead—an impulse that is universal, however differently loss and the communal response to it are experienced across cultures. . . . Yet I was still afraid I'd be attacked for "essentializing"—for supposing that there are features, shared across cultures, that constitute the essence of being human.[15]

Surely "essentializing"—a poor choice of word for an acknowledgement of shared humanity—is necessary in the imaginative work involved in recognizing the existence of someone else. As a novelist like George Eliot reminds us, that recognition is difficult and demands a leap into empathy that is facilitated by the imaginative demands of literature. The real-world value of great and complex art can accustom us to the intricate and often painful ambiguities of the commingled—or mutilated—world. The aesthetic disposition, we would argue, is actually much less quietist than theoretically convoluted dispositions that see everything as "always already" inscribed; much less quietist, indeed, than a social constructivism that regards individuals as importantly or even definitively constrained by the particularities of their race, class, and gender.

On the contrary, the experience of beauty cultivates confidence in one's *own* perceptions and preferences. Nehamas has this very accomplishment of individuality in mind when he writes that a life of aesthetic experiences and choices is one in which he has been able to "put things together in my own manner and form." The judgment of beauty, he writes, "is a judgment of value," implicating us "in a web of relationships with people and things." The conscious choices behind this implication "lead toward individuality."[16] In that achieved individuality, with its bracing sense of independence, authenticity, and personal agency, resides beauty's promise of happiness, for implicit in this accomplishment of autonomy and agency is a larger reassurance about the ability of humanity in general to shape and improve the world.

Critics of aesthetics may, of course, dismiss the "better world" orientation that often accompanies a serious interest in beauty as sentimental, religious, and naïve, an indulgent distraction from the hard truths of our time. But they are mistaken. The ability to establish strong personal agency and then project certain futures, certain human potentialities, as novelists often do, and the ability to enter into and respond emotionally to those projections, as strong readers do, is a realistic and mature way of expressing faith in the possibility of humanity's capacity to improve itself.

Dmitri Tymoczko, in describing Beethoven's brilliance, evokes precisely this disposition of passion and reason:

> [We] can have tremendous, Beethovenian passions without losing all sense of our own limitation. (As one can have powerful political convictions while still recognizing that reasonable people may disagree.) Beethoven himself may not have achieved the perfect synthesis of these two, complementary qualities. But the evidence of both his music and his life suggests that he tried. Passionate maturity, neither resignation nor moderation nor fanaticism: that, perhaps, is what is truly sublime.[17]

The display of "passionate maturity" may be the best that we could ever hope for in our teaching of literature. The centrality of aesthetic experience in the struggle toward adaptation to a world forever changed, and in the struggle toward the creation of a more humane world, means that professors of literature have a special, even extraordinary, responsibility. In conveying the fullness of powerful aesthetic gestures, they must convey more than the form and content of particular poems, plays, and novels. They must embody in their very mode of teaching the paradox of passionate control that so often characterizes the greatest works of art, and they must embody the moral value for each individual of this dynamic act of balance. If the humanities really are caught up, as William Arrowsmith says, in the "chaos of living,"[18] then surely emotions have a part to play in the classroom. A former student of Wayne Booth's at the University of Chicago recalled, "During our last meeting [of a class on *Ulysses*], Mr. Booth read the final section of Molly's soliloquy. As he approached the end, his voice began to tremble. I looked up from my text to see Wayne Booth crying as he read 'yes I said yes I will yes.'"[19]

Weeping's not required for great teaching, of course; but there's nothing wrong with professors expressing to their students the way in which sustaining fictive truths suffer into being. Indeed, as Booth's student notes, "the memory of that moment confirms the deep power of great art and pushes me onward." And for those who have carried their literary affections with them through a long life, it may actually be impossible to keep private emotion at bay when a work recalls vividly moments from that life. Paul Fussell writes movingly about the difficulty of keeping his emotions checked when teaching certain works: "During my final years of teaching, I had to be very careful what I talked about, and quoted, in front of a class, for I found I could not navigate unmoved through certain things."[20] In our age of distance learning and downloaded lecture content, it's all the more important that humanities professors resist the mechanization of the classroom and take more seriously than ever their function as living embodiments of the power of beauty. Raimond Gaita, a moral philosopher, puts the matter most strongly: "Critical thinking can be taught. How and why really to care for the truth can't be, not, at any rate, in the same way. For that you need example in your teachers and in the texts that you study. The examples won't all come from the humanities, but only the humanities can give what you need to reflect on their significance."[21] It is an interesting idea that the humanities might nurture moral seriousness and that such seriousness is required if one is to be more than merely clever or well versed in one's subject. The return of beauty to literary studies, which we think to be both underway and overdue, is one step toward the revitalization of the liberal arts. That will be its grand, social, public accomplishment.

Just as important as restoring vigor and honesty to the formal discipline of literature, however, is acknowledging why study in the humanities at all should matter to the individual person. In *The Future of Aesthetics*, Francis Sparshott writes that

> [t]he power of beauty, and the place of something like beauty among values; the function of the artistic activities of adornment, fiction, and play in the life of the mind; the logic whereby criticism gets from description to evaluation and back—these three deep, underlying problems seem certain to persist as recurrent perplexities for the philosophical mind, in one form or another, even if no discipline is devoted to them and no organized philosophy has a home prepared for them. And the three problems will continue to lead into each other, as they always have when people really think about them.[22]

Sparshott is right that a neglect of beauty by contemporary philosophy is in some ways unimportant, since people will inevitably return to the subject "as they always have." The philosophical problems associated with beauty do not disappear because we cease to attend to them. But in departments of literature, our neglect of beauty as a subject for discussion has implied that the kinds of problems Sparshott identifies—the place of beauty among values; the function of aesthetic play in the life of the mind; how to evaluate a work—are less important to us than the many other issues with which we have been content to occupy our students. What, however, could be more important than the evolution of "moral seriousness"? What greater opportunity as a teacher could there be than to give a student the tools, as Gaita says, to reflect on the significance of all that the humanities represents?

It is possible that such ambition strikes some professors as overly romantic or grandiose. But it does nobody any good to assume false modesty about what literary studies might be able to accomplish. Besides, the theorist whose focus is exclusively, for example, on gender surely has his or her own ambitious vision for what his or her study and promotion of literature might accomplish.

Perhaps it is time for a disclaimer. Should we ever be in the unlikely position of repopulating our English department, we would not replace all our theorists with aestheticians. We would *not* suggest that all lines of inquiry pursued in English departments, other than the aesthetic, should be done away with. There is a place for theory, but that place is not everywhere. Theory, as Mark Edmundson argues, is "crucial for a culture of criticism." But "we are doing harm to ourselves and others if we theorize literature and leave it at that."[23] Thus along with theory we would always hope to find wonder, noting that wonder is, as Charles Baxter puts it, "at the opposite pole of worldliness" and that wonder "puts aside the known and accepted, along with sophistication, and instead serves us an intelligent naïveté."[24]

Perhaps intelligent naïveté is really the best state of mind with which to approach any work of art; it's surely more likely than worldliness to accommodate the wonder that should be part of any important aesthetic encounter. It is wonder that causes us to regard the poem or the play or the novel that we're reading as something other than a mere historical document. And therefore we *do* suggest that scholarly consideration of a work of literature should acknowledge its status as a work of art. And we *do* suggest that while English professors should be intellectually free to wander at will, we should nonetheless abandon our pretense of expertise in areas other than our own and instead embrace more fully and more publicly what we can actually do rather well, which is read; and we should recognize how extraordinarily important that contribution can be to the university. The return of beauty to literary studies will only be fully accomplished when professors of literature recapture their own lost aesthetic responsiveness and when they work to convey that responsiveness, in its passionate maturity, to students eager to share in it.

It is our belief that part of that responsiveness necessarily involves paying attention to a work's formal shape. This is no methodology to be reserved for formalists or New Critics (should there be any of them still about). The relevance of aesthetics to cultural studies, for example, has been vigorously demonstrated by several scholars.[25] Paying attention to form is simply part of the reading process—something that should, in the classroom exploration of the work, be acknowledged *before* there is further discussion of the proposed method for reading or the ideology of what is read.

Similarly, the emotional impact of the work—its beauty—is part of the reading experience of *every* person who pays attention, and it therefore warrants close and primary attention in our discussion of what a work does. A work of literature can do many things, but before everything else, it makes us read it. This is something to discuss; it is something to make a place for in our teaching of the work; it is something that might in fact destabilize other parts of the planned interpretive practice, but it is nonetheless something that should not be passed over or ignored. There is no need to replace our theorists with aesthetes, no need to hire or fire anyone at all, because everyone who ever loved literature enough to study it for a living is probably a believer in beauty anyway. They've just been hiding it.

Coda

There is a generative joy in aesthetic experience. As we move responsively through our lives, we are compelled, as Sanders observes, to "answer the beauty we find with the beauty we make."[26] But when we began this book, the dark cloud hanging in the blue sky of September 11, 2001, was visible from our classroom. What of the horror we find in the world? How are we to answer that? How, as Stanley Kunitz's poem asks, is the heart to be reconciled to its "feast of losses"? Is it possible to answer the horror we find with the beauty we have made—and continue to make?

Our answer—yes—is an expression of radical aesthetic optimism. Radical aesthetic optimism is always to be found in works of great literature, which embody their authors' faith in the transformative possibilities of writing. And in the course of writing this book, our bleak views concerning the absence of beauty in the classroom have been similarly transformed, or at least brightened, by the evident aesthetic optimism of many contemporary writers, critics, and teachers. Notwithstanding the mainstream turn away from literary aesthetics in American universities, we have been encouraged to find varieties of aesthetic optimism present in the works of a growing number of critics and teachers, many of whom we have quoted here.

The return to beauty is, we think, a timely one, for beauty, as we have noted, can be lifesaving; it has "everything to do with survival."[27] Viewed in this way, beauty is grand; it evokes and partakes in the weighty philosophical questions from which, as teachers, we have too often shied away but that every class of incoming students we have ever taught appears ready and eager to explore. As teachers we have been too timid, too relativist in our thinking, to argue, as Frederick Turner unapologetically does, that beauty "is central to all meaningful human life and achievement, it gives access to the objective reality of the universe, it is an independent and powerful experience in its own right, and it is culturally universal both in its general characteristics and in many details."[28] Professors of literature have in recent years made scant use of the phrases that come so easily to Turner—phrases such as "objective reality" or "meaningful human life." To claim that something is "culturally universal" does not win one tenure these days. And indeed, when Turner writes that something beautiful may have in it "a strong rush of the imagined joy of paradise,"[29] we too cringe, though through no fault of Turner: the word "paradise" for the modern mind has in recent times been coupled to the suicide bomber, and the word for some ears now conjures both violence and delusion.

Yet it is precisely because of this new linguistic coupling, as well as the ages-old imagistic yoking of the beautiful with the terrible, that beauty itself needs to be addressed more urgently than ever. The darker side of beauty undeniably exists in the aesthetic appeal of morally bankrupt ideologies.[30] But in teaching our students about beauty—by sharing it, making a space for it, drawing attention to it; in revealing it where perhaps it is not obviously present; and above all, by acknowledging it—we help them in their resistance as well as in their survival. In this we are both realists and idealists, subscribers, as surely all teachers of literature should be, to Isaac Rosenfeld's principle. It is what he called "the principle of New York and of all great cities"; it is a principle that comes to us as a mission, and that mission is to find "the everlasting in the ephemeral things: not in iron, stone, brick, concrete, steel, and chrome, but in paper, ink, pigment, sound, voice, gesture, and graceful leaping, for it is of such things that the ultimate realities, of the mind and the heart, are made."[31]

Notes

Preface

1. Kunitz, "The Layers," 217.
2. There are, happily, exceptions. James Wood, senior editor of *The New Republic* and chief literary critic for *The Guardian*, currently teaches in the English department at Harvard and continues to write informed, accessible, and widely read literary criticism. Louis Menand, also of Harvard, and Michael Wood at Princeton are, similarly, "crossovers" whose work reaches a wide audience and remains fully identifiable as literary criticism.
3. If we are teachers, we must judge what is worth teaching; and as readers, we must presumably decide what is worth our time. Why should a class on British literature make space for Virginia Woolf and E. M. Forster but not for the far more widely read Marie Corelli? One obvious answer: life is short. Emory Elliott effectively expresses the problem: "As long as people review and evaluate cultural expression and make choices about what to preserve, study, and recommend . . . they will seek to define standards of judgment and thereby fall back into aesthetics. The issue then is . . . how to redefine the parameters of 'art' and formulate new questions for evaluating cultural expression in ways that are fair and just to all" (See Elliott, introduction, p. 9).
4. Rorty, *Achieving Our Country*, 139.

Introduction

1. Files, "A 178-Foot Surprise Rises Over Washington."
2. Jefferson Airplane, *Surrealistic Pillow*.
3. Bernstein, *The Unanswered Question*, 318.
4. Wat, "Reading Proust in Lubyanka," 250.
5. Koestenbaum, *The Queen's Throat*, 103.
6. Bacon, "Of Beauty," qtd. in "A Note on Performance" by Edmunds in *Purcell Songs*, n.p.
7. Said, *Musical Elaborations*, 86.

8. Bernstein, *The Unanswered Question*, 317–18.

9. Orwell, "Inside the Whale," 112.

10. Whitman, "Song of Myself," *Leaves of Grass*, 88.

11. Jarrell, *Poetry and the Age*, 128.

12. Agee and Evans, *Let Us Now Praise Famous Men*, 204.

13. It stands to reason that the reverse may also be true—that is, if one argues that art is in some way good for you, then one must be prepared to defend the notion that other kinds of art may be harmful. It is understandable that such a position makes Americans uncomfortable given its potential for a tilt toward censorship. Harold Bloom is probably most adamant in his position that art does nothing other than teach us how best to be alone, an attractive position because it allows its proponents to avoid the flip side of the "art can be good for you" equation. Given that many aesthetic experiences take place in a community or that after the solitary Bloomian art experience we often must rejoin a community, the issue of whether or how art may shape or alter that rejoining—the role it plays in our construction as social entities—is one to be addressed rather than ducked. While Bloom avoids getting bogged down in questions regarding the therapeutic role of art, we have found ourselves plagued during the course of writing this book with the question of whether art may not also have negative consequences; despite our fear of both plagues and bogs, we will later attempt to address that question as a relevant if highly problematic element in aesthetic judgment and evaluation.

14. Murdoch, *Existentialists and Mystics*, 14.

15. Henry James, qtd. in Alvarez, *The Savage God*, 273.

16. Mack, *Everybody's Shakespeare*, 111.

17. Dmitri Tymoczko, "The Sublime Beethoven," 42.

18. Edmunds, "A Note on Performance," 64.

19. Ibid.

20. Schopenhauer, *The World as Will and Representation*, 258.

21. Purcell, "Music for a While," 28.

22. Hopkins, "Henry Purcell," 80.

23. Doty, *Heaven's Coast*, 65.

24. Merrill, *A Different Person*, 199.

25. Kundera, *The Unbearable Lightness of Being*, 153.

26. *What Dreams May Come*.

27. Hampshire, "The Eye of the Beholder," 44.

28. Giles, "Sharps and Flats," 2.

29. Murdoch, *Existentialists and Mystics*, 26.

30. Doty, *Heaven's Coast*, 97.

31. Bloom, *The Western Canon*, 28.

32. Murdoch, *Existentialists and Mystics*, 10.

33. Ibid., 7.

34. Scruton, 437.

35. Bernstein, *The Unanswered Question*, 39.

36. Klein, *Cigarettes are Sublime*, xi.

37. Bernstein, *The Unanswered Question*, 209.
38. Rochberg, *The Aesthetics of Survival*, 13.
39. Nehamas, "An Essay on Beauty and Judgment," 7.
40. Godignon and Thiriet, "The Rebirth of Voluntary Servitude," 231.
41. Cooper, citing Burke, 57.
42. Lane, "The Joyless Polity," 329–70.
43. *American Beauty*.

Chapter 1

1. Qtd. in Edel, *Henry James: A Life*, 697.
2. Elkins, "The Ivory Tower of Tearlessness," B7–B10. For more of Elkins's work, see http://www.jameselkins.com/html/books.html.
3. Mannheim, "Utopia in the Contemporary Situation," 23–26.
4. Pipes, "Misinterpreting the Cold War," 156.
5. Ibid., 160.
6. Rorty, *Achieving Our Country*, 127.
7. Schjeldahl, "Beauty Is Back," 161.
8. Handy, *The Age of Paradox*, 260.
9. Star, *Feed* magazine (defunct; no longer available online).
10. Clayton, "Deep Thinkers Missing in Action."
11. Schor, *The Overworked American*.
12. Easterbrook, "Axle of Evil," 35.
13. Schjeldahl, "Beauty Is Back," 161.
14. Donoghue, "Speaking of Beauty," 13.
15. Gilbert-Rolfe, "Beauty."
16. Sontag, "An Argument About Beauty," 23.
17. Clark, "Arguments About Modernism," 247.
18. Shawn, "The Fever," 179, 202.
19. Yelavich, "Beauty's Back in Town."
20. James, *The Varieties of Religious Experience*.
21. Griffiths, *The Golden String*, 32–33.
22. "Blanchot and Weil's Notion of Sacred Language."
23. Cullinan, "A Treasure Worth Preserving."
24. Roberts, "A Little Protector," 118.
25. Qtd. in Edel, *Henry James: A Life*, 51.
26. Segalen, *Essay on Exoticism*, 28.
27. Doty, *Heaven's Coast*, 88.
28. Farmelo, *It Must Be Beautiful*, xii, 28.
29. Wassarman, "Channels of Communication in the Ovary," 57.
30. Agee, *Let Us Now Praise Famous Men*, 117.
31. Merrill, *A Different Person*, 198–99.
32. Rorty, *Philosophy and Social Hope*, 7–8.

33. Joyce, *A Portrait of the Artist as a Young Man*, 144–45.
34. Stearns, "The Sound of Consolation."
35. Doty, *Heaven's Coast*, 97.
36. Stearns, "The Sound of Consolation."
37. Conradi, *Iris Murdoch: A Life*, 120.
38. Koestenbaum, *The Queen's Throat*, 137.
39. Kosman, "Our Shared Humanity Given A Voice in Arts," E1.
40. DeLillo, "In the Ruins of the Future," 1–2.
41. Ibid.
42. Adorno, *Minima Moralia*, 25.
43. Bernstein, *The Unanswered Question*, 313.
44. Ibid., 321.
45. Gray, *Straw Dogs*, 120.
46. Ibid., 115.
47. Ibid., 30.
48. Hickey, "Buying the World," 73.
49. Carlson, "Aesthetic Appreciation of the Natural Environment," 39.
50. Donoghue, "Speaking of Beauty," 17.
51. The statement, Stockhausen, says, was misconstrued. See online, http://www.stockhausen.org/message_from_karlheinz.html.
52. Clark, "Arguments About Modernism," 247.
53. Schjeldahl, "Notes on Beauty," 53–60.
54. Miller, *The Tropic of Cancer*, 74.
55. Murdoch, *Existentialists and Mystics*, 215.
56. Ibid., 228.
57. Barthes, *The Responsibility of Forms*, 192.
58. Pepys, *The Diary of Samuel Pepys*, 94.
59. Schweitzer, *An Anthology*, xxvi.
60. Qtd. in Danto, "The Abuse of Beauty," 39.
61. Hickey, "Buying the World," 73.
62. Konrad, *The Melancholy of Rebirth*, 154.
63. Hickey, "Buying the World," 87.
64. Segalen, *Essay on Exoticism*, p. 44.
65. Hampshire, "The Eye of the Beholder," 44.
66. BBC UK online, "The Elaborate Pearls of the Voice."
67. Qtd. in Sontag, "An Argument About Beauty," 25.
68. Graves, *Goodbye to All That*, 115.
69. Elkins, "The Ivory Tower of Tearlessness," 9–10.
70. Qtd. in Danto, "The Abuse of Beauty," 54.
71. Miller, *Tropic of Cancer*, 74.
72. Lentricchia, "Last Will and Testament of an Ex-Literary Critic," 28.
73. Poulet, "Criticism and the Experience of Interiority," 62.
74. Schweitzer, *An Anthology*, 58.
75. Koestenbaum, *The Queen's Throat*, 42.

76. Barthes, *The Responsibility of Forms*, 295.
77. Rilke, *Sonnets to Orpheus*, 21.
78. Barthes, *The Responsibility of Forms*, 265.
79. Merrill, "After Greece," in *Selected Poems 1946–1985*, 62.
80. Ibid., 63.
81. Jakobson, "A Postscript to the Discussion on Grammar of Poetry," 21–35.
82. Bloom, *The Western Canon*, 3.
83. Segalen, *Essay on Exoticism*, 21.
84. Poulet, "Criticism," 72.
85. Fried, "How Modernism Works," 248. In a striking change of tone and position, Fried's intellectual combatant on this subject twenty years ago, T. J. Clark, who then found Fried's love of beauty reactionary, a regressive indulgence of people aching for the certainty and exultation that a now-absconded God gave them, now finds the over-politicization of aesthetic objects the real problem. Having surveyed the results of a relentlessly social and historical approach to art, Clark admits to second thoughts, as Michael J. Lewis, in an essay in *The New Criterion*, notes: "Clark recognizes that something has gone badly wrong. Under the reign of formalism, the art object was a kind of cloistered virgin, its aesthetic integrity guarded against any kind of political or social agenda that might taint it. But in an age of agenda art, the object had lost its purity, as it were, to become a play-thing of any political agenda that might claim it." Lewis then goes on to quote Clark: "In the beginning . . . the argument was with certain modes of formalism, and the main effort in my writing went into making the painting fully part of a world of transactions, interests, disputes, beliefs, 'politics.' But who now thinks it is not? The enemy now is not the old picture of visual imaging as pursued in a state of trance-like removal from human concerns, but the parody notion we have come to live with of its belonging to the world, its incorporation into it, its being 'fully part' of a certain image regime. 'Being fully part' means, it turns out in practice, being at any tawdry ideology's service." Lewis, "T. J. Clark in Winter," 4.

Chapter 2

1. Halberstam, "The Death of English."
2. DeLillo, *White Noise*, 10.
3. Menand, "The Marketplace of Ideas."
4. Benton, "Life After the Death of Theory," C4.
5. Menand, "The Marketplace of Ideas."
6. Ibid.
7. Halberstam, "The Death of English"
8. Mangino, "A Feminist Teacher 'Overreacts.'"
9. Garelick, "Career Girls," A14.
10. Adorno, *Minima Moralia*, 132–33.
11. Delbanco, "The Decline and Fall of Literature," 36.

12. Scholes, "Does English Matter?" 37.
13. Chopin, *The Awakening and Other Stories.*
14. Perloff, "Something is Happening, Mr. Jones."
15. Edmundson, *Literature Against Philosophy, Plato to Derrida.*
16. Johnson, *A World of Difference*, 184–99.
17. Ibid., 184.
18. Ibid., 191.
19. Ibid., 199.
20. DeLillo, *White Noise*, 67.
21. Dickson, "Plagiarism Plagues College Campuses."
22. Posner, "Plagiarism—Posner Post."
23. See, for example, Lacan, *Écrits: A Selection.* See also Baudrillard, "The Evil Demon of Images and the Precession of Simulacra."
24. DeLillo, *Mao II*, 45.
25. Bromell, "Summa Cum Avartia," 74.
26. Qtd. in Hitchens, "The Captive Mind Now."
27. Ibid.
28. Allitt, "Professors, Stop Your Microchips," B38.
29. Teachout, "The Return of Beauty."
30. Ibid.

Chapter 3

1. Donoghue, *Speaking of Beauty*, 85.
2. Our comments here are directed specifically at college students. When children are learning to read, and when reading is painful and laborious, it seems logical that the best choice of reading material is whatever they are most interested in reading. We are concerned with students who already presume themselves to be good readers and perhaps have even identified themselves as English majors. Serving up works to college students *because* they will be able relate to the material is condescending.
3. Murdoch, "The Sovereignty of Good over Other Concepts," in *Existentialists and Mystics*, 385.
4. Bishop Butler's epigraph to G. E. Moore's *Principia Ethica*, 1903.
5. Rorty, *Achieving Our Country*, 126.
6. Denby, *Great Books*, 31–32.
7. Greenblatt, "Resonance and Wonder," 161–83.
8. Bloom, *The Western Canon*, 28.
9. Scarry, *On Beauty and Being Just*, 3.
10. "Beauty is an unstable property because it is not a property at all. It is the name of a particular interaction between two beings, a 'self' and an 'Other'." Steiner, *Venus in Exile*, xxi.
11. See Caughie, "How Do We Keep Desire from Passing with Beauty?" 269–84.

12. Emory Elliott, qtd. in Heller, "Wearying of Cultural Studies, Some Scholars Rediscover Beauty," 15. Elliott has done his part to redress the balance, however; see his introduction to *Aesthetics in a Multicultural Age* for a nuanced discussion of the issue.
13. Weinstein, *A Scream Goes Through the House*, 394.
14. Ibid., 395.
15. Murdoch, *Existentialists and Mystics*, 29.
16. Ibid., 369.
17. Scarry, *On Beauty and Being Just*, 114.
18. Murdoch, *Existentialists and Mystics*, 369.
19. Ibid., 373.
20. Ibid., 385.
21. Donoghue, *Speaking of Beauty*, 46.
22. Ibid., 47.
23. Greenblatt, "Resonance and Wonder," 170.
24. Ibid., 170.
25. Ibid., 181.
26. Donoghue, *Speaking of Beauty*, 122.
27. Jarvis, qtd. in Donoghue, *Speaking of Beauty*, 122.
28. Murdoch, *Existentialists and Mystics*, 379.
29. Murdoch's immediate qualification should, in fairness, also be noted: "At least this can seem to be so, though I would feel that the artist had at least got a starting point [for being wise] and that on closer inspection the concentration camp guard might prove to have his limitations as a family man. The scene remains disparate and complex beyond the hopes of any system." *Existentialists and Mystics*, 379–80.
30. In this we part company from Murdoch, whose vision of great art is more independent of its subject perceivers than our own. Murdoch writes that "Good art . . . is something pre-eminently outside us and resistant to our consciousness. We surrender ourselves . . . with a love which is unpossessive and unselfish." *Existentialists and Mystics*, 372.
31. "A serious scholar has great merits. But a serious scholar who is also a good man knows not only his subject but the proper place of his subject in the whole of his life." Murdoch, *Existentialists and Mystics*, 379.
32. Murdoch, *Existentialists and Mystics*, 370.
33. Weinstein, *A Scream Goes Through the House*, xxxvi.
34. May, "A Will and a Way."

Chapter 4

1. Woolf, *Mrs. Dalloway*, 120.
2. Emily Dickinson, letter to Colonel T. W. Higginson, *The Life and Letters of Emily Dickinson*, 276.

3. Woolf, *Mrs. Dalloway*, 13.
4. Woolf, *To the Lighthouse*, 19.
5. Woolf, *The Diary of Virginia Woolf*, 53.
6. Qtd. in Caughie, "How Do We Keep Desire from Passing with Beauty?" 269–70.
7. Caughie, "How Do We Keep Desire from Passing with Beauty?" 270. Caughie is wrong, however, in some of her readings of Scarry's book. Scarry does not argue that "We hold these truths to be self-evident" is "just precisely because it scans" (273; see Scarry, *On Beauty and Being Just*, 102). Nor does Scarry claim to find contemporary theory indifferent to social justice because theory is ugly, or obscurely written, as Caughie suggests (275).
8. Caughie, "How Do We Keep Desire from Passing with Beauty?" 274.
9. Ibid., 279.
10. Ibid., 279.
11. Murdoch, *Existentialists and Mystics*, 9.
12. Caughie, "How Do We Keep Desire from Passing with Beauty?" 280.
13. Ibid., 273.
14. Here Caughie paraphrases George Steiner's point in his 1978 essay, "On Difficulty" (Caughie, "How Do We Keep Desire from Passing with Beauty?" 275).
15. Caughie, "How Do We keep Desire from Passing with Beauty?" 277.
16. Caughie, "How Do We Keep Desire from Passing with Beauty?" quoting Berger, 280.
17. Caughie, "How Do We Keep Desire from Passing with Beauty?" 280.
18. Bell, *Art*, 18.
19. Reed, "Through Formalism," 32.
20. Steiner, *Venus in Exile*, xxiii.
21. Caughie, "How Do We Keep Desire from Passing with Beauty?" 280.
22. Finding something morally repugnant to be formally beautiful is problematic. Walker Evans's haunting photography for James Agee's *Let Us Now Praise Famous Men* is a case in point. How are we to respond to these images? What is beautiful about poverty? Must we efface the subject matter to find the photographs beautiful, or should we argue instead for the magnificence of the works as documents and foreground our own lack of ethical clarity in regarding them as aesthetic objects? Agee's triumph lies in his refusal to make such questions easy or merely academic. His determination to confront the ethical problems of his work and the resulting convoluted torture of his prose leave us as uneasy and ultimately as implicated as he himself is. See Agee and Evans, *Let Us Now Praise Famous Men*.
23. Murdoch, "Interview with Bryan McGee," in *Existentialists and Mystics*, 10.
24. Woolf, *Mrs. Dalloway*, 163.
25. Caws, *Reading Frames in Modern Fiction*.
26. Peter's "That was interesting" is later echoed by the similarly detached yet aesthetically engaged Lily Briscoe as she completes her painting in *To the Lighthouse*. Working with the shadow on the step, that may or may not be cast by the ghost/ memory of Mrs. Ramsay, Lily notes without emotion that "It was interesting. It might be useful." Woolf, *To the Lighthouse*, 201.

27. Sufficiency is an abiding theme where beauty is concerned in Woolf. See, for example, Mrs. Ramsay's thoughts of mortality tempered by her pleasure in beauty as the lighthouse beam rolls over the waves: "It is enough! It is enough!" Woolf, *To the Lighthouse*, 65.

28. James, "The Art of Fiction," 32. James elaborates on this idea in *Portrait of a Lady* (1881), when Isobel Archer perceives the true relations between her husband and Mme Merle. See also Fry's well-known defense of this theory as it takes shape in the visual arts: Fry, "The Philosophy of Impressionism," in *A Roger Fry Reader*, 12–20.

29. Peter in fact recalls nobody so much as Walter Pater in his recognition that life is too short "to extract every ounce of pleasure, every shade of meaning." Woolf, *Mrs. Dalloway*, 79.

30. Donoghue, *Speaking of Beauty*, 21.

31. Ibid., 22.

32. Sanders, *Hunting for Hope*, 146.

33. See Elaine Scarry's elaboration on the experience of making an error in beauty, and of beauty's role in bringing to our attention our capacity for error, in part one of *On Beauty and Being Just*.

34. Woolf, *Mrs. Dalloway*, 69.

35. Ibid., 46.

36. Ibid., 139–40.

37. Green, "The Right Thing in the Right Place," 91.

38. Hardy, *Tess of the D'Urbervilles* (1891) and *A Pair of Blue Eyes* (1873).

39. Sanders, *Hunting for Hope*, 146.

40. "They both smiled, standing there. They both felt a common hilarity, excited by the moving waves; and then by the swift cutting race of a sailing boat, which, having sliced a curve in the bay, stopped; shivered; let its sails drop down; and then, with a natural instinct to complete the picture, after this swift movement, both of them looked at the dunes far away, and instead of merriment felt come over them some sadness—because the thing was completed partly, and partly because distant views seem to outlast by a million years (Lily thought) the gazer." Woolf, *To the Lighthouse*, 20.

41. A later interview with Sanders on this subject confirms his sense of the similarity of response: "While I was looking at [my daughter's] wedding photos, I was also looking at images from the Hubble Space Telescope, and I realized that both sets of images aroused the same emotions in me. I wondered where those emotions might come from, and whether this correlation between intimate and cosmic beauty was accidental or whether it might point toward some congruence between our minds and the universe. I ended up arguing that what we call beauty—whether found in a person's face, a mathematical formula, a piece of music, or anywhere else—is an intimation of the harmony between ourselves and the underlying order of things. Beauty is a momentary glimpse of that order, a reconciliation of inner and outer space." Perry and Zade, "Something Durable and Whole," 22.

42. Sanders, *Hunting for Hope*, 144.
43. Woolf, *To the Lighthouse*, 141.
44. Woolf, "Reading," in *The Essays of Virginia Woolf*, 3:142.
45. Woolf, *To the Lighthouse*, 97.

Chapter 5

1. Merrill, *Selected Poems, 1946–1985, 332–39*.
2. Tuttleton, "William Arrowsmith," *90*.
3. Adorno, *Minima Moralia*, 77.
4. Murdoch, *Existentialists and Mystics*, 203.
5. Merrill, *Late Settings*.
6. Merrill, "Santorini," in *Selected Poems*, 337.
7. Merrill, "The Thousand and Second Night," in *Collected Poems*, 182.
8. Rose, *Love's Work: A Reckoning With Life*, 105.
9. Merrill, *Selected Poems*, 337.
10. Merrill, *The Inner Room*, 57.
11. Willard Spiegelman, qtd. in Rotella, ed. *Critical Essays on American Literature Series*, 17.
12. Arnold, "To Marguerite—Continued," 1479.
13. Merrill, *Selected Poems*, 293–94.
14. Merrill, *Selected Poems*, 294.
15. Auden, *Collected Poems*, 112.
16. Kipling, "Broken Men," 109.
17. Merrill, *Selected Poems*, 333.
18. Ibid., 332.
19. Merrill, *The Changing Light at Sandover*, 213.
20. Merrill, "Santorini," *Selected Poems*, 332.
21. Merrill, *Selected Poems*, 332.
22. Ibid., 333.
23. Merrill, "Little Fanfare for Felix Magowan," in *Selected Poems*, 113.
24. Shelley, "A Defense of Poetry," 798.
25. Lowry, *Under the Volcano*, 249.
26. Lehman, "Elemental Bravery: The Unity of James Merrill's Poetry," in *James Merrill: Essays in Criticism*, 23.
27. Lowry, *Under the Volcano*, 57.
28. Merrill, "Santorini," *Selected Poems*, 333.
29. Ibid., 333.
30. Ibid.
31. Ibid., 334.
32. Ibid., 335.
33. Ibid.
34. Ibid., 336.
35. Ibid., 337.

36. Ibid.
37. Ibid., 338.
38. Ibid.
39. Ibid., 338–39.
40. Shelley, "Ode to the West Wind," 730.
41. Merrill, *Selected Poems*, 339.
42. Merrill, *Inner Room*, 70.
43. Merrill, "Santorini," *Selected Poems*, 339.
44. Smith, "Fail Better."

Chapter 6

1. DeLillo "In the Ruins of the Future," 1–2.
2. Amis, "The Voice of the Lonely Crowd."
3. Rorty, *Philosophy and Social Hope*, 14.
4. DeLillo, "In the Ruins of the Future," 2.
5. Aiken, "The Revolt Against Ideology," 254.
6. DeLillo, "In the Ruins of the Future," 2.
7. DeLillo, *Falling Man*, 42.
8. DeLillo, *The Names*, 3.
9. Ibid., 330.
10. DeLillo, *Mao II*, 215.
11. See Nehamas, "A Promise of Happiness." These lectures were subsequently published in book form as *A Promise of Happiness: The Place of Beauty in a World of Art* (Princeton, NJ: Princeton University Press, 2007).
12. Rose, *Mourning Becomes the Law*, 146.
13. Friedman, "A Failure to Imagine," 15.
14. Gitlin, "The Ordinariness of American Feelings."
15. DeLillo, *The Names*, 317.
16. Ibid., 114.
17. Ibid., 297.
18. Engles and Duvall, eds. *Approaches to Teaching White Noise*.
19. Passaro, "Dangerous Don DeLillo."
20. DeLillo, "Interviews with Don DeLillo."
21. Ibid.
22. Ibid.
23. Comte-Sponville, "The Brute, the Sophist, and the Aesthete: Art in the Service of Illusion," 61.
24. Said, *Musical Elaborations*, 96.
25. Scruton, *The Aesthetics of Music*, 499.
26. DeLillo, *Great Jones Street*, 2.
27. Ibid., 104–5.
28. Ibid., 45–46.
29. Ibid., 12.

30. Ibid., 62, 90.
31. Ibid., 264.
32. Ibid., 263.
33. Rose, *Mourning Becomes the Law*, 141.
34. Wood, "Americans on the Prowl."
35. Gitlin, "The Ordinariness of American Feelings."
36. Passaro, "Dangerous Don DeLillo."
37. DeLillo, *The Names*, 295.
38. Ibid., 307.
39. Ibid., 52–53.
40. DeLillo, "Baader-Meinhof," 78–82.
41. Rose, *Mourning Becomes the Law*, 52.
42. Perl, "Saint Gerhard of the Sorrows of Painting," 27, 28, 29.
43. Kafka, "Letter to Oskar Pollak," 16.
44. Rose, *Mourning Becomes the Law*, 36.
45. Camus, "Helen's Exile," 153.
46. Wordsworth, "Lines Written a Few Miles Above Tintern Abbey," 237.
47. DeLillo, "In the Ruins of the Future," 1–2.
48. Passaro, "Dangerous Don DeLillo."
49. Rose, *Mourning Becomes the Law*, 9.
50. DeLillo, *Mao II*, 200.

Chapter 7

1. One of the more embarrassing signals of the shift from English departments to those of cultural studies has been the pretense of expertise in a range of areas in which the scholar of literature has, in most cases, no training. Frank Lentricchia observes that "An advanced literature department is the place where you can write a dissertation on Wittgenstein and never have to face an examiner from the philosophy department. . . . [It is] the place where you may speak endlessly about gender and never have to face the scrutiny of a biologist, because gender is just a social construction and nature doesn't exist." Lentricchia, "Last Will and Testament of an ex-Literary Critic," 32.
2. Newton, *The Meaning of Beauty*, 9.
3. Ibid., 10.
4. Ibid., 9.
5. Bell, *Art*, 18.
6. Steiner, *The Scandal of Pleasure*, 7.
7. Bloom, *The Western Canon*, 28. Notwithstanding the beauty of his phrasing, Bloom's bleak vision of the English department is grimmer than our own.
8. Lentricchia, "Last Will and Testament of an Ex-Literary Critic."
9. Scarry, *On Beauty and Being Just*.
10. Lentricchia, "Last Will and Testament of an Ex-Literary Critic," 31.
11. Fjellestad, "Frank Lentricchia's Critical Confession," 406.

12. Tompkins, "Me and My Shadow," 169–78.
13. Ibid.,178.
14. Ibid., 173.
15. Ibid., 174–75.
16. Lentricchia, "Last Will and Testament of an Ex-Literary Critic," 26.
17. Rorty, *Achieving Our Country*, 125–40.
18. Ibid., 128.
19. Rorty's *bête noir* in this essay is Frederic Jameson, identified by Rorty as "profoundly antiromantic." *Achieving Our Country*, 125, 126.
20. Rorty, *Achieving Our Country*, 126–27.
21. Rorty, *Achieving Our Country*, 133.
22. Lentricchia, "Last Will and Testament of an Ex-Literary Critic," 31.
23. Allison, "Believing in Literature," in *Skin*, 181.
24. Lentricchia, "Last Will and Testament of an Ex-Literary Critic," 27.
25. Rorty, *Achieving Our Country*, 129.
26. Murdoch, "Against Dryness," in *Existentialists and Mystics*, 287–95.
27. Rorty, *Achieving Our Country*, 133.
28. Fish, "Why Literary Criticism is Like Virtue," 11–16.
29. Daniel O'Hara assumes this "someone" to be Rorty, but this seems unlikely, given Rorty's affinity for Murdoch and her call for a turn *away from* the self. Rorty moreover laments the withering of connections between academics and a wider public, while Fish, by contrast, assents to a version of literary criticism even more narcissistic in practice than Lentricchia's and similarly minimizes the consequences of teaching literature. See O'Hara, "Lentricchia's Frankness," 40–62.
30. O'Hara, "Lentricchia's Frankness," 45.
31. Ibid., 46.
32. Of course, some academics believe the death of the English department to be an overdue and welcome event. See the previously mentioned article by Judith Halberstam, "The Death of English."
33. It should be clear that this comment is addressed to the opinions expressed in Fish's essay and cannot speak to his actual in-class performance. One assumes he is a fine teacher, but this piece, at least, makes no space for the discussion of how teaching as a practice might be affected by the altered ambitions of the literary critic.
34. O'Hara, "Lentricchia's Frankness," 46.
35. Ibid., 50.
36. Ibid., 51.
37. Lentricchia, *The Edge of Night*, 89; qtd. in O'Hara, "Lentricchia's Frankness," 51.
38. O'Hara, "Lentricchia's Frankness," 62.
39. Ibid., 41.
40. Lodge, "Goodbye to All That," 39.
41. MacCabe, qtd. in Lodge, 39.

42. Lodge, "Goodbye to All That," 39. Lodge's comments arise in a review of Terry Eagleton's *After Theory*. Eagleton's name cannot really be added to Lodge's list because his work is neither fully confessional nor creative. It does offer, however, its own "devastating criticism" of theory; see Lodge, 41.

43. O'Hara, "Lentricchia's Frankness," 62.

44. Rorty, *Achieving Our Country*, 139–140.

45. O'Hara, "Lentricchia's Frankness," 49.

46. Hassan, "Confessions of a Reluctant Critic," 1.

47. Ibid., 13.

48. Ibid., 14.

49. Ibid., 2.

50. Ibid., 14.

51. Greenblatt, "Resonance and Wonder," 170.

52. Star, "Stealing Beauty."

53. Allison, "Believing in Literature," 165.

54. Steiner, *The Scandal of Pleasure*, 8.

55. Bell makes the claim that butterflies and cathedrals evoke clearly different kinds of emotions in the viewer, and that it is in this way that we know art to be distinct from nature. But distinguishing among the types of emotional response is trickier than Bell concedes, and the analogy falters for various reasons, most obviously those of scale. See Bell, "The Aesthetic Hypothesis." *Art*, 15–34.

56. Our position, that beauty depends in part on the perceiving subject, is closer to that of Steiner, who argues that "[b]eauty is an unstable property because it is not a property at all. It is the name of a particular interaction between two beings, a 'self' and an 'Other.'" *Venus in Exile*, xxi.

57. Scarry, *On Beauty and Being Just*, 58.

58. Ibid., 58.

59. Ibid., 60.

60. One problem with this point of view is that it doesn't address the reasons why a person might be emotionally sensitive to, say, music but insensitive to human suffering. The torturer who is soothed by opera as he works; the young soldiers who admire a pianist's skill as they systematically mow down the inhabitants of a ghetto; such images have rightly given pause to those who would insist that an appreciation for great beauty is in itself morally therapeutic.

61. Arnold, "The Function of Criticism at the Present Time," 1–25; and Wilde, "The Critic as Artist," 341–407.

62. Scarry, *On Beauty and Being Just*, 62.

63. Ibid., 81.

64. Ibid., 94–95.

65. Ibid., 52.

66. Ibid., 95.

67. Ibid., 98.

68. Ibid., 110.

69. Murdoch, qtd. in Scarry, *On Beauty and Being Just*, 112–3.

70. Scarry, *On Beauty and Being Just*, 114.
71. Murdoch, "Literature and Philosophy," in *Existentialists and Mystics*, 29.
72. Murdoch, *Existentialists and Mystics*, 14.
73. Turner, *Beauty*, 1; Murdoch, *Existentialists and Mystics*, 10.
74. Turner, *Beauty*, 3.
75. Ibid., 1.
76. Weinstein, *A Scream Goes Through the House*, ix.
77. Ibid.
78. Ibid., xii.
79. Ibid., xxiv.
80. Turner, *Beauty*, 4–5.
81. Ibid., 15.
82. Ibid., 15–16.
83. Ibid., 35.
84. Ibid., 135.
85. Donoghue, *Speaking of Beauty*, 3.
86. Ibid., 6.
87. Ibid., 7.
88. Ibid., 9.
89. Ibid., 8.
90. Ibid., 23.
91. Ibid., 24.
92. Ibid., 23.
93. Ibid., 48.
94. Eagleton, *After Theory*, 101–2.
95. Donoghue, *Speaking of Beauty*, 86.

Conclusion

1. Eliot, "The Waste Land," 43–44.
2. Woolf, *Mrs. Dalloway*, 58.
3. Stearns, "The Sound of Consolation."
4. Sanders, *Hunting for Hope*, 152–53.
5. Lewis-Krause, "In the Penthouse of the Ivory Tower."
6. Hirsch, *How to Read a Poem*, 1.
7. Qtd. in Conradi, *Iris Murdoch*, 171.
8. Wood, "Comment."
9. Zagajewski, "Try to Praise the Mutilated World," 60.
10. Hirsch, *How to Read a Poem*, 86.
11. Ibid., 84.
12. Nehamas, *A Promise of Happiness*, 228.
13. Malebranche, qtd. in Hirsch, *How to Read a Poem*, 1.
14. Of course there are notable exceptions. Edward Hirsch's magnificent *How to Read a Poem* has a chapter titled "The Soul in Action." Hirsch acknowledges,

however, the gradual disappearance of this word from the study of literature: "For many it has felt like a concept whose usefulness waned along with the nineteenth century" (246). Yet, as Gaston Bachelard writes, "the word *soul* is an immortal word. In certain poems it cannot be effaced, for it is a word born of our breath" (qtd. in Hirsch, *How to Read a Poem*, 246).

15. Ruddick, "The Near Enemy of the Humanities is Professionalism," B7.
16. Nehamas, *A Promise of Happiness*, 215–16.
17. Tymoczko, "The Sublime Beethoven," 43.
18. Tuttleton, "William Arrowsmith," 90.
19. Hesser, "Remembering Wayne Booth," 1.
20. Fussell, *Doing Battle*, 296. Of his research for *The Great War and Modern Memory* (New York: Oxford University Press, 1975), Fussell writes, "I had cried so often while writing the book that to steady myself I often had to take a long walk and breathe deeply after writing some heartrending passage. And sometimes I compressed my lips tightly so that those close to me wouldn't know what I was feeling. But as I worked I grew unashamed of my tears and regarded them as part of what I was doing." Fussell, *Doing Battle*, 267.
21. Gaita, qtd. in Rood and Shaw, "Why Go to University?" 11.
22. Sparshott, *The Future of Aesthetics*, 83.
23. Edmundson, *Literature against Philosophy, Plato to Derrida*, 3.
24. Baxter, qtd. in Hirsch, *How to Read a Poem*, 257.
25. See, for example, Emory Elliott et al., *Aesthetics in a Multicultural Age*.
26. Sanders, *Hunting for Hope*, p.148.
27. Ibid., 153. Sanders is in good company: as Elaine Scarry points out, "Homer is not alone in seeing beauty as lifesaving. Augustine described it as 'a plank amid the waves of the sea'." Scarry, *On Beauty and Being Just*, 24.
28. Turner, *Beauty*, 15.
29. Ibid., 8.
30. For a fine discussion of this problem, see Devereaux, "Beauty and Evil," 227–56.
31. Rosenfeld, "Life in Chicago," 534.

Bibliography

Adorno, Theodor. *Minima Moralia: Reflections from a Damaged Life*. Trans. E. F. N. Jephcott. London: NLB, 1974.

Agee, James, and Walker Evans. *Let Us Now Praise Famous Men: Three Tenant Families*. New York: Houghton Mifflin, 1988.

Aiken, Henry David. "The Revolt Against Ideology." In *The End of Ideology Debate*, edited by Chaim I. Waxman, 229–58. New York: Simon and Schuster, 1969.

Allison, Dorothy. "Believing in Literature." In *Skin: Talking About Sex, Class and Literature*, 165–81. Ithaca, NY: Firebrand Books, 1994.

Allitt, Patrick. "Professors, Stop Your Microchips." *Chronicle of Higher Education* 51, no. 42 (June 24, 2005): B38.

Alvarez, A. *The Savage God: A Study of Suicide*. New York: Bantam, 1973.

American Beauty. DVD. Directed by Sam Mendes. Los Angeles, CA: Dream Works SKG, Jinks/Cohen production, 1999.

Amis, Martin. "The Voice of the Lonely Crowd." *The Guardian Unlimited* (online), June 1, 2002. http://books.guardian.co.uk/review/story/0,12084,725608,00.html (accessed October 15, 2007).

Arnold, Matthew. "The Function of Criticism at the Present Time." *Essays Literary and Critical by Matthew Arnold*, edited by Ernest Rhys, 1–25. London: J. M. Dent, and New York: E. P. Dutton, 1907.

———. "To Marguerite—Continued." In *The Norton Anthology of English Literature*, edited by M. H. Abrams, vol. 2, 1479–1480. 7th ed. New York: Norton, 2000.

Auden, W. H. *Collected Poems*. Edited by Edward Mendelson. New York: Random House, 1976.

Bacon, Francis. Quoted in "A Note on Performance," by John Edmunds. In *Henry Purcell Songs, With Realizations of the Figured Bass*, edited by John Edmunds. New York: R. D. Row Music Company, 1960.

Barthes, Roland. *The Responsibility of Forms: Critical Essays on Music, Art, and Representation*. Berkeley: University of California Press, 1991.

Baudrillard, Jean. "The Evil Demon of Images and the Precession of Simulacra." In *Postmodernism: A Reader*, edited by Thomas Docherty, 194–200. New York: Columbia University Press, 1993.

BBC UK online. "The Elaborate Pearls of the Voice." April 16, 2002. http://www.bbc.co.uk/dna/h2g2/A694631 (accessed October 15, 2007).

Bell, Clive. *Art*. New York: Capricorn, 1958.

Benton, Thomas Hart. "Life After the Death of Theory." *Chronicle of Higher Education* 51, no. 34 (April 29, 2005): C1–C4.

Bernstein, Leonard. *The Unanswered Question: Six Talks at Harvard*. Cambridge and London: Harvard University Press, 1976.

"Blanchot and Weil's Notion of Sacred Language." About Simone Weil. http://simone .weil.free.fr/languagesacre.htm (accessed October 15, 2007).

Bloom, Harold. *The Western Canon: The Books and School of the Ages*. New York: Riverhead, 1995.

Bromell, Nick. "Summa Cum Avartia: Plucking a Profit from the Groves of Academe." *Harper's Magazine* 304, no. 1821 (February 2002): 71–76.

Camus, Albert. "Helen's Exile." In *Lyrical and Critical Essays*, edited by Philip Thody and translated by Ellen Conroy Kennedy, 148–153. New York: Knopf, 1968.

Carlson, Allen. "Aesthetic Appreciation of the Natural Environment." In *Aesthetics*, edited by S. Feagin and P. Maynard, 30–40. New York: Oxford University Press, 1997.

Caughie, Pamela. "How Do We Keep Desire from Passing with Beauty?" *Tulsa Studies in Women's Literature* 19, no. 2 (Autumn 2000): 269–84.

Caws, Mary Ann. *Reading Frames in Modern Fiction*. Princeton, NJ: Princeton University Press, 1985.

Chopin, Kate. *The Awakening and Other Stories*. Edited by Nina Baym. New York: Modern Library, 2000.

Clark, T. J. "Arguments About Modernism: A Reply to Michael Fried." In *The Politics of Interpretation*, edited by W. J. T Mitchell, 217–34. Chicago and London: University of Chicago Press, 1983.

Clayton, Mark. "Deep Thinkers Missing in Action." *Christian Science Monitor Online*, January 21, 2003. http://www.csmonitor.com/2003/0121/p17s02-lehl .html (accessed October 15, 2007).

Comte-Sponville, André. "The Brute, the Sophist, and the Aesthete: Art in the Service of Illusion." In *Why We are Not Nietzcheans*, edited by Luc Ferry, 21–69. Chicago and London: University of Chicago Press, 1997.

Conradi, Peter J. *Iris Murdoch: A Life*. New York: Norton, 2001.

Cooper, David E., ed. *A Companion to Aesthetics*. London: Blackwell, 1995.

Cullinan, M. P. F. "A Treasure Worth Preserving." Latin Mass Society. http://www .latin-mass-society.org/cullinan.htm (accessed October 15, 2007).

Danto, Arthur C. "The Abuse of Beauty." *Daedalus* 131, no. 4 (Fall 2002): 35–56.

Delbanco, Andrew. "The Decline and Fall of Literature." *New York Review of Books* 46, no. 17 (November 4, 1999): 32–38.

DeLillo, Don. "Baader-Meinhoff." *New Yorker*, April 1, 2002, 78–82.

———. *Falling Man*. New York: Scribner, 2007.

———. *Great Jones Street*. New York: Penguin, 1994.

———. "Interviews with Don DeLillo: Don DeLillo's America." Don DeLillo's America—A Don DeLillo page. February 17, 2005. http://perival.com/delillo/ delillo.html (accessed October 15, 2007).

———. "In the Ruins of the Future." *The Guardian*, December 22, 2001, 1–2.

———. *Mao II*. New York: Penguin, 1991.

———. *The Names*. New York: Vintage, 1989.

———. *White Noise*. New York: Penguin, 1985.

Denby, David. *Great Books: My Adventures with Homer, Rousseau, Woolf, and Other Indestructible Writers of the Western World*. New York: Touchstone, 1997.

Devereaux, Mary. "Beauty and Evil: The Case of Leni Riefenstahl's *Triumph of the Will*." In *Aesthetics and Ethics: Essays at the Intersection*, edited by Jerrold Levinson, 227–56. Cambridge: Cambridge University Press, 1998.

Dickinson, Emily. "Letter to Colonel T. W. Higginson." In *The Life and Letters of Emily Dickinson*, edited by Martha Dickinson Bianchi, 276. New York: Biblo and Tannen, 1971.

Dickson, Virgil. "Plagiarism Plagues College Campuses." *The DePaulia*. http://www.thedepaulia.com/story.asp?artid=1346&sectid=1 (accessed October 15, 2007).

Donoghue, Denis. "Speaking of Beauty." *Daedalus* 131, no. 4 (Fall 2002): 11–20.

———. *Speaking of Beauty*. New Haven and London: Yale University Press, 2003.

Doty, Mark. *Heaven's Coast*. New York: Harper Collins, 1997.

Eagleton, Terry. *After Theory*. New York: Basic Books, 2004.

Easterbrook, Gregg. "Axle of Evil." *The New Republic* 228, no. 2 (January 20, 2003): 27–35.

Edel, Leon. *Henry James: A Life*. New York: HarperCollins, 1987.

Edmunds, John. "A Note on Performance." In *Henry Purcell Songs With Realizations of the Figured Bass*, edited by John Edmunds. New York: R. D. Dow Music Company, 1960.

Edmunds, John, ed. *Henry Purcell Songs: With Realizations of the Figured Bass*. New York: R. D. Row Music Company, 1960.

Edmundson, Mark. *Literature Against Philosophy, Plato to Derrida: A Defence of Poetry*. Cambridge: Cambridge University Press, 1995.

Eliot, T. S. "The Waste Land." In *The Wasteland and Other Poems*, 27–54. New York: Harcourt, Brace, 1962.

Elkins, James. "The Ivory Tower of Tearlessness." *Chronicle of Higher Education* 48, no. 11 (November 9, 2001): B7–B10.

Elliott, Emory, Louis Freitas Caton, and Jeffrey Rhyne, eds. *Aesthetics in a Multicultural Age*. New York: Oxford University Press, 2002.

Engles, Tim, and John N. Duvall, eds. *Approaches to Teaching White Noise*. New York: Modern Language Association of America, 2006.

Farmelo, Graham, ed. *It Must Be Beautiful: Great Equations of Modern Science*. London: Granta Books, 2003.

Files, John. "A 178-Foot Surprise Rises Over Washington." *New York Times*, September 30, 2004, late edition, A16.

Fish, Stanley. "Why Literary Criticism is Like Virtue." *London Review of Books* 15, no. 11 (June 10, 1993): 11–16.

Fjellestad, Danuta. "Frank Lentricchia's Critical Confession, or, the Traumas of Teaching Theory." *Style* 33, no. 3 (Fall 1999): 406–13.

Fried, Michael. "How Modernism Works: A Response to T. J. Clark." In *Politics of Interpretation*, edited by W. J. T. Mitchell, 221–48. Chicago and London: University of Chicago Press, 1982.

Friedman, Thomas L. "A Failure to Imagine." *New York Times*, May 19, 2002, late edition, section 4, 15.

Fry, Roger. *A Roger Fry Reader*. Edited by Christopher Reed. Chicago and London: University of Chicago Press, 1996.

Fussell, Paul. *Doing Battle: The Making of a Skeptic*. Boston and New York: Little Brown, 1996.

Garelick, Rhonda. "Career Girls." *New York Times*, January 24, 2004, late edition, A14.

Gilbert-Rolfe, Jeremy. "Beauty." *X-Tra* 2, no. 3 (2000). http://strikingdistance.com/xtra/XTra100/v2n3/jgr.html (accessed December 1, 2007).

Giles, Patrick. "Sharps and Flats." *Salon*, November 18, 1999. http://www.salon.com/ent/music/review/1999/11/18/tabula/index.html (accessed October 15, 2007).

Gitlin, Todd. "The Ordinariness of American Feelings." *Open Democracy*, October 10, 2001. http://www.opendemocracy.net/conflict-us911/article_105.jsp (accessed October 15, 2007).

Godignon, Anne, and Jean-Louis Thiriet. "The Rebirth of Voluntary Servitude." In *New French Thought: Political Philosophy*, edited by Mark Lilla, 226–31. Princeton, NJ: Princeton University Press, 1994.

Graves, Robert. *Goodbye to All That*. New York: Doubleday, 1985.

Gray, John. *Straw Dogs: Thoughts on Human and Other Animals*. New York: Farrar, Straus, and Giroux, 2003.

Green, Daniel. The Reading Experience Blog. July 22, 2005. http://noggs.typepad.com/the _reading_experience/2005/07/james.html

Green, Jennifer M. "The Right Thing in the Right Place: P. H. Emerson and the Picturesque Photograph." In *Victorian Literature and the Victorian Visual Imagination*, edited by John O. Jordan and Carol Christ, 88–110. Berkeley: University of California Press, 1995.

Greenblatt, Stephen. "Resonance and Wonder." In *Learning to Curse: Essays in Early Modern Culture*, 161–183. New York and London: Routledge, 1992.

Griffiths, Bede. *The Golden String*. New York: P. J. Kenedy and Sons, 1955.

Halberstam, Judith. "The Death of English." *Inside Higher Education*, May 9, 2005. http://insidehighered.com/views/2005/05/09/halberstam (accessed October 15, 2007).

Hampshire, Stuart. "The Eye of the Beholder." *New York Review of Books* 46, no. 18 (November 18, 1999): 44.

Handy, Charles. *The Age of Paradox*. Cambridge: Harvard Business School Press, 1995.

Hassan, Ihab. "Confessions of a Reluctant Critic or, the Resistance to Literature." *New Literary History* 24 (1993): 1–15.

Heller, Scott. "Wearying of Cultural Studies, Some Scholars Rediscover Beauty." *Chronicle of Higher Education* 14, no. 15 (December 4, 1998): A15–A16.

Hesser, Jeffrey. "Remembering Wayne Booth." Letter. *University of Chicago Magazine* 98, no. 2 (December 2005): 1–2. http://magazine.uchicago.edu/0512/issue/letters.shtml (accessed June 7, 2007).

Hickey, Dave. "Buying the World." *Daedalus* 131, no. 4 (Fall 2002): 69–87.

Hirsch, Edward. *How to Read a Poem and Fall in Love with Poetry.* San Diego, New York, and London: Harcourt, 1999.

Hitchens, Christopher. "The Captive Mind Now." *Slate*, August 30, 2004. http://www.slate.com/id/2105821/ (accessed October 15, 2007).

Hopkins, Gerard Manley. "Henry Purcell." In *The Poems of Gerard Manley Hopkins*, edited by W. H. Gardner and N. H. Mackenzie, 80. New York: Oxford University Press, 1967.

Jakobson, Roman. "A Postscript to the Discussion on Grammar of Poetry." *Diacritics* 10, no. 1 (1980): 21–35.

James, Henry. "The Art of Fiction." In *The House of Fiction: Essays on the Novel by Henry James*, edited by Leon Edel, 23–45. London: Rupert Hart Davis, 1957.

James, William. *The Varieties of Religious Experience.* New York: Modern Library, 1999.

Jarrell, Randall. *Poetry and the Age.* New York: Farrar, Straus, and Giroux, 1953.

Jefferson Airplane. *Surrealistic Pillow.* Audio CD. RCA, 2003.

Johnson, Barbara. *A World of Difference.* Baltimore: Johns Hopkins University Press, 1987.

Joyce, James. *A Portrait of the Artist as a Young Man.* Edited by Jeri Johnson. Oxford: Oxford University Press, 2000.

Kafka, Franz. "Letter to Oskar Pollak." January 27, 1904. In *Letters to Family, Friends, and Editors*, edited by Max Brod, translated by Richard Winston and Clara Winston, 15–16. New York: Schocken, 1977.

Kipling, Rudyard. "Broken Men." In *Rudyard Kipling's Verse: Inclusive Edition, 1885–1926*, 108–9. New York: Doubleday, 1928.

Klein, Richard. *Cigarettes are Sublime.* Durham, NC: Duke University Press, 1993.

Koestenbaum, Wayne. *The Queen's Throat: Opera, Homosexuality, and the Mystery of Desire.* New York: Vintage Books, 1994.

Konrad, George. *The Melancholy of Rebirth: Essays from Post-Communist Central Europe, 1989–1994.* New York: Harcourt Brace, 1995.

Kosman, Joshua. "Our Shared Humanity Given A Voice in Arts." *San Francisco Chronicle*, September 18, 2001, E1.

Kundera, Milan. *The Unbearable Lightness of Being.* Translated by Michael Henry Heim. New York: Harper Perennial, 1999.

Kunitz, Stanley. "The Layers." In *The Collected Poems of Stanley Kunitz*, 217. New York: Norton, 2000.

Lacan, Jacques. *Écrits: A Selection.* Translated by Alan Sheridan. New York: Norton, 1977.

Lane, Robert. "The Joyless Polity." In *Citizen Competence and Democratic Institutions*, edited by S. E. Elkin and K. E. Soltan, 329–70. University Park: Pennsylvania State University Press, 1999.

Lee, Hermione. *Virginia Woolf.* New York: Vintage Books, 1999.

Lehman, David. "Elemental Bravery: The Unity of James Merrill's Poetry." In *James Merrill: Essays in Criticism,* edited by David Lehman and Charles Berger, 23–61. Ithaca, NY: Cornell University Press, 1983.

Lentricchia, Frank. "Last Will and Testament of an Ex-Literary Critic." In *Quick Studies: The Best of Lingua Franca,* edited by Alexander Star, 25–35. New York: Farrar, Straus, and Giroux, 2002.

———. *The Edge of Night: A Confession.* New York: Random House, 1994.

Lewis, Michael J. "T. J. Clark in Winter." *The New Criterion* 25 (December 2006): 4–8.

Lewis-Krause, Gideon. "In the Penthouse of the Ivory Tower." *The Believer,* July 2004. http://www.believermag.com/issues/200407/?read=article_lewis-kraus (accessed October 15, 2007).

Lodge, David. "Goodbye to All That." *New York Review of Books* 51, no. 9 (May 27, 2004): 39–43.

Lowry, Malcolm. *Under the Volcano.* New York: Harper Perennial, 2000.

Mack, Maynard. *Everybody's Shakespeare: Reflections Chiefly on the Tragedies.* Lincoln: University of Nebraska Press, 1994.

Mangino, Robin. "A Feminist Teacher 'Overreacts'." *Tufts Daily,* December 1, 2005. http://media.www.tuftsdaily.com/media/storage/paper856/news/2005/12/01/viewpoints/A.feminist.teacher.overreacts-1492244.shtml.

Mannheim, Karl. "Utopia in the Contemporary Situation." In *The End of Ideology Debate,* edited by Chaim Waxman, 10–26. New York: Simon and Schuster, 1969.

May, Thomas. "A Will and a Way: An Interview with Stephen Greenblatt." Amazon.com. http://www.amazon.com/exec/obidos/tg/feature/-/551085 (accessed October 15, 2007).

Menand, Louis. "The Marketplace of Ideas." *ACLS Occasional Paper no. 49,* 2001. http://www.acls.org/op49.htm.

Merrill, James. *A Different Person: A Memoir.* New York: HarperCollins, 1993.

———. *The Changing Light at Sandover.* New York: Knopf, 2006.

———. *Collected Poems.* Edited by J. O. McClatchy and Stephen Yenser. New York: Knopf, 2002.

———. *The Inner Room.* New York: Knopf, 1988.

———. *Late Settings.* New York: Atheneum, 1985.

———. *Selected Poems, 1946–1985.* New York: Knopf, 1992.

Miller, Henry. *The Tropic of Cancer.* New York: Grove Weidenfeld, 1992.

Moore, G. E. *Principia Ethica.* Cambridge: Cambridge University Press, 1903.

Murdoch, Iris. *Existentialists and Mystics: Writings on Philosophy and Literature.* Edited by Peter Conradi. New York: Penguin, 1999.

Nehamas, Alexander. "A Promise of Happiness: The Place of Beauty in a World of Art." *The Tanner Lectures in Human Values* 23 (April 2001). http://www.tannerlectures.utah.edu/lectures/Nehamas_02.pdf (accessed October 15, 2007).

———. "An Essay on Beauty and Judgment." *Threepenny Review,* no. 80 (Winter 2000): 4–7.

Newton, Eric. *The Meaning of Beauty.* New York: Whittlesey House, 1950.

O'Hara, Daniel T. "Lentricchia's Frankness." *Boundary 2* 21, no. 2 (Summer 1994): 40–62.

Orwell, George. "Inside the Whale." In *The Complete Works of George Orwell,* edited by Peter Davison, vol. 12, 86–112. London: Secker and Warburg, 1997.

Passaro, Vincent. "Dangerous Don DeLillo." *New York Times Magazine,* May 19, 1991. http://www.nytimes.com/books/97/03/16/lifetimes/del-v-dangerous.html (accessed October 15, 2007).

Perl, Jed. "Saint Gerhard of the Sorrows of Painting." *The New Republic* 226, no. 12 (March 29, 2002): 27–32.

Pepys, Samuel. *The Diary of Samuel Pepys.* Edited by Robert Latham and William Matthews. Vol. 9. Berkeley: University of California Press, 1976.

Perloff, Marjorie. "Something Is Happening, Mr. Jones." *Electronic Book Review,* April 1, 2004. http://www.electronicbookreview.com/thread/criticaleulogies/elitism (accessed December 10, 2007).

Perry, Carolyn, and Wayne Zade. "Something Durable and Whole." Interview with Scott Russell Sanders. *Kenyon Review* 12, no.1 (Winter 2000): 10–24.

Pipes, Richard. "Misinterpreting the Cold War: The Hardliners Had it Right." *Foreign Affairs* 74, no. 1 (January/February 1995): 154–160.

Posner, Richard. "On Plagiarism, Ghost Writing, and Falsities." *IPBIZ.* http://ipbiz.com/blogspot.com/2004/10/on-plagiarism-ghost-writing-and.html (accessed December 7, 2007).

Poulet, Georges. "Criticism and the Experience of Interiority." In *The Structuralist Controversy,* edited by Richard Macksey and Eugenio Donato, 56–88. Baltimore, MD: Johns Hopkins University Press, 1972.

Purcell, Henry. "Music for a While." In *Henry Purcell Songs: With Realizations of the Figured Bass,* edited by John Edmunds, 28. New York: R. D. Row Music Company, 1960.

Reed, Christopher. "Through Formalism: Feminism and Virginia Woolf's Relation to Bloomsbury Aesthetics." *Twentieth Century Literature* 38, no.1 (Spring 1992): 20–43.

Rilke, Rainer Maria. *Sonnets to Orpheus.* Translated by M. D. Herter. New York: Norton, 1992.

Roberts, Robert C. "A Little Protector." In *God and the Philosophers: The Reconciliation of Faith and Reason,* edited by Thomas V. Morris, 113–27. New York: Oxford University Press, 1996.

Rochberg, George. *The Aesthetics of Survival: A Composer's View of 20th century Music.* Ann Arbor: University of Michigan Press, 2004.

Rood, David, and Meaghan Shaw. "Why Go to University?" *The Age* (Australia), December 19, 2005, 11.

Rorty, Richard. *Achieving Our Country: Leftist Thought in Twentieth-Century America.* Cambridge, MA: Harvard University Press, 1998.

———. *Philosophy and Social Hope.* New York: Penguin, 2000.

Rose, Gillian. *Love's Work: A Reckoning With Life.* New York: Schocken, 1997.

———. *Mourning Becomes the Law: Philosophy and Representation*. Cambridge: Cambridge University Press, 1996.

Rosenfeld, Isaac. "Life in Chicago." *Commentary* 23, no. 6 (June 1957): 523–34.

Rotella, Guy, ed. *Critical Essays on American Literature Series: James Merrill*. New York: Twayne, 1996.

Ruddick, Lisa. "The Near Enemy of the Humanities is Professionalism." *Chronicle of Higher Education* 48, no. 13 (November 21, 2001): B7.

Said, Edward. *Musical Elaborations*. New York: Columbia University Press, 1993.

Sanders, Scott Russell. *Hunting for Hope: A Father's Journeys*. Boston: Beacon Press, 1998.

Scarry, Elaine. *On Beauty and Being Just*. Princeton, NJ: Princeton University Press, 1999.

Schjeldahl, Peter. "Beauty Is Back: A Trampled Esthetic Blooms Again." *New York Times Magazine*, September 29, 1996, 161.

———. "Notes on Beauty." In *Uncontrollable Beauty: Toward a New Aesthetics*, edited by Bill Beckley and David Shapiro, 53–60. New York: Allworth Press, 2001.

Scholes, Robert. "Does English Matter?" *Brown Alumni Magazine* 99, no. 1 (Sept/Oct 1998): 34–39.

Schopenhauer, Arthur. *The World as Will and Representation*. Vol. 1. New York: Dover, 1969.

Schor, Juliet. *The Overworked American: The Unexpected Decline of Leisure*. New York: Basic Books, 1992.

Schweitzer, Albert. *An Anthology*. Edited by Charles R. Joy. Boston: Beacon Press, 1947.

Scruton, Roger. *The Aesthetics of Music*. Oxford: Clarendon Press, 1997.

Segalen, Victor. *Essay on Exoticism: An Aesthetics of Diversity*. Durham, NC: Duke University Press, 2002.

Shawn, Wallace. "The Fever." In *Four Plays*. New York: Farrar, Straus, and Giroux, 1998.

Shelley, Percy Bysshe. "A Defence of Poetry." In *Norton Anthology of English Literature*, edited by M. H. Abrams, vol. 2, 798–802. 7th ed. New York: Norton, 2000.

———. "Ode to the West Wind." In *Norton Anthology of English Literature*, edited by M. H. Abrams, vol. 2, 730. 7th ed. New York: Norton, 2000.

Smith, Zadie. "Fail Better." *The Guardian*, January 13, 2007. Audio download. http://www.audible.com/adbl/entry/offers/productPromo2.jsp?BV_UseBVCookie=Yes&productID=SP_NYEV_000061 (accessed October 15, 2007).

Sontag, Susan. "An Argument About Beauty." *Daedalus* 131, no. 4 (Fall 2002): 21–26.

Sparshott, Francis. *The Future of Aesthetics*. Toronto, Buffalo, New York, and London: University of Toronto Press, 1998.

Star, Alexander. "Stealing Beauty: The Joy of Reading Returns to the Classroom." *Slate*, September 18, 1996. http://www.slate.com/id/3117/# (accessed October 15, 2007).

Stearns, Daniel Patrick. "The Sound of Consolation." *Andante Magazine*, September 2001. http://www.andante.com/article/article.cfm?id=14258 (accessed October 15, 2007).

Steiner, Wendy. *The Scandal of Pleasure: Art in an Age of Fundamentalism*. Chicago and London: University of Chicago Press, 1995.

————. *Venus in Exile: The Rejection of Beauty in 20th-Century Art*. New York: Free Press, 2001.

Teachout, Terry. "The Return of Beauty." *U.S. Society and Values* 8, no. 1 (April 2003). http://usinfo.state.gov/journals/itsv/0403/ijse/teachout.htm (accessed October 15, 2007).

Tompkins, Jane. "Me and My Shadow." *New Literary History* 19, no. 1 (Autumn 1987): 169–78.

Turner, Frederick. *Beauty: The Value of Values*. Charlottesville: University of Virginia Press, 1992.

Tuttleton, James W. "William Arrowsmith: A Recollection." *New Criterion* 12, no. 10 (June 1994): 85–90.

Tymoczko, Dmitri. "The Sublime Beethoven." *Boston Review* 6 (December 1999/ January 2000): 40–43.

Wassarman, Paul M. "Channels of Communication in the Ovary." *Nature Medicine* 8 (October 1, 2002): 57–59.

Wat, Aleksander. "Reading Proust in Lubyanka." In *Four Decades of Polish Essays*. edited by Jan Kott, 245–54. Evanston, IL: Northwestern University Press, 1990.

Weinstein, Arnold. *A Scream Goes Through the House: What Literature Teaches Us About Life*. New York: Random House, 2003.

What Dreams May Come. Directed by Vincent Ward. Los Angeles, CA: USA Films, Polygram Production Company, 1998.

Whitman, Walt. *Leaves of Grass*, edited by Harold Bloom, 28–160. New York: Penguin, 2005.

Wilde, Oscar. "The Critic as Artist." In *The Artist as Critic: Critical Writings of Oscar Wilde*, edited by Richard Ellmann, 341–407. Chicago and London: University of Chicago Press, 1998.

Wood, James. "Comment." The Reading Experience Blog by Daniel Green. http://noggs.typepad.com/the_reading_experience/2005/07/james.html.

Wood, Michael. "Americans on the Prowl." *New York Times*, October 10, 1982, section 7, 1.

Woolf, Virginia. *The Diary of Virginia Woolf*. Vol. 4. Edited by Anne Olivier Bell and assistant editor Andrew McNeillie. 5 vols. London: Hogarth Press, 1982.

————. *Mrs. Dalloway*. New York: Harcourt Brace Jovanovich, 1981.

————. "Reading." In *The Essays of Virginia Woolf*, edited by Andrew McNeillie, vol. 3, 141–61. London: Hogarth Press, 1986.

————. *To the Lighthouse*. New York: Harcourt Brace Jovanovich, 1981.

Wordsworth, William. "Lines Written a Few Miles Above Tintern Abbey." In *The Norton Anthology of English Literature*, edited by M. H. Abrans, vol. 2, 235–38. 7th ed. New York: Norton, 2000.

Yelavich, Susan. "Beauty's Back in Town; or, Design Gets a Hickey." *High Ground Design*, 2000. http://www.highgrounddesign.com/design/dcessay997.htm (accessed October 15, 2007).

Zagajewski, Adam. "Try to Praise the Mutilated World." Translated by Clare Cavanagh. In *Without End: New and Selected Poems*, 60. New York: Farrar, Straus, and Giroux, 2002.

Index